DP GOES A-ROVING

Nicholas M. Romano

The Book Guild Ltd

First published in Great Britain in 2017 by
The Book Guild Ltd
9 Priory Business Park
Wistow Road, Kibworth
Leicestershire, LE8 0RX
Freephone: 0800 999 2982
www.bookguild.co.uk
Email: info@bookguild.co.uk
Twitter: @bookguild

This work is entirely fictitious and bears no resemblance to any persons living or dead.

Typeset in Minion Pro

Printed and bound in the UK by TJ International, Padstow, Cornwall

ISBN 978 1911320 838

British Library Cataloguing in Publication Data.
A catalogue record for this book is available from the British Library.

Hearty thanks to the authors who have been a source and a prop to me, in the regretful awareness that most of them are no longer in a position to say, "Don't mention it".

To the DPs of this world

Play up! Play up! And play the game!
Sir Henry Newbolt

CONTENTS

PART I

1

NUT FARM

Uncle Raffaello had disappeared in the dead of night. Nut Farm had been lying idle, waiting, hoping against hope...

Standing at the core of an expanse of wheat, a boy lets his hand touch a spike braving the fiery sun; the plant feels woolly and the fingers dart back, but, lo, a butterfly is dancing, black and yellow, amidst the grainy heads! The kid's clenched fist stays motionless while his hazel eyes fill with the sensuous flutter of spotted wings. "If only I had my uncle's arms!" he sighs.

Uncle Raffaello, endearingly called by all and sundry Raf, had welcomed his mum and him as escapees from the native little town which would soon be bristling with soldiers. "The lads are coming," roly-poly Gigi, installed as usual in his salt-and-tobacco shop, had announced in his innate high nasal voice, his podgy neck spinning. "Aha, they will need my ciggies!" he had gushed, languorously lowering his eyelids. He had proved prophetic: a good-looking youngster in uniform had been spotted inside his place of trade before long, holding a packet of cigarettes in his hands and letting the tobacconist's fingers graze his cheeks. A couple of weeks later Romeo, a local lanky all-rounder, had cropped up in his gig, and hey presto! Nut Farm had heaved into view.

A string of scorching days and balmy nights had rolled on and not a solitary word had been said by the villagers about tanks and men in combat gear encroaching upon the freedom of folk living in a peaceable corner of the earth; even his well-informed, black-beshirted uncle, on being asked about the goings-on, had pushed out his under lip and waved a dismissive hand. Not long afterwards, his long-limbed body had moved beyond the outer edge of the hamlet, his black shirt merging into the darkness of the night.

The boy's short arms go akimbo, his eyes close and his ears prick up in case a familiar voice should lash the cobs as it had done when the long hot summer was still young…

"Dino-o-o!" The imperious call lost its momentum inside the grain; a deep-throated moo floated along in response; olive-brown dungarees squeezed through the wonky door of the barn and came to a halt in front of the little lad leaning over the farm sole cow and fingering her maroon-streaked fur.

"Didn't you hear my voice, kid? Rosa did." The tone was harsh, the stare cold.

"Rosa's ears are longer than mine, Uncle."

"Never mind her ears. I want you to come with me." A whiff of wartime tobacco hit the boy in the nostrils.

"Where to?"

"Up to the village."

"But why now?"

"Ugh! Don't but and why me! I'll have none of it from a cheeky nipper. Shake a leg and you will see." Tungsten flecks lit up beady eyes while a long forefinger and a massive thumb pinched the nipper's cheek. Then, poker-faced, the man was on his way out.

"Just as you say, Uncle." Both hands firmly in the pockets of his frayed cords, Dino came away and shuffled on, his lips letting out a low-pitched whistle. A few steps later, he aimed his left foot at a milk pail in the way, but a vibrant lowing sound from Rosa now standing stationary on the shed threshold made him jib. In the next breath, his short legs cleared, scissors-like, the bucket.

Man and boy galloped to a glossy black Balilla, the jewel in the crown of the national motor industry and a fount of visible pride and joy for the owner of Nut Farm. Dino saw his parched hand crank the engine energetically and heard the awesome piece of machinery roar into life. Within seconds both were on board and the vehicle was progressing sedately up the gravel path.

The rumbling ride came to the child as a thrilling novelty which made him sit without a stir and agog with expectations. A peek at the driver's foot jerking on and off the clutch and yet causing no more than the occasional judder gave him a fillip; the spectacle of arms handling the steering wheel with apparently consummate ease made him flash a supercilious smile at the villagers he saw step aside speedily while the vehicle grazed brick walls whose rustic greyness had stood the test of time. Holding his head high, he threw a sidelong glance in the direction of old men sitting at their café tables in front of glassfuls of wine and making inaudible sounds through their wide-open mouths: were they having a sunny chat about the storm raging somewhere else and, like the sweeping-by Balilla, outside their reach? If that was the case, wasn't holding a goblet of carmine wine preferable to touching the grey handle of a gun?

The watcher's gaze shifted to a decrepit balcony on which a young woman was up to the elbows with a mattress and, as the motion of her mouth and the vibrations in her neck intimated, in the middle of a song while the pad was rhythmically hit. Could the tune be the one he had heard on the wireless and was all about a young couple snogging by the edge of the sea? Adalgisa, Gigi's niece, had been crooning it while beating her own flowered mattress, but her mouth had taken the shape of Giotto's perfect O, which was the centrepiece on his classroom ageing walls, whereas the lips of the woman standing on the balcony reminded him of the grey mullet's gills he had once watched gasping for breath on the plank of a fishing boat.

The prestigious automobile came to a standstill on the verge of the village square and the two occupants emerged into the full light of the day. The boy felt the roughness of cobblestones underneath his exceedingly thin-soled shoes and, awestruck by the sight of people flocking into the curiously elliptical enclosure, he clung to his relative: the pungent aroma of Rosa on the man's fustian suit invaded his nose as the two of them wormed their way through the throng. "Fighting for a place in the sun, my friend?" a dumpy man was heard asking, and he squinted at the tonsure-like bareness on the crown of his head, the mature strawberry blotch on one cheek, and the twins being suckled by their lupine mother in the cute embroidery on his hip-length jacket.

"It's mainly for the sake of my lucky nephew, headmaster," Uncle Raf replied through gritted teeth while pointed fingers poked the lucky nephew in the ribs.

A congenial smile surfaced and expanded beneath the headmaster's round, silver-framed spectacles; his right hand extended to a time-worn plaque on the wall; his mouth dropped at an angle and grazed the child's earlobe. "The plate up there is a tribute to intrepid men who wore red shirts," he whispered. "Prepare for a few more shirts, boy, but they won't be red this time."

Aha, the flaming shirts of the one thousand Garibaldini who had fought heroically to make his country into a unified boot! Dino had seen a batch of them depicted in his history book. Another time, another place, of course, but hadn't wars fought by soldiers with differently coloured uniforms been coming and going with equally bloodstained effects? The thought sent shivers down his spine, and they felt like the flu that, regular as clockwork, would pay him a visit in the dead of winter.

Cymbals, drums and trombones sprang up and filed past – their beats more or less in harmony with the stepping of men not necessarily of military age and sporting a pitch-dark shirt.

6

"Youth, youth, spring of beauty!" a band struck up and ears stretched, eyelids narrowed, mouths stirred like cauldrons on the boil.

"Do you believe they will reach the place in the sun we are all dreaming of, Raf?" asked the headmaster, his head bizarrely askew.

"I surely do, as God is my witness!" An assertive smile played around fleshy lips.

Dino's peeled eyes descried the marchers wind up the dusty road and fade into the orange hue of the late afternoon in the guise of darksome earthworms. Lagging behind and on his knees, a boy looked taken up with his shoelaces, and wasn't he Piero, the grocer's son? He waved vigorously until he saw the nipper spring to his feet and skitter away to catch up with the men, a satchel bouncing on his backside. The watcher's eyes turned away and met the lean shape of Padre Orsino framed in the window of his recently done-up parish house. Two V-shaped fingers were slowly circling, and the face looked pervaded by pallor offset by the blackness of a soutane: dark upon dark, but what had a priest's garment in common with a shirt on the march? He had often watched the cassock ripple in the street and give its wearer the complexion of a raven on an exploratory errand; how much more pleasing to the eye was the white surplice the man of God would put on for the Holy Mass attended by regular faithful and saintly fixtures ensconced in wall niches!

The *oompah-oompah* was now almost out of earshot; the boy veered round to his uncle and waited for a signal, which promptly came as, "Time to go home, kid", followed by a bounce in the direction of his swish four-wheeled acquisition.

The drive homewards was uneventful save for a minor incident caused by a flock of sheep leisurely crossing the road. The driver's bushy eyebrows flicked upwards while a 'he-e-e!' flew through pursed-up lips in tune with hairy hands tightening their grip on the wheel and jerking as if in an effort to pull it upwards. Taken aback, the passenger slew around in his seat: was the seasoned carter still alive and kicking inside the novice driver? The onlooker scratched his head, but no other sound was heard; the ovine hindrance was adroitly dealt with and the Balilla progressed stately to the farm.

Emerging at an angle from the vehicle, Uncle Raffaello stretched his legs and went on his knees. "Mother Earth. O good Mother Earth," he sighed while kissing a pair of clods. "We humans have a short memory, but thou rememberest," he added to the accompaniment of solemn nods. Then he stood up and threw out his hairy chest. A strip of shirt peeped out from under his jacket. It had an unmitigated black colour.

Dino turned his attention to the farmhouse, and there she was, his mother, standing at the door and screening her eyes with her little hands. Her head formed a cobnut in the wooden frame.

"Thank you, Uncle," he blurted, and hared off to the waiting woman.

"Where on earth have you been?" she inquired in her wonted anxious strain; her searching dark eyes pinned him to his tiny patch of grass.

"To the village, Ma… to see a parade of men wearing black shirts."

"Ah! Don't do that again, son." Granules of sourness in her voice had the tang of the crab apple at which he'd had a bite in the teeth of Romeo's warning to leave the fruit well alone for the sake of his tender guts.

"But I… Uncle Raf, I mean," he started just as the man himself loped in, casting an expanding shadow on the doorway.

"I say, driving my boy to the show offered by a bunch of stuffed shirts, eh?" she snapped, her hands tapping her folded arms at a fast tempo.

"He took a gander at the march of youths who make a

beautiful spring. It has done him no harm, sister." A lopsided, foxy smile pervaded the creases around his fierce eyes beneath beetling eyelids.

"Shall we leave the beautiful spring to one side for now, brother?" She handed the child a meagre portion of brown bread and pale yellow smoked cheese. "Go out and have a bite. War is a game for grown-ups, darling."

Her darling slouched out to a giant sun on the down path and to the monotone of invisible cicadas. Entranced, he looked skywards and dearly wished he could fly off into the wide blue yonder. A powerful smell of hay made his nostrils twitch. Closing his eyes as he would while receiving the wafer from Father Orsino's outstretched hand, he let a crumb of the valuable hunk fall on his tongue. It tasted good.

From the far end of the field, the silhouette of his moderately older cousin Lando came into view. Darksome, sinewy, it advanced by leaps and bounds on the quick-growing grass. The lad had been scarcely more than a name in a list of relations who belonged to the soil and were supposed to stay on it as their fathers and forefathers had done, but evacuation to Nut Farm had brought a change. In the course of a visit to Lando's duck-egg blue cottage, there had been indications of a mind at loggerheads with a twill-patterned, badly-fitting suit and in harmony with things like Pythagoras' theorem, the Punic Wars, and the one now being fought up and down the country. 'They're coming and will carry the day before too long,' he had prophesied on one occasion, and Dino had cottoned-on without much effort to who the prospective victors were. And there was another thing: his cousin had disclosed a soft spot for knights-errant and damsels. 'Sweeties' he had called them once or twice in the appreciative tone of the schoolmaster, who had hinted at shirts of a hue very unlike that of the men on the march. While playing at soldiers, he had challenged an invisible foe to single combat: "I am Orlando, villain!" he had cried out and made his fellow player associate the name with that of the paladin fighting murky infidels in the colourful pages of the strip cartoon he would devour week in week out in his room at home.

The grub disappeared into his pocket just as Lando reached him. "I say, where on earth were you this afternoon?" the arrival inquired.

"Ah, my uncle took me to see the recruits in the big square."

Ripples of frown flooded Lando's brow. "Your uncle didn't invite me, and I know why. Only the other day he was telling off a young man wearing a red scarf around his neck. Mind you, the black shirt he gave me as a present last Christmas is hanging, still unused, in my wardrobe."

"I saw Piero in the piazza, and he was marching with the men."

"Piero? Ha-ha! This stupid war will be over and done with before he can become a soldier and…" His ears leant over to have a listen at a male voice floating down the field from a banger trundling on the road. *O Sun who rise free and jocund*, the voice warbled, and "Sure!" Lando squeaked before screwing up his dark brown eyes and focusing them on a girl en route to them, her sable tresses streaming down her angular shoulders, her polka-dot skirt fluttering in the breeze. An orange cockerel could be heard squawking as it peeped out from under her arm. "We're having company, cousin," he chuckled.

"Oh, that's Ange. She often comes and plays with me. Haven't you met her?"

The girl had now reached the farm. "I saw you in the piazza the other day, Dino," she said by way of a greeting. "You were waving like mad to the men in black shirts." She sucked air into her nose; sniffles seemed to be inherent in her thin organ of smell.

"Cool it! I was only waving at my friend Piero. He was following the men."

Her almond-shaped eyes sparkled with bemusement. "Is he, too, going to the war?"

"No, silly, he isn't. Hasn't your mum told you that war is a game for grown-ups?" He paused briefly before adding, "wait a sec, there was a boy soldier in a story I read not long ago, and this boy helped other soldiers up in the Alps by taking messages around the trenches. They called him Mercury. It's a marvellous story, and..."

"Never heard of a boy soldier called Mercury," Ange chipped in. A mischievous smile cropped up on her small face. "Tell me, what d'you want to do when you grow up?"

"Ahem, I don't know yet... but I'll never be a soldier, cross my heart." His left hand leapt onto his chest.

She swivelled round to Lando. "And you?"

"Aha, I'd like to see a bit of the world." He sounded like one envisaging a host of virgin lands waiting to be explored.

She held on to her smile, but the impish tinge in it had vanished. "I for one am dreaming of growing like a butterfly. Your uncle calls me Pupa when he is in a good mood – doesn't he, Tesorino?" A couple of vigorous taps on the crest of the cockerel prompted a long squawk. "I must go now," she announced and skittered along the grass, her spotted skirt in full swing anew.

"Whew! The chick has given me a bit of a tingle," Lando revealed as soon as she was out of earshot. His long finger pointed at his belly, or the region in the vicinity of it. "What about you?" A blush coloured the other's cheeks. "Oh, well. I can see that you're still wearing short trousers. Now, listen carefully, cousin," he went on, "I'm going into the hills tonight. A few men are hiding in caves up there, and they are desperate for news, booze and a bit of grub. But mum's the word, eh?" he added, lowering his voice and producing a wink that vied with the size of his face. Dino's response was a slow, conspiratorial nod, which was rewarded with a couple of emphatic pats on the shoulder and followed by the departure of the Mercury in the family. His mother's food came out of his pocket in a flash and he lashed out at it.

The magenta car that emerged through the mist the following morning looked as if competing with Uncle Raffaello's Balilla in a beauty contest. While Dino gawked at it, the back door swung open and Aldo, a classmate of his since primary school days, sprang out waving at the chauffeur and shouting, "Hail!" with a winsome smile and an outstretched right hand. His peacock-blue eyes scrutinised the farm. "Nice," he hissed.

By Jove, he looked taller and smart in his green plus fours above long socks and boots, but also, he looked older by virtue of his blond hair slicked down and backwards in a Blackshirt style – a fine Son of the Fasces at first blush! And ho, he really took after his dad, the man Dino had passed by in the street more than once and who had made him dart an awe-stricken glance at his craggy face adorned with a neatly trimmed moustache, a countenance fitting to a tee the charcoal greyness of the tunic falling over baggy trousers as well as the cap covering a modicum of hair combed *de rigueur*.

"I can see a pretty little cow, too," the visitor went on to say while pointing at the mammal which was standing at a short distance with perked-up ears.

"Come and meet Rosa," said the host.

They moved to the heifer. Aldo's fingers slid along her streaky back. "Dear Rosa," he murmured into her big ear, "we all live in a land flowing with milk and honey now; and aren't you pleased?"

A basso continuo 'mo-o-o' wafted along. "I hear the voice of a patriotic creature. Believe, obey, fight," Aldo continued while unleashing a string of assertive nods. The last three words had been spurted out staccato, and they sounded familiar to his classmate because he'd heard them being roared out on the wireless by their national leader in a strikingly similar cadence. The exhortation had also put in an appearance in the shape of enormous graffiti on more than one dilapidated wall in the village, close to the message that a single-day life as a lion was preferable to a-hundred-day life as a sheep. Come to that, how would the grass-eating ovine creatures that shared the field with Rosa have felt about the statement if they'd been able to decode it? On the other hand Romeo, too, had failed to decipher the official communication exempting him from military duties on grounds of age and been obliged to turn to Uncle Raf for a proper read: regrettably, he wouldn't be going places in a sunny country on the other side of the Med. "There must be a few nice lizards out there. You have a bow at hand by any chance?" he heard Aldo say and shook his head apologetically. "Don't worry, mate. All I need is a piece of good string," he was told.

No sooner said than done! Romeo, who'd been standing by, was seen darting into a shed and coming out of it armed with a bow-shaped woody stem equipped with a reedy arrow. "Abracadabra, lads!" he cried while proffering the item all smiles. Lando gave a tight salute in response and grabbed the tool. "I am not a child of the Capitoline she-wolf for nothing," he stated with a quiet laugh while scanning the field.

The handyman gave a low bow and disappeared behind the farm fence. On cue the pointed body of a pygmy reptile appeared, squatting on a stone and flicking its tongue. The hunter tiptoed to it, and his stick darted off. "La-la-la!" he cried and dashed forward. "Victory! Victory!" he crowed as he came back by leaps and bounds, holding a little grey-green body writhing at the tip of the bow-head. With mixed feelings, the other saw him ease the lizard into a jar. Would the victor now display magnanimity and restore the captured creature to freedom? There and then a piercing cry and the crackle of firearms stirred the somnolent air. From the far end of the farm a couple of male shapes appeared and vanished like lightning.

"Let's get out of here," Dino pleaded, but Aldo nonchalantly grabbed a withered twig and placed the jar on it. An oblong matchbox cutely ornamented with two X-shaped little fasces appeared from inside his pocket. He struck a long stick and studiously set the leaves on fire: pretty soon the prisoner would be jumping up and down like a deranged frog inside its glass abode. Agog, he stared and waited. His playmate made off, and, on entering at a run the spinney adjacent to the farm, caught sight of two blokes moving at full tilt away from a young body dangling from an olive branch. A fleeting squint allowed him to see the human frame wriggle, kick the air convulsively and, after a couple of jerks, sink into immobility while the baggy trousers the youth wore, his flowered shirt, and his quaint straw hat danced in tune with the breeze. The mesmerised witness felt his heart thump like mad and two hands grip his shoulders. His head whirled and his body flattened like a deflated balloon, but within a couple of minutes he was clear-headed enough to perceive that he'd been confined to a small shed. He squatted on his haunches and whimpered, "Dad! If only you were here!" while breaking out in a cold sweat, wiping his fevered brow and going dry with panic. Then, as the wooden puppet-boy to whom he he'd taken a shine had done when ambushed by a murderous fox and a like-minded cat, he shut his eyes, straightened his legs, and froze. When his eyes reopened, he pricked them up into the dimness and his round face twitched with terror at the sound of a scratch at the door and the sight of the latch being gingerly lifted up, but the pupils reverted to their ordinary size as soon as Ange's voice reached him in a whisper: "Come out before they are back!" it was saying on a par with the urgency conveyed by the sloe-shaped eye glaring through a chink. When, on all fours, he crawled out of the cage his saviour was gone. "Bravo, bravo, Ange," he murmured while, massaging his sore neck, he moved apace on the road. Yet, how come she'd been at the scene of the crime? His head swayed: had the horrible thing really happened,

14

or had he just awoken from a nightmare? His sloping shoulders went into a repeated shrug. The panic into which he'd been thrown inside the shed had left him now that he'd been restored to the world of the free. He breathed deeply in and out. Should he go and tell the Carabinieri about the felony inside the grove? A startling recollection of what had befallen the puppet-boy when the Law had caught up with him put the idea to flight. *Lando, none other than Lando, would be informed*, he said to himself, but the next moment he slapped his forehead: his cousin was as likely as not somewhere in the hills at that very instant! The sudden sound of church bells made him stop and place a finger on the tip of his nose. Aha, Don Orsino! He'd go to confession and spill the beans; the man of God would understand in spite of his crow-like cassock. A tentative smile crept up and chased out a bout of spasm on his warming cheeks as he trotted all the way to the church.

The holy place felt cool and soothing. A woman was on her knees at the confessional, and an ebony cat was slinking into the vestry. On tiptoe, he moved in, and there it was, the quaint feline, squatting on a chasuble. He sidled up to it and stroked its fluffy head, waiting for the inborn purr, but no joy: he was confronted with an arching body and burning malignant eyes. Seconds later, the furry creature was making a beeline for the door; there, one leg went up and a stream of yellow liquid spurted out; then the graceless beast disappeared. He swung around and found himself close to the very one he'd come for: Don Orsino, his surplice comfortingly hiding the soutane, towered over him while asking in his ingrained soft voice, "Anything the matter, child?"

"P-P-Padre, I…" he sobbed, but a pale hand descended onto his head, and it had the tender feel of his father's limb the night he had left home to go… where? He rose and trudged to the door, shaking his head.

In the glittering street, a loudly familiar, "Ciao, comrade!"

hit his ears and whipped his round-shouldered body back into shape. He looked up: his classmate's right hand was sticking out of the window of his dad's high-powered car and expanding into a Roman salute. Willy-nilly, he waved back.

Soon enough, Rosa was apprised of the heart-breaking moment inside the copse. Keeping his lips within an inch of her fleshy ear, he let her know in the hush-hush tone he would regularly sink into at the confessional about the young man swinging at Nut Farm and himself roughly bundled into a shed until Ange had come to the rescue. "You know, she saved my life," he whispered in a tremulous voice. "I really thought I was seeing a little fairy with blue hair... I mean the one who had a wooden boy taken down from the tree on which two assassins had hung him." He paused for a sigh. "But no little fairy had the young man taken down," then he moaned and saw his confidante's liquid eyes glitter against the light filtering through the barn little window, one hoof go up and then come down with a thud. His mouth opened into an oval shape; a harsh scream bubbled out and reverberated across his body. His own, abruptly broken, voice caught him on the hop.

When he re-entered the farmhouse, a stocky bloke encased in a shabby tracksuit was sitting sprawled out in his uncle's exclusive wickerwork chair, and he looked pretty busy quaffing wine from a pot-bellied brown bottle. Whence on earth had he sprung?! Oh well, Romeo had hinted at deserters lurking about at night like jackals and then exclaimed with a growl of anger, "The bloody cowards will hang for this, mark my words!" Was this man a deserter? The boy's eyes glanced off in the direction of his mother seated close to the inglenook and ostensibly taken up with the task of adjusting her oyster-shaped hair slide on the nape. He shot an inquiring look, saw her eyes peremptorily point at his room and reluctantly clumped upstairs. By making dexterous use of his short arms and legs he ensconced himself in the massive oak-boarded double bed he'd been sharing with his uncle and lay at ease while focusing on the picture book that portrayed the ups and down in the extraordinary life of the wooden boy that was now a boon companion. Not for long though. The silent spell came to an abrupt end when his legs jerked off the sheets, slid into his frayed cords and moved gingerly downstairs. The intruder was still occupying the usurped chair, his head aslant in a slumberous posture, and his arms hanging over the sides; then he was leaping off his seat and making a beeline on the creaky planks for his mother. Dino saw him paw her cheeks, and in the twinkling of an eye surged forward and kicked the brute in his massive buttocks. A wave of disbelief swept over the stranger's pockmarked face; a fierce light glinted in his bulging eyes; an arching hand landed on the assailant's body, and two strong arms lifted it up and dragged it to the floor.

"Stop messing him about!" his mum cried, and the ogre slouched back to her, his eyes now bursting with a fiendish look; his hands fluffed her hair and tampered with her slide. She responded with utter contempt by pushing his limbs off, and the attacker recoiled and made for Dino, but, "Run, son, run!" she shrieked with outstretched arms, and he darted to the door just in time to bump into Aunt Eulalia, Raffaello's nicely plump wife, on her way in. As she stood befuddled and wide-legged in the doorway, he squeezed through the gap and scarpered out into the field.

The night teemed with invisible crickets. He sat on a soft bale and raised his head to a moon on the wane. With half an eye, he spotted shadows slinking along the edge of the farm: were they inhabitants of a fairyland? One of them wore a veil exposing a beetle nose, which strikingly conjured up his uncle's organ of smell. He rubbed his eyes and screwed them up: wrapped in attire which resembled a cassock and twinkled in the faint light emanating from the meagre slice of moon, a lean body was moving on the trail of the spectral forms. The onlooker pinched himself to make sure he wasn't dreaming, sprang to his feet and scurried back into the house. His mother was still sitting in front of the hearth and keeping her arms limply on her legs. She was on her own, now. "Go to bed, there's a good boy," she murmured with a smile that seemed to be fighting its way through the muddle of creases on her angular face.

He slouched away and headed for the stairs but, on reaching the first step, he swivelled round and asked, "Ma, where is Pa?"

"I don't know, sonny, honest to God" she replied with a sigh while staring into the sheaf of crackling logs. He kept motionless, asking himself whether grasshoppers were rubbing their legs against their bodies at the corners of the inglenook. When he looked at his mother again, her eyes were still glued to the log fire: she seemed to have entered a fairyland of her very own.

The sun-drenched summer was drawing to a close when, early in the hazy morning, a jeep pulled up at the top of Nut Farm. Dino dropped the bag of feed intended for Rosa and drooled over a star-spangled banner stuck on a pole on one side of the jeep. "The Americans! The Americans!" a female voice yelled in a visible transport, and he cast a puzzled look: had the war finally come to the village? And had not Uncle Raf told him that the Americans were their sworn enemies? If so, why the thrill of joy in the woman's voice? Was she crazy? He saw her trot away, her arms flailing wildly. *Yes, she must have a screw loose*, he said to himself while twirling his forefinger on his temple and staring at the combatants hailing from an immensely distant country. He had watched men dwelling in what Don Orsino had called 'The New World' do their deeds in some film or other being shown at the parish community centre: they would ride on horseback equipped with cowboy hats and fight Red Indians in the boundless prairies of the Far West. They killed the redskins like flies, these guys, yet, occasionally, they fell prey to them. In one of those 'Westerns', as the priest would call them, a paleface was tied to a torture pole, and a watcher in the packed hall had shouted, "Moron! How on earth did you fail to see the redskin behind you? It serves you right." And ugh! the captive's screams! His own eyes had misted, but within seconds he'd been sighing with relief and smiling broadly at the spectacle of uniformed cattlemen riding at breakneck speed and coming to the rescue of their comrade at the eleventh hour. "Hallelujah! Our men are arriving!" the chiding chap had yelled, and the audience had clapped in unison while, at the back of the enthralled flock, skinny arms concealed by the cassock were rising towards the ceiling and the Presence beyond it.

Dino edged to a few paces' distance from the arrivals and stood with arms akimbo on his patch of yellow grass. Utterly captivated by the chequered uniforms of young men dressed in full combat gear, he gaped at them as they stepped to and fro, busily taking green padded flasks to the spout of the spluttering fountain at the roadside and letting long cigarettes dangle at an angle from their lips. Had they, too, got the weed from Gigi? He heard them laugh like a drain: were soldiers, too, capable of a hearty laughter, then? He was filled with pleasure by the sight of their fresh faces sparkling in tune with their boots and giving him the impression that they were challenging the brilliance in the sky. He saw them brandish their long guns. Ah, what would his uncle say if he were there!

One of the soldiers emerged from behind the jeep and, while rubbing his hands with a rag, hollered, "Ciao, bud. Me, too, mo-o-o in America." His sea-green eyes shone in small flashes as they turned to Rosa now making her way towards them. "Me Ron," he added while tapping on his chest with greasy fingers. "And you? Benito, eh?"

The boy's chin went up slowly for a negative signal. "Dino," he replied, "Dino Puppi."

Keeping his heavy gun in the palm of his hand, the visitor made for Rosa, and the little lad encircled the mammal's head as if prompted by protective feelings. "Wow!" the other gushed and cupped his hand around his mouth as though preparing for a louder cry, but a peremptory call from a fellow combatant made him step back and hop onto the jeep. The sturdy motor vehicle jugged off and the GI stood upright while maintaining eye contact with Dino and Rosa; then his arm moved up, something flitted birdlike in the air and landed a few metres away from the boy and the cow. He rushed to pick up the item: it was a packet of chewing gums, ho-ho! he had come into possession of the fabulous nuggets! Smiling broadly, he waved Ron off. "So long, puppy kid. *Io amico*," his departing friend roared, while his grinning face and patterned body receded into a blur.

Holding the gift in a vicelike grip, Dino skipped to Rosa and leant against her, flaunting his share of the chicle and laughing heartily, but choral sounds made him turn his neck and have a careful listen: the servicemen were singing on their way to battle! He recognised the tune because Lando had been humming the lyrics, and they were all about a pretty young woman called Susanna. He heard the Americans chirp them out in harmony with the host of cicadas judiciously nestling in their secluded barracks; their military voices oozed a charming confidence and the sound of it gave the listener a big fillip. He swung back to Rosa and saw her chew her well-deserved cud. A gum dropped into his wide-open mouth, and he chomped in sync.

Late in the evening, and as the sole occupier of his uncle's double bed, he relished the white linen expanse a good deal more than the feel of hard springs and the whiffs redolent of the mothball odour he had inhaled while crawling behind his relative's square shoulders for a display of the youth that was the spring of beauty. With a sniff, he shifted in search of an odourless spot, found none and sank into immobility, his face up to the flaky ceiling. Seconds later, muttering voices from the kitchen rolled over him like sea wavelets encroaching on the farm: "Benito on the run…

the Krauts… the Yanks… the Tommies… Monte Cassino… a deluge of bombs… rivers of blood… carcasses everywhere." He leapt up and tiptoed to the window: the cicadas had called it a day, but no crickets were rubbing their forewings; one solitary gun thundered from afar, and a plane droned heavily behind dark thick clouds. He regained his bed, threw the rough upper sheet over his head, and tossed and turned in an effort to enter a world light years away from a planet that seemed keen on pricking him like the puzzles in the crossword weekly Aunt Eulalia would hand him now and then as an alternative to the story of the wooden puppet. One of the word games had actually put him on the rack and at long last relented: 'it's a doggone world', it meant.

Slicing through the thick daylight, Romeo sauntered into the kitchen and took a place at the table where Dino's mother was sitting. His face was straight; his farm-nurtured, obdurately bony body hang at an angle because of his stoop. "Up at the village everybody is talking of Raffaello and of death squads skulking under cover of darkness," he announced in a voice that jarred with the clamour of bells from the parish church. "Your brother has sneaked off in the middle of the night like a fox. He was last seen at the wheel of his Balilla, and the car was chock-a-block with blokes wearing shirts of a colour I don't care to mention. They were heading for the hills. Now, it's hawked about that a good number of men are keeping themselves inside caves up there, and that their shirts are of a different colour. See what I mean?"

From the opposite side of the table Dino's mother crossed herself. "We had better pray for my reckless brother and the likes of him," she suggested with a deep sigh.

"Aye, but what are you thinking of doing now?"

"I'm only waiting to see which way the wind blows."

"It won't be a long wait by the lie of the land."

21

"For goodness' sake keep as silent as the grave, Romeo. Haven't you read the poster on the wall?"

"Ha, my reading is no better than a dead dog. Besides, I don't care a fig about all them posters." His statement was enhanced by a shrug. Knowing glances were exchanged before a pipe emerged, a mammoth match sparked above a horse-head shaped bowl, and between sucking noises the odd-job chap mentioned the stranger who had lately cropped up at the farmhouse.

"He looked a wretch and I did my best to help him," his interlocutor rejoined composedly.

Silence fell again and spiralled up in line with puffs of smoke, but it was dispersed by Romeo saying, "And there's more news. People are also talking about the youngster who early in the summer dangled all night from a tree in the olive grove. Christ, not even the king of Ai swung for so long! The word at the village is that it was done by your brother's friends." The forceful tone intimated a guy with a stoop outweighed by an upright frame of mind. "The star-crossed lad stood up there without the ghost of a smile while, good God, a bright spark was standing down in here merry as a cricket. Some people think that the intruder came to the farm hoping for a bit of low-down on your husband as well as on the men who've taken to the hills. 'Two women in a house and no man in sight: what could be better than that for a one-night stand?' somebody chortled in the bar last night." His scrawny fingers tapped on the horse head. "*La-a calunnia è un ventice-ello,*" he struck up, echoing with moderate success Basilio's musical metaphor in *Il Barbiere di Siiviglia.*

The metaphorical link between slander and a breeze set alight the woman's dark eyes. "We'll be leaving the farm before we get blown off," she announced.

The prospect of leaving Nut Farm was the last straw for her child noiselessly sitting at the top of the wooden stairs. "I don't want to go home, Ma. I don't want to see the war," he whined.

Her face flushed with unease. "We must go home, Dino, and the sooner the better."

"All right then, if we really must. But I'm not leaving without Rosa. Surely she can be taken to our garden."

"No problem, kid; no problem at all," was the handyman's response to the plea in a voice that sounded as if coming out of the farm humus. His eyes flashed a paternal smile made more intense by his slightly boss-eyed stare. "I'll tell you what – you go home and get the figurines and the star out for your Christmas crib. This war is almost over. Peace will be soon with us again and things will be just as they were before."

Dino wheeled round to face his mother and saw a hazy beam cross her visage. Pulling a face, he got to his feet and scampered up into his uncle's room. Shafts of a vacancy shrouded in mystery pierced his bemused features.

***

"Dino! Where the devil are you hiding?" The voice is high-pitched, taut like a mandolin string, demanding. Engulfed in a sea of spikes, the boy reopens his eyes: the butterfly is gone. Weaving his way through the maze, he heads for the maternal sound.

***

It wasn't long before Romeo's big cart, crammed with fresh local produce and luggage, rattled its way towards the railway station. Bouncing up and down in sync with his mother, Dino launched a long farewell look at the barn inside which Rosa was as likely as not munching away at her cherished feed. She had been informed of his departure as well as of the verdant garden ready to accommodate her at his little town, and her response had been some longer-than-usual lowing. His feelings fluctuated between elation and fear whilst his bleary eyes advanced across the contiguous farm: it made a desolate landscape apart from the presence of Tesorino, who could be seen scratching about without a squawk.

When the cart entered the piazza, nobody was in it. Up in the parish house a head was bent over a book behind a window pane, and it displayed an impressive tonsure. Two fingers went up, and were they not circling in the air? Dino's peeled eyes left the question suspended in the early beam of light hitting the plate glass.

Minutes later, the squat frame of the village station came into view. Mother and son helped Romeo with some of the load and plodded up the craggy stairs that led to the tracks and to a train not to be missed. The leaden colour of the brick-and-mortar rural building was pathetically relieved by tufts of green grass peeping through disconnected slabs and carnations stuck in colourless pots on the scuffed windowsill of the stationmaster's room. A solid phalanx of human bodies stood on the long platform, and it was heard to murmur to a crescendo as soon as a raucous bell announced an oncoming train. Droves surged forward in answer to a loud, prolonged whistle and gusts of white smoke leaping skywards. Brakes screeched to a halt. The endless line of coaches had made it. Sucked into a vortex of arms and legs, Dino landed close to a caffèllatte-coloured carriage and a high windowpane. Strong, benevolent arms whisked him up to a woman's pastoral face and spaced-out yellowing teeth. He hurriedly secured two seats and rushed back to the window. Oh yes! Discernible in the multitude, his mother's sharp face was approaching the carriage. "Bravo, my son," she mumbled as she waddled in, a single suitcase firmly in her hand. "Don't worry. Romeo will take care of the whole lot," she reassuringly added while adjusting her hair slide with a laboured smile. He turned his head: untold people, boxes, and caged fowl could be seen converging onto the platform and it looked an endless procession. He held on and waited for the train to resume its march. It was ages before, with a hoot and a jolt, the caffèllatte chain was on the move again. His eyes searched into the reeling crowd left behind and yes, yes! there she was, Ange, her saffron tresses cascading down her shoulders and, beneath her arm, a void which Tesorino had regularly filled. A sudden flush of warmth made him wave his hands excitedly, but hers kept motionless, and a blank look seemed to be filling her speckled features. In a space of seconds she was a tiny contour receding in a pattern of interlaced bodies and blurred faces.

He shuffled away from the window and caught sight of two men conversing in the chock-full gangway. He heard them talk of women allegedly offering their bodily wares for a quick buck in the backstreets of the nearby seaside city as well as of urchins endowed with a knack of making the boots of well-oiled GI's shiny as a beryl and then relieving them of their valuable footgear. Oh, God, was his latest friend Ron now marching barefooted? "I doubt that the Yankees will let their mammas know about the whole shoot when they're back home, hee-hee!" one of the two croaked with a funny foreign accent, and Dino recognised him at once because he lived only a couple of doors away in the narrow street to which he was returning: the guy had become American by virtue of a long spell in Brooklyn, which he'd left soon after an army of his new fellow countrymen had landed at the heel of his boot-shaped country – or so his mother had recounted. Romeo probably knew a good deal about the affair, for on one occasion he had stated sarcastically, "I'm sure the Americano came back to give the GI's a good hand on the sly; a few guys of his stamp have been taken out of jail for that very same purpose. A brilliant move, I say."

In the dim light suffusing the corridor, the reddish-yellow scar crossing the fellow's cheekbone resembled a narrow slice of a deep-baked pizza, and, like a streak of lightning, an image of the werewolf who'd been heard to howl at the full moon in

25

the secret garden adjacent to his own flashed across his mind: what if the Americano was none other than the bewitched creature? He turned his gaze to the locomotive: it was puffing on and inexorably taking him back to the place where Adalgisa would sing ever and anon about billing and cooing close to the lapping sea, and paunchy Gigi would still be welcoming lads dressed in grey and green into his shop smelling of weed and bonbons. Besides, if Romeo was true to his word, Rosa would join them all and chew the good grass luxuriantly growing in his spacious garden. And who else was he going back to? Oh yes, there would be the other Rosa – or, for the record, Rosina as she was affectionately called by her street neighbours – the immensely old, toothless, gorgon-like woman he had once caught in the act of hitching up her skirt and revealing a furry splodge underneath.

He glanced sideways and oh, no, his mum had succumbed to sleep! At close quarters her symmetrically open mouth reminded him again of Giotto's O hanging close to two little fasces on the ashen wall of the hardly symmetrical classroom he would soon be compelled to regain. He felt sick at heart and asked himself if the milk-white little lamb he had once espied being carried by his uncle to the abattoir had felt any worse. A series of jolts made his parent's eyes flick open and fleetingly focus on him before coming to a close again. Had she, too, detected the proximity of the guy from Brooklyn? Also, was she aware of her son's pent-up emotions eager to surface like the lava bubbling inside the volcano on the island to which the patriotic expat had been welcomed back with open arms? He tiptoed quietly to her, sat close to her dormant body and rested his head on her lap: it was redolent of the good earth at Nut Farm and he breathed in the scent with the enraptured countenance of a nursling clinging to a primordial fount of wellbeing.

26

2

THE CHAIR

Lying in bed half-awake, Dino descried images shifting like varicoloured pieces of glass in a kaleidoscope: a field of wheat under the sway of a despotic sun and a thickset man wearing an ebony shirt in the midst of the flaxen growth; a maroon-streaked heifer trotting along and a black-and-yellow butterfly fluttering away; a farmhouse door and an apprehensive woman screening her eyes with her little hands. Lingering memories; wheels within wheels; traces marking a twisting path; the illusory pursuit of an irrecoverable moment of being. A few years had slipped by since myriad men had been killed or maimed in battle, and young soldiers had left his little town for keeps; but then, had they lingered on, there would have been no further oodles of cigarettes for them because the obliging supplier had been found sitting against the wall in a corner of the courtyard, dead as a doornail and displaying a nasty gash in his fat neck. Yes, the affable bloke had finally deserted his sweet-smelling shop and taken with him a face telling a story of its own in the midst of folk with faces and stories of their own – all gone with the wind that had blown with a vengeance up and down their boot-shaped country. By the grace of God, a seemingly endless war was now a back number.

Inside the Palladian edifice where he was now attending high school (a middle rung of the ladder conducive to higher things in the eyes of his parents) none of his sagging-cheeked teachers had so far mentioned the military events; only the one-armed podgy caretaker had hinted at them when, during one of the only too-short breaks for a badly needed leg stretch (and a surreptitious puff or two at a cig in the loo), he had owned to leaving his other limb in a foreign field while taking part in a scramble for a place in the sun. "Lost forever," he had sighed without clarifying whether he was referring to his missing arm or to the sun-baked country where little ebony faces had been promised a new bridegroom and a new sovereign with a little help from a catchy melody coming from the land of bel canto...

One eye flicked open and perceived the hour on a loudly ticking old alarm clock. It was about time he prepared for school. With a yawn, he deserted his bed, got rid of his checked pyjamas and slipped into baggy trousers that, from the aesthetic point of view of one of his cousins, afforded him the cute looks of a teddy bear.

He reached school on time and stood at the entrance of the room to which he and his classmates were confined six days a week – the four or five hours of constraint being mercifully shortened on Saturdays as they had been for twenty-odd years by courtesy of a regime keen on weekend parades. The poky enclosure evoked his primary school classroom but for the absence of Giotto's flawless O and of the stylish little fasces he recalled hanging on the wall beneath the mastiff face of the national leader. While his eyes converged on the long passage ahead his neck sensed the proximity of Aldo, the classmate who seemed to have been his shadow since they had shared a rather small desk.

Dino heard him recite, a textbook in his hand, "Then in came Corinna in a long loose gown, her white neck hid by tresses hanging down", in his customary staccato manner and with a mischievous glint in his duck-egg blue eyes. In the next breath he was saying, "Corinna reminds me of Zaza", while his free hand slid along dark hair which had in earlier days been soberly flattened in compliance with macho aesthetics and was now as shiny as Clark Gable's threadlike mane in *Gone with the Wind*. The enticing Corinna had been the apple of the elegiac poet Ovid's eye, yet for some reason Dino felt drawn to Dido, the Phoenician princess abandoned by Aeneas and in the aftermath of the desertion taking leave of life on a pyre.

Aldo appeared determined to play with the fire kindled by the classy mistress of yore in remembrance of the local scarlet woman who had stood beneath a blush-pink lamp along Orchard Lane – her Alsatian Amore by her side and her large yellow-green catty eyes defying the tease of men. Zaza, a figure of indefinable age, had made her presence a constant in the rotation of the seasons until a stray bomb from a starry sky had left her room in a shambles and the occupant lying at rest in a double bed with a gory hole in her cupola breasts and crimson patches on her perennially golden hair. Early in the hazy morning a handful of grateful men, walking huddled together and aslant, their collars held up against a persistent drizzle, had dutifully escorted the departed companion to her final abode – Amore trotting in their wake.

Aldo let the lovesick Ovid and the royal Corinna thud onto his desk while Dino transferred his concern to the fading cream window and the ashen wall on which the crucified Man God had pride of place. "D'you remember Zaza?" Aldo chuckled, but "Hush!" he hissed while he kept his ear askew towards the tap-tap of a walking stick and his eyes on a squat man feeling his way to the door, finding the gap in the wall as was his wont and stepping in with the confident gait of a conqueror. Instants later, he was installed in his chair with a vacant smile on his pudding face and his fingers adjacent to raised round marks which protruded like tiny nipples. Seconds balanced on a knife edge ticked away while his hands formed cups over the sides of his fleshy features and his bulky dark glasses focussed on a bunch of pupils anxious to tune into the discreet sounds issuing from his throat: all done to death, yet ever so alive.

"Georg Hegel," the gentleman struck up in the drowsy last hour of the school day, and the guttural name filled up the vacancy in his lingering smile. "You have just heard the name of a supreme Idealist; the Absolute Spirit he saw riding in the shape of Napoleon on a white steed is still with us. This thinker from Stuttgart set the pace of philosophy, and the best we can do is to try and cope with it. Hegel knew that a lot more was to happen in the course of the journey of humanity into the unknown, but, nothing daunted, he suggested that we should refrain from mentioning the future, for the destiny of mankind lies in the lap of the gods. He was solely offering a synoptic picture of the condition of the human race, and if at times the picture was hazy, well, so be it. Did not the owl of Minerva fly only at dusk?" The teacher rose, stepped to the only, flaky window in the room and stood against the panes, taking well-timed drags on a severely docked cigarette, his hollow eyes up to a congenial sun. Pens dropped noiselessly onto tops that bore the scars of arrow-transfixed hearts; fingers fumbled pincer-wise; eyes glowered at the pre-war chair on which the pupil selected for the oral test would soon be seated with his hands clasped at the back – doubt being a less idealistic yet handy method under the circumstances. On tenterhooks, the unhappy lot waited, but the end-of-class bell rang sonorously and, "That's all for the day, gentlemen," the speaker announced, using an appellative which seemed to be an ingrained habit of his, for he had not discarded it even when a pleasingly lavender-scented female specimen had entered the male preserve – an event of hardly any moment now because in the wake of a few suspicious looks at the chair the comely intruder had vanished and taken the fragrance with her. "We stay on the Stuttgart theorist for the rest of the week," the Hegelian conjurer let the audience know before leaving the classroom at a well-rehearsed pace. His exit left, as it customarily would, more than one rhetorical question hovering and a few fingers wiggling.

Within minutes Aldo and Dino were strolling along the public gardens at the core of their brick-and-mortar little town. They paused at the fountain basin that was the centrepiece of the green oasis and, leaning against the circular edge, watched the scatter of fawn fish darting in and out of the reflection of broken clouds in the water.

"D'you think they are aware of the mirror image in the basin?" Aldo asked while stirring the liquid.

"Most likely. They aren't blind like good old Tiresias, you see."

"Hang on a minute, mate. Eyeless as the ancient chap was, Zeus and Hera often turned to him for advice. And why did they? Simply because the Theban soothsayer was widely believed to be endowed with both attributes of Love." There followed a ripple of laughter and then, "by the way, I'm dying to find out if our Hegel fan has experienced love in the same way as Tiresias did."

The other dipped his hand into the water, upset the liquid with increasing oomph and contemplated the dazzle of flitting fins. "I believe that the fish are quite content with their own image of the sky," he finally asserted.

A couple of days later the Hegelian pundit came into view at the far end of the corridor, and wasn't he walking hand in hand with Tiresias? At close quarters the escorting figure exhibited the more familiar contours of the man's wife, and she could be seen to be holding gently his body by the arm, her fluffy red hair falling over her shoulders on either side of spirited green eyes – a beauty spot and a conspicuous touch of rouge on her cheeks striking a balance with her rounded, full-bosomed body:

doubtfully a Corinna look-alike, but not altogether devoid of feminine charm. "Our man's better half, he-he!" Aldo remarked and added promptly, "The only question is: which half?"

The woman let go of her less-deserving half smoothly and, flashing a smile at the appreciative onlookers, walked away wagging her bottom in glamorous Josephine Baker's fashion. Her consort sailed into the room, keeping the void at bay with outstretched hands, his pointed chin stretched up, his vacuous smile set in. Straight as an arrow, he made for his chair and took possession of it in front of an abruptly dumb class; his Braille-trained fingers and resonant voice checked up on present and absent and then he singled out a name.

Complying with the call, Aldo replaced the teacher on the seat, intertwined his hands at the rear of it and let his eyes follow the educator's steady steps up and down the room until "Do you see Hegel as a religious philosopher?" hit him at point-blank range. He pushed out the under lip, pondered and replied, "Hegel made use of Christian terms and praised the Christian religion for seeing God as a spiritual entity; yet he did not believe in a transcendent, omniscient being. In all frankness, I find his attitude a bit puzzling."

The examiner leant over and discreetly touched the lad's hands. "To be equally frank, you do seem to miss the point," he said. An explanation was given: "The fact is, Hegel made no great fuss of the Creator worshipped as the Father of Jesus worldwide. What mattered to him was that God is transcendent and as such entitled to a place in his system because the Spirit is everything." He moved to the window and stood at ease, his back facing an audience still engulfed in silence.

The lull was displaced by words bubbling out at a tempo as fast as the wriggle of Aldo's hands: "Likewise, the State is kind of intangible. Nobody can be a real somebody without the State because... because it, too, is everything. A power as such wants a strong leader... someone like..."

The questioner snapped his fingers. "Never mind the strong leader you are so eager to mention. You keep missing the main point, young man," he chipped in while moving two joined fingers with rhythmical strokes in the manner of a barber handling a cutthroat razor. His carefully measured pacing was resumed with a shake of the head. "The main point is that only the philosophical road leads to the realm of the Spirit, which is the Absolute". The man's forefinger went up in a lofty professional fashion. "Well above art and religion, philosophy holds the key to the casket of truth. That's what Hegel told the world, and I've done my best to pass the message on to you. Regrettably, it would appear that I have failed to get it across."

Aldo produced a quickly aborted smile and faltered out, "I… I've taken notes to the top of my bent and my fingers have been aching more than ever."

A sympathetic smile illuminated the other's face and was followed by "Quite honestly, I'm sorry to hear that." There was a brief pause and then, "although it's not a question of fingers, I daresay. Grey matter seems to be the culprit here. The crux of the matter lies in *Being*, *Nonbeing*, and *Becoming*. Unfortunately, I'm duty bound to suspect that you've been moving from the first stage to the second one, and, to be still absolutely honest, I dread to think what sort of thing your Becoming will be. You may regain your seat, dear fellow."

It sounded a chillingly mild statement. Aldo stood up with a hint of reluctance and traipsed back to his desk. Then and there, cheerfully insistent, the bell rang, but he gave little sign of sharing his classmates' elation.

Out in the street Dino was moving briskly along the cobbled street that would take him to a well-deserved repast when a finger poked him in the ribs and a voice affected by a dreadful test asked, "What about having a little stroll in the woods this Sunday?"

Conveniently located at several removes from the urban area, San Vito's Wood had been since the year dot a favourite haunt of nature-loving ramblers as well as of poets chasing elusive rhymes, butterfly collectors on a netting spree, and young couples escaping from family ties into the safety of bushy nooks. In the late afternoon, Aldo and Dino sauntered amidst aged boles – a legacy, the old story ran, of the illustrious folk from the Tiber – and the former's impromptu whistling and capering conveyed a thorough appreciation of things historical to the latter. Most wondrous of all was a somersault in sync with a strident laugh at the sight of a lizard, and the pleasing appearance was followed by the performer's recollection of the quaint little reptile he had captured at Uncle Raffaello's farm on a wartime hot summer afternoon. "It looked like a salamander to me, and salamanders thrive in the fire, don't they?" Aldo pressed on, and good gracious! wasn't he suddenly tall and ugly, endowed with a straggly beard, a mouth widening like jaws of a yawning crocodile, and eyes red like burning lanterns? Yes, there he was again, the fire-eater that had scared stiff a hapless wooden boy, and Dino had a sudden urge to cry "Have mercy, your Excellency!", but his chum sneezed once, twice, and owned that unfortunately the little beast was a cheat. A cheap and most popular cigarette leapt onto his lips; he lit it and took a long, ostensibly pleasurable, draw.

A sudden rustle of leaves made both peer through a bush: inside the foliage, a muscular male body lay sprawled out, submerging a shapely female form supine on the ferny soil. Blissfully oblivious to the inquisitive eyes, the pair was engaged in tossing and jerking of a quality that would have probably earned the blessing of the past master Ovid. Their mouths agape, the intruders stared at the ruddy mass of hair and the beauty spot on the woman's rouged face; then Dino shrank back and kept himself half concealed behind a tree until he saw his fellow stroller step nonchalantly on dry twigs and heard him titter, "Our visit is over. I think it was worth it, don't you? Now you know, and that makes two of us – unless he, too, knows, ha-ha."

The listener had a sense that the two of them had just been offered a display of human nature partly dressed in a not altogether idealistic fashion: surely Hegel had not minced his words when he had stated that only an objective spirit can aspire after an ethical life and entertain an idea of the Absolute; to all appearances the duo performing inside the bush were subjective spirits bound to comply with the urgent importunities of their empirical minds. Visibly disconcerted, he set off at a trot.

Aldo fell in step but came to a halt as soon as they reached the edge of the wood. "The Spirit is everything indeed. Alleluia!" he gushed while swerving to an oak tree; a beaver stream aimed at the sky and arched down to earth. When the steamy flow ceased, there was the sound of deep relief, and in quick succession something like "it's a black endless knight for Tiresias, mate." His classmate broke into a gallop.

Dino was a trifle late the following morning and tiptoed into the classroom, but his wary steps were perceived by the philosophy master and acknowledged with a little turn of the neck and a bow of the head accompanied by signs of assent in the direction of the whey-faced pupil occupying the chair in the prescribed posture. By the look of it the fearsome test was going swimmingly: "The Spirit Absolute is the pinnacle of the philosophical ascent," the examinee was heard to assert and, the marvel of it, a sunny smile was suffusing the face of the ardent Hegel acolyte; shortly afterwards, a chuckle brought a little cloud onto his radiant features and a slightly louder giggle made them whirl around and face the desk; dark sunglasses settled on its scratched panel and the tiny scrap of paper defiantly pinned to it. Dino gaped at the snippet and then gave a hard stare at the crater-like notch on the temple where a bullet had probably hit: by common consent the man was a casualty of war, but the surmise of a DIY botch-up broke there and then through the haze in the mind of the intrigued observer: he had never thought of it before, viz. of a doubtfully Hegelian response to a betrayal of a strictly personal – domestic? – nature. Like a runner all set for a spring he bent his body and closed his eyes. When they reopened, Aldo had already made the desk and was gingerly removing the paper, but the feeble sound did not escape the antennae of the eyeless man. "Continue," he said in a voice as thin as a saw blade whilst his features revelled in a feast of grimaces.

"The Spirit Absolute is everything," the chair-bound youth burst out. "And..."

A booming "Worm, miserable earthworm! I see Idealism going down the drain!" made the student sink into silence while the fingers of the philosopher-turned-inquisitor felt around his body. On a par with the contemptible burrowing creature, the captive squirmed and finally wriggled free. The vacated chair crashed to the floor and stayed on the tiles belly up like a mutilated octopus laying bare the remnants of its awesome tentacles. Boohoos that sounded like the asthmatic chugs of an old pump drawing up a well rent the thick air and mingled with spluttering cries about the Spirit Absolute that was everything.

Sedately, his meaningful features now a blank, the teacher headed for the window, groping about like a latter-day Cyclops outwitted by a blinding Odysseus. On reaching the shabby panes, his jerking hands pushed the frames outwards and his protruding head sniffed the air in the manner of a fish surfacing to catch a mirror image of the sky in its stone cage – or so it seemed to Dino. A packet of cigarettes emerged from a pocket in the gentleman's faded dun jacket, and it looked very much like another specimen of the cheap and exceedingly popular make cherished by Aldo. The off-white cylinder was set alight, and rings of bluish smoke spiralled up, flying arguably towards the transcendent being.

Inside the public gardens once more, Dino leant over the fountain basin and sank his eyes into the frothy water. Aldo, who had sneaked up on him and was now moving around the edge, would breathe a word about the philosophical accident in the classroom, at an educated guess, but no, "Have you ever bumped again into your Nut Farm sweetheart?" he was asking in a razor-sharp tone of voice and then adding, "you know, the little wench had something in common with my sister Brada."

Dino's adamant wagging of the head was followed by a sour-cream smile on his ball-shaped face and "I bet my boots that I will never see her again."

"Never say never. *Being, Nonbeing,* and *Becoming* – don't forget the dialectic, comrade!" The imperious manner made the listener suspect that the survivor of the Hegelian ordeal was, like the teacher puffing smoke into the atmosphere, endeavouring to make contact with the Spirit that was everything, absolutely everything.

3

THE NAME OF THE GAME

It was in the air and then it was on it: people were rioting up and down the streets of the provincial capital in the aftermath of the failure of the local soccer team to achieve promotion to the upper league. In the eyes of its supporters the referee's decision not to award a glaring penalty in stoppage time had signalled nothing short of a sell-out. The news of the official's misdeed had spread like wildfire, and "Betrayal! Betrayal" devoted fans were now chanting in the normally drowsy town; in a matter of hours, wavelets of indignation had grown into breakers.

Dino was quietly savouring a generous dose of risotto Bolognese when the extraordinary event pierced the silence in his room. The troubled spot was not far from home, and the proximity gave him itchy feet; admittedly, the feeling that had killed the cat in the well-known story was largely to blame for the peculiar sensation, but honest to God his entire body was burning with the desire of being a witness of history in the making (well, local history to say the least) as well as of complying with the ethical Kant's categorical imperative drummed into him by his idealistic philosophy teacher and still ringing in his ears. Furthermore, nobody else was at home – and this meant that the coast was clear as crystal.

Alas, the road looked far from clear while he cycled strenuously on his way to the place in turmoil: cars and motorbikes were moving fast and furious in the same direction, presumably steered by people incensed by the behaviour of the pipsqueak credited with enough sense to be in charge of the beautiful game. The bumbling fellow had manifestly never heard of Immanuel Kant, or he wouldn't have turned a deaf ear to his guidelines: surely they were applicable to the duties of football referees!

On reaching the leafy outskirts of the town at issue he saw fit to pursue his investigation on foot and tied his beloved Bianchi to a tree. A great number of men and, surprisingly, women were heading for the centre, and he felt it was his duty to follow the herd. In the high street leading to the showpiece Versailles-style edifice that had been a Royal Palace in dynastic times droves of marchers came within view and he judiciously kept his distance until he found himself drawn into a whirling motion of bodies, engulfed in a sea of faces roughened by the hue and cry, and in the midst of arms holding placards on which the word *VIVA* was followed by the name of the unfortunate team in question writ equally large above a caricature of the referee seen as a cuckold as well as a fraud. Apart from that, everything appeared to be in tune with the occasion; well, nearly everything: what about, say, the host of flags whose redness did not necessarily relate to the colour of the team logo, or about the profuseness of T-shirts embroidered with a big *A* on the front? Was it because when it comes to a crucial matter of justice, reason and emotions go hand in hand? If so, why were dark police vans disgorging young men equipped with uniforms, helmets and batons? Aha, where there's smoke there's fire! Granted, but who had started the smoke?

It wasn't long before the Law got engaged in a brisk confrontation with flag wavers and more than one *A*-logo wearer was seen up to the elbows in throwing pebbles at the cadets with the plastic gesture of ancient disc throwers. Dino glanced at his empty hands and weaved his way out of the crowd: he had come as an observer of history, and that was that!

Within minutes it just so happened that the youngster's flair for detachment failed to reach the consciousness of guardians of the nation's sense of law and order: whilst the observer of history leant as stiff as a board against the nearest wall, his pumpkin face aglow and his horn-framed eyes alight, a handful of uniformed striplings came at him, batons at the ready; before he could say Jack Robinson a hail of blows fell on adeptly chosen vulnerable parts of his compact body, strong hands grabbed him by the scruff of the neck and shoved him into a Black Maria on standby. In an instant, he was seated on a ledge which felt tangibly unkind to his buttocks and discerning the blurred shape of a few lads as well as, how marvellous but also perplexing, a small number of gals: visibly taken aback, as he himself had been, by the far-reaching and far from gentle arm of the Law, they were making the most of it by staring blankly at nothing in particular and presumably wallowing in muddy streams of thought. Then the engine roared into life and the van rolled away from the hot spot, heading at a slow but steady pace for a probably cooler destination.

It was no lengthy journey. The vehicle safely achieved its goal and a large yet scarcely heart-warming room received the unhappy lot. Long, tense minutes elapsed before the door opened with a derisive squeak, a ginger-haired head poked through the gap and eyes embedded in a stony face scrutinised the troublemakers now in sheltered accommodation. Dino scratched his head while considering himself in luck of sorts: after the perilous hullabaloo in the open, the poky enclosure had a cocooning feel about it. He addressed the inquisitive fellow: "I'd like very much to make a call to mum and dad, sir," he said. "Mind you, it's only to let them know that I am in safe hands." The tone was that of a considerate son and a law-abiding citizen.

"I do appreciate your fine sentiments, young man, but I'm in no position to oblige you. The thing is, you are not checking in at a hotel," came as an answer before the blank face withdrew and the door looked an impenetrable panel again.

Inching his way through the little crowd, Dino shuffled to a handy wall and leant against it, pondering over a sleepless night in the divine yet not very pleasurable arms of Themis.

In the hazy stillness of the dawn the newcomers were dislodged and requested to climb onto a metallic large van which looked as if it had been exempted for the nonce from its usual cattle carrier duty. En route some of the passengers, a couple of them manifestly past their prime (where were the girls now?), were heard to mutter about the way they were being treated by a self-styled civil authority. Sitting on yet another uncongenial plank, Dino peeped through a judas hole at the world now out of his reach: people were walking on the pavement, probably on their way to their legitimate places of work. Would they notice the official conveyance and spare a thought, if not a prayer, for the wretched creatures caged inside? Ahem, wishful thinking. None of the passers-by were casting even a cursory glance at the van: they were flitting by, obviously wrapped in their humdrum preoccupations. Dear! Dear! What was the world coming to? How could human beings concern themselves exclusively with their run-of-the-mill engagements as if no history-making event had occurred and no fellow creatures were being dragged to a place of segregation and punishment? "Come on, say it. None of your business, eh?" he growled in an undertone at the insensitive lot and heard an inner voice rejoin, *Ah, but a crime has been committed! There's no denying that.* He sniffed and countered, *Hold your horses. Whose crime? What about the referee's misbehaviour? The silly billy failed to blow his whistle, didn't he? Will he now receive a deserved rap over the knuckles from the supporters of civic virtues for his*

41

shameful conduct? But there! A sudden jolt and a screech of brakes prompted the captured lad to let an eye go through the peephole again: massive characters were inscribed on the front of an imposing ochre brick building. STATE PRISON, they read. The pathetically subservient lorry had made it.

The inside brought less than a modicum of comfort. Blinking eyes shifted along a narrow corridor flanked by walls crying out for a coat of decent paint and leading to a hall which looked exceedingly level with the passage. At the far end of the large room a hefty bloke abundantly past his prime sat behind an incongruously royal-blue desk, wearing a polka-dot shirt which enhanced tortoise-shell glasses and sporting a lump of grey hair slicked back in a style reminiscent of not too distant dreams of imperial grandeur. The contact with the arrivals was totally uninspiring: the official entered names and addresses in a thick margin-ruled register with the punctiliousness of a duteous accountant and subsequently requested peremptorily that the transgressors should surrender their personal belongings: belts, shoelaces and all. It might well prove a little tough on the owners, he conceded, but it was for a good cause, and the items would be returned to them in due course. The procedure was, needless to point out, strictly in agreement with the law they had so brashly contravened. Among the items which Dino handed in ruefully was his bicycle lock key. He rubbed his straggly hair and spouted, "Dear me! I've left my beautiful pushbike fastened to a tree. Could an officer kindly go and retrieve it for me? You see, it was my parents' present on the occasion of my finals, and I'm rather fond of it."

The receptionist gave him a penetrating look. "I'm sure your parents' gift is pretty safe just where you left it. Besides, it's against the rules to cycle anywhere inside this establishment," he let him know in dulcet tones.

The preliminaries over and done with, the uncalled-for

guests were escorted to a huge bluish-purple tinged room lamenting the passing of the years and invited to take possession of one or other of the straw mattresses that filled the place to capacity. Spoilt for choice, Dino picked up one at random and sat upright on it, waiting for things to happen, the story to unfold.

Before too long he was in the grip of a compound of anxiety and boredom and, as soon as a guard passed by, "Excuse me, chief, what's the next item on the agenda?" he inquired.

"A proper interrogation. That's what the next item on the agenda is, squire," the officer replied, fingering his clipped moustache. "But take it easy. You've got all the time in the world to get the feel of the place."

Before long a proper feel of the place was provided by the tickle of rather tepid water flowing by fits and starts from a communal shower tap while a guard stood, yawning, at the door; following that, by the taste of a similarly lukewarm as well as indifferent cappuccino served in a suspiciously off-white mug. Hours of tense idleness passed slowly and then it was time for lunch, which turned out to consist of a modest portion of spuds and desiccated meat to be washed down with water which had a tang of fluoride and saccharine in it. Dino touched his belly, and it felt as though a brick had replaced the pangs of hunger he remembered invariably experiencing on his way home at the end of the daily stint at his Palladio-style school.

The remainder of the day went by without the interrogation anticipated by the guard and when night finally came, the lad was only too glad to lie on his pallet with one arm at an angle across his forehead. Visual memories of the recent goings-on flooded in, and a lingering ache in his back reminded him of energetic cadets' limbs in full swing, but the images and the sensation paled into insignificance as soon as he thought of his parents and of how they must be seeing the occurrence as a misfortune bringing pain-cum-dishonour to the family.

43

He crinkled his sensitive nose and was assailed by a twinge of regret which was only assuaged by the consideration that there were extenuating circumstances in his case: apart from the pressure from an unconditional moral principle, being present where the feelings of a sport-conscious community had been trampled underfoot was the trademark of a conscientious citizen and no judge in his or her senses would regard his socially motivated behaviour as a crime. Surely his parents would presently know the truth, only the truth and nothing but the truth, and on the strength of it conclude that there was method in their son's seeming act of madness? Yes, mum and dad would confidently wait for a happy ending to the unhappy story. Well, then. In the teeth of the springless old sack he would sleep on the unfortunate incident. Come to think of it, he would be following the good example set by everybody else in the dormitory.

Well, almost everybody, to set the record straight: not much later his thoroughly deserved slumber was broken into by fitful bursts of snivel issuing from the bed adjacent to his own. He jerked up and peered into the semidarkness: a wisp-like teenager was sobbing. "Shush," he whispered, "or you'll have the whole dorm up in arms. Don't you see they are all peacefully sleeping?" By way of a confirmation, an assertive snore coming from the far end of the large room blended with the boy's gasps. "Come on," he went on with the demeanour of a solicitous elder brother, "there's no cause for worry. Neither you nor I will end up in front of a firing squad for having been on a demo." He fell silent and waited for a sober response, but in the absence of one he resumed his little sermon: "Though, to be candid about it, I'd rather face the squad than the music from my folks when I return home." It was a bit weak as a joke, he sensed immediately, but it did the trick: arguably, the thin-skinned fellow suspect was not one to be appeased only by a refined brand of humour, or, more likely, the way he felt about his own family was too deep

44

for tears. Whatever the reason, the sobs petered away, and pretty soon the snoring variations were making the only sound in the entire dormitory.

Dino was on his way back from the meal he had come to see as a travesty of justice when the prophetic guard stopped him with a request to report to the examining magistrate forthwith. He saw the sword of Damocles hang over him and stepped sideways, but in the twinkling of an eye he was in the presence of a middle-aged gentleman casually dressed and sporting the air of a dutiful servant of the Law. Little time was wasted in formalities. "Let's get down to bedrock," said the official, "have you joined the throng solely out of a passion for the unlucky team you presumably support?" Dino pursed his lips. A string of equally probing queries provoked answers that came through guttural sounds of assent and with the help of the mime that is the natural means of communication of an articulated puppet. A silent perusal of thickly typewritten notes, accompanied by a sequence of gentle strokes of the silvery-white growth of beard adorning the gent's judicial face, gave the watcher the heebie-jeebies, but they subsided as soon as he was told that, albeit under a cloud, he appeared to have an immaculate record; besides, a snapshot taken by one of the vociferous crowd and submitted by a cadet showed him standing well away from the protesters and innocent of a T-shirt with an *A* printed on it; he was a wolf in sheep's clothing, perhaps, but still the son of a professional man held in high esteem by his fellow citizens, including, needless to say, himself as a judge and a friend. Antecedents of the kind would undoubtedly speed up the ongoing investigation, and a remand in custody was not necessarily on the cards. The investigator released a full-blown smile while his hand sank into his briefcase and re-emerged holding a brown envelope. "It's for you, and do take a look at its content if you so wish. It would be absolutely legal," he said. "You will notice that the item is

45

open. *Dura lex, sed lex*, he added with a measured nod which intimated regretful recognition of the importance of the Roman dictum about the law being the law, harsh though it might be.

Dino lifted the flap of the envelope gingerly and brought out a record of '*Va, Pensiero*', the Hebrew slaves' choral song from Verdi's *Nabucco*. A tiny label stuck on the round piece of plastic read, "See you soon, dear son." So much for the silly joke he'd cracked to buck up the distressed boy the night before! The music he'd talked about had now come to him, and it contained notes of an altogether different quality. He cast a sheepish smile at the latter-day Solomon, but the smile broadened when he was informed that the quizzing was over and he was free to go – in a manner of speaking, naturally. He stood up, gave a low bow and dragged his heels out of the room, heading for the freedom of the courtyard.

A football match was in progress, and the spectacle brought a wry smile onto Dino's face. "Oh no, not again," he muttered. "Be a good sport and join the fray!" one of the inmates shouted, and he responded by getting rid of his bulky specs and mingling with the players. His short legs ran nimbly up and down the gravelly pitch until the foot of a half-back tripped him up and made him lose his balance; a hard look at his aching ankle gave him scant solace, but on second thoughts his face broke into a tidy smile: the accident had a silver-lining by virtue of having occurred inside the penalty area. On cue, the sound of a whistle was heard, and, "Go on and kick the ball into the back of the net, chief!" a member of his team bellowed, but he waved a dismissive hand, tapped a finger on his naked eye, and let the chap have a go. The outcome of the kick was a goal whose technical beauty was barely spoiled by the goalkeeper's index and little fingers stuck up hornlike. Regrettably, it turned out to be the only score in the match, for soon it was time to leave the flagged ground and return to the encampment. Dripping with sweat, Dino went to retrieve his glasses, but where were they? Swaying his head, he embarked on a hectic search supported by roars of laughter from his fellow players. Cut to the quick, he boomed: "We'll soon see who's having the last laugh. I intend to report this shameful thing to the proper authorities, and the culprit will end up in jail, I promise you." The joke might well have the quality of a punch line in a not very sophisticated farce, and yet it proved no dud; he wondered if the electrifying atmosphere of a cooler had kindled bright sparks when he saw the penalty scorer come to him, waving the bone of contention and saying with a grin on his suntanned face, "You're in the company of honest people in here, you know, and allow me tell you that if the duffer on the pitch in the town everybody's talking about had blown his whistle as promptly as our referee has just done, we wouldn't have the pleasure of your company now, he-he-he." The hearer acknowledged that the guy was talking a good deal of sense and fully deserved a tap on the shoulder. By the looks of it, he was making friends.

In the small hours of the following day he caught a glimpse of an attempt at a doubtfully orthodox kind of friendship. While resting on his pallet in a sea of sleepiness dotted with blue tiny lights regularly spaced out on the walls, he wondered whether he was actually occupying a makeshift bed inside a tent at a jamboree campsite and lying close to a boy with whom he had just played Cub Scout games. He screwed up his eyes against the softly lit background: a dark silhouette was moving with the sinuous grace of a prairie wolf, and didn't it belong to the Scout leader engaged in a routine night patrol? The conjecture was nipped in the bud by a voice muttering, "Hey, what the deuce d'you think you are doing?" Peering into the penumbra, he discerned the shape of a hand sliding along the still fully-dressed body of the boy and then moving jerkily away from it with a gesture that strikingly resembled that of the goalkeeper in the aftermath of the violating penalty kick; a harder look captured the intruder's vanishing form. "The body is the soul," he remembered being told by Don Orsino while discoursing on the integrity of human bodies being violated by men at each other's throats; "It may well be so, Padre, but the fact remains that I've had enough of the body as well as the soul for one night," he mumbled and kept as quiet as a mouse while waiting for a deep slumber that would put him out of his misery.

The compound was covered in mist, and when he went outdoors for a constitutional, low cotton wool clouds gave him a sense of being lost along a Milky Way all of his own. In a bid to work out his position he spun round and stretched out his arms, hoping that they would eventually point to the magnetic north, and he had almost completed the gyration when somebody else's arms came into contact with his own. A forehead surmounted by a remarkable quiff materialised trough the haze and a grating albeit benevolent voice said, "Having a workout? Well, then the gym is the place you want, young man." He felt that offering a geomagnetic explanation of his jerks to the uniformed author of the suggestion was somewhat out of order; mumbling thanks, he turned the corner and, keeping his eyes shut, moved in the direction indicated by his inborn needle. His eyes reopened within an inch of a collision with the inmate who had reunited him with his spectacles on the makeshift pitch.

"Tell me, do you ever indulge in a bit of snout?" asked the man through a chink in fleshy lips holding a cigarette at an angle.

"Well, I, er, don't mind the occasional cig," he burbled.

The tube of paper came off the mouth and was handed over with words such as, "The fag is all yours, but don't smoke it. Just take a gander at the inside."

Goggling in amazement, Dino obliged and, wonders will never cease, a flimsy scrap lay in the midst of the crushed leaves. "Jesus!" he gasped out. "It beggars belief, I must say."

48

"It comes from the female wing, you know," the donor revealed with a 'see-what-I-mean' wink which intimated one in the eye for the prison apparatchiks.

In the grip of excitement, the recipient extracted the tiny roll and unfolded it. A message jutted down in minuscule characters leapt out at him: "I've heard of you from A," it read. "As soon as both of us are out of this bog there will be an old pals' reunion. Join the party, comrade. B."

"Phew!" he breathed out: who could B and A possibly be? "I wonder who…" he began with feigned composure.

"Let's have a word on the quiet, my friend," the other chipped in, and the word that followed was about a tight-knit fraternity sadly misunderstood by too many people up and down the country. He happened to be one of the brothers and hell-bent on fighting for a fair share of the big national cake: it was a matter of pure business and nothing personal, of course; all the rumours about trafficking in drugs and humans, especially girls, on top of money laundering, were nothing but the slander of venomous politicians in league with judges and cops. Besides, what about the wheeling and dealing of those on high? "We are no shit. We have nothing in common with the fat cats that prowl about in the corridors of power, I tell you!" the bloke stated with a smirk. "Still, it's good to see some of them purr as soon as we stroke them with a hand full of dough," he added in a crescendo. "There's more to it than meets the eye!", he exclaimed while his forefinger pulled down his lower eyelid, and in the next breath Dino was told how the authorities knew only too well that the members of the Family to which he belonged were the heirs of the brave *picciotti* – 'young pigeons', he explained for good measure – who had followed Don Peppino and fought for the liberation and unification of the country. Don Peppino, it became clear in the context, was none other than Giuseppe Garibaldi. Sure enough, the organisation was a secret one, but then had not the other great Giuseppe – Mazzini, he meant (no

Don before the name this time) – resorted to secret societies for the good of the nation about to be born?

It sounded like an intriguing historical analysis and therefore well deserving of an appreciative nod, which was duly given. Soon afterwards, the assenting listener felt as if he'd been hit by a bombshell, for he was being warmly invited to join the confraternity. "I've a hunch that you are just the type we're after, and you have my word of honour that my blood brothers would welcome you with open arms," the chap continued. "You see, I've been informed that you are a well-educated young man, someone who does not take part in a demo only because a dickhead posing as a referee has turned a blind eye to a big foot put out to trip a fellow player. And we have lot of time for brains of your sort. A pep-talk to less educated young men would be of great help, I'm sure. Are you giving us a hand, brother?" He paused, but his beady eyes signified a burning desire for a positive reply.

"I hope there will be a new, big society in our country," the reply was.

"Ha-ha, this new, this big society will never be, will never be," the other countered, echoing a smash hit. "Now, will you take my offer?"

In consonance with the sacred oath sworn by members of the brotherhood epitomised by his interlocutor, Dino opted for silence. Suppose, just suppose that, after being received by the Family as one of them, he, by virtue of being quick on the uptake, were to get higher and higher on the promotion ladder and, goodness knows, end up as a Don one fine day! Well, well, well. It was a perplexing prospect, to put it mildly. He tightened his lips, and they felt as dry as sandpaper. He looked upwards as though praying for assistance from those quarters.

His pleading face appeared to warm the cockles of the jailbird's heart. "No cause for concern, guv. We are all men of honour, as everybody in our country as well as in every other country on earth knows only too well," he asserted with a grin which displayed long sharp teeth.

"I… I'm s-sure you are", he managed as a comment.

Bravo! *Bravissimo*! Please give me an answer before you leave the slammer. They will allow you to go out of here very soon, you can count on that, but I'll let you have a phone number in no time. Only, don't be a schmuck. It's between you, me, and the gatepost, *capisci*?" The bloke touched the lad on the shoulder with a stick in a quasi-ceremonial fashion, and the dubbed conspirator bowed his head and gave a reassuring nod: was he complying with a moral obligation engendered by someone who belonged to an updated secret and just as honourable society? "*Arrivederci*, brother," the principled member whooped, his jagged teeth on full display once more, and moved on, whistling another popular tune, which was about evil-life boys singing a serenade to a comely girl and finally bursting into tears.

The abruptly 'made' brother walked back to his allocated pallet, stretched his body out on the uncongenial mattress and while tuning in resignedly to a relentless snore thought deeply about the encounter in the misty courtyard. It had been a remarkable episode and no mistake, but who on earth were B and A? He snorted and worked himself into a fluster until the idea sprang into his mind that 'A' might well stand for Aldo. Had not his former classmate told him that he had a little sister called Brada, who might just as likely be the scribbling B? The conjecture put him at ease. Still, the question was: could the girl be seen as a passionate supporter of the unfortunate team? Or was she having a go at a political version of the game? He extended his arms and made them move in a circle while breathing deeply in and out. Come to think of it, the prospect of meeting B was a far cry from a bore; as to a renewed contact with A, well, that was another kettle of fish.

One day later, the detainee was bound to acknowledge that the expectations of the secret fraternity member were well founded: the official wearing a polka-dot shirt and tortoise-shell glasses approached him with the news that he would set free in the morning. He was indeed and walked out of the place of confinement on a cushion of air. When he bestowed a farewell glance on the barred windows in the upper building, a loud cry hit his ears. He shot a keener look, and there he was, the brotherhood fellow, flashing a winsome beam and flailing his arms. He responded with a moderate wave of the hand, and it dawned on him that the 'brother' had failed to give him his phone number. So be it: he wouldn't dream of being granted another opportunity of securing the key to an entry into a tight-knit family.

It wasn't long before his parents welcomed him back with tears in their eyes, as the members of a no less closely integrated family were expected to do. He savoured the homecoming and the regained liberty, not to mention the tidings that his cherished pushbike had been retrieved and was waiting for collection at the nearest police station. As soon as he was back in his room he had a proper listen to the Hebrew slaves' appeal to Thought immortalized by Verdi (another Giuseppe, come to think of it). The poignant lament over the beautiful country the captives had lost made the penny drop, and it sounded the nearest thing to a Kantian category: penalty was the name of the game.

4

OF KNIGHTS AND BUTTERFLIES

More than one year had elapsed, and where were now all the old familiar faces? Had they vanished into Tiresias' night and stayed there like actors waiting in the wings for their next turn on the stage? Time after time, Dino mulled over the clandestine invitation he had received while feeling the arm of the law, and one morning he came out of bed with half a mind to make a closed book of the conundrum. The book was shut and stayed so until a letter from Aldo landed on the hall floor: could he join him and his sister Brada on a houseboat, the sender was asking? They might have a chat on the long school years they had shared and even reminisce about Nut Farm; moreover, a little surprise was in store. Directions were duly enclosed. "Whoopee!" the recipient squawked while making the letter flit up to the ceiling: his guess about A and B had been far from wild. "Aldo and Brada, here I come!" he croaked in anticipation.

At the weekend, he stood close to the siblings on the upper deck of the boat the twosome had occupied while it squatted, forlorn and pregnant with the salt tang of the sea, on the fringe of a cove. Aldo struck him as the eternal schoolboy clinging to a realm of bygone certainties, Brada as a truncated Amazonian specimen equipped with aggressive fawn eyes. And there they were, the three of them, imbibing more than a snifter of whisky and soda while looking at one another in the manner of survivors of a shipwreck.

"I'm curious to know if our philosophy teacher is still pacing up and down our classroom," Dino said as they chewed the fat, and his former classmate gave him an amused look at the same time as, lying back awkwardly on a decrepit sofa, his sister disclosed that she'd been thinking long and hard about the system as a manipulator of their lives and had concluded that delivering a good kick in the leviathan's buttocks was an absolute must; she sounded old as Socrates and young as the guerrilla affectionately known as Che. Her eyes focussed on a book peeping through a chink in the sofa. "Fancy that!" she whooped, "isn't it the old romance my spinster teacher thrust upon me when I was under her sway? In all frankness, I came to like it – especially the bit where Orlando goes nuts."

Off at a tangent, her brother pointed to a stuffed, life-size clown lolling in a drab rocking chair and tittered, "I'm sure he kept his master in high spirits." He paused briefly. "Incidentally, I wonder what Gero's doing with himself these days. Any recent news from his quarter?"

Her reply was a haughty laugh coupled with the info that the character in question had galloped away on the steed he was exceedingly fond of, started up a manège, lost his fabulous quadruped and not long after that gone one better by mislaying the ring that Angelica, his sweetheart, had given him. "Fortune to the lovers is unkind," she remarked, sounding kind of epic; then, turning to Dino who was sitting on a frayed hearthrug in a corner of the lounge, she hissed, "good job the quizzing chap loosened his clutches on you, comrade. I wasn't so lucky; I went on trial, was found guilty and put on probation."

Her lucky comrade pulled a long face, but his features regained their customary roundness quick as a flash. "A snap and a police cadet helped me out, you see," he said.

"Handy to have a cop on your side, isn't it?" she countered with a shrinking smile. "Now, to hark back to Orlando et al, what did you make of all those knights and maidens when you were at school?"

His lineaments tensed up again: knights and damsels were a thing of the past, yet the name of the young woman facing him rang a bell. "No fun intended, Brada, but did your parents give your name a bit of a clip when you were little?"

"Not to my knowledge. I've been Brada all my life, as far as I remember."

He sought refuge in Aldo and saw flecks take place on the face of the former son of the fasces. Seconds later he heard him say, "I can see someone from your extended family" and turned round: Lando, his country cousin of old, was stepping down from a pearly-grey motorbike and approaching with a smile which seemed to have lost none of the young sweet-corn flavour. The appearance out of the blue made him feel happy as an earwig in a ripe apricot.

"How's everybody?" the arrival asked before veering round to Dino and chiming, "Ciao, cousin. It's great to see you again."

"Lando! You surely catch me on the hop. I, er, I…"

"Welcome, comrade!" Brada chipped in, gay as a lark. "There will be plenty of time for a tête-à-tête with your cousin. Feeling peckish? There's some nice grub to hand."

The stuffed timbale she promptly doled out with the gusto of a solicitous hostess had gone cold, but the carmine wine from the Etna region felt as warm as a sunbeam from the Apollo-blessed isle. A few swigs had been swallowed and utterly relished when she intoned, *"El pueblo unido jamas serà vencido"*, while her eyes, masked by dark lashes, swept the audience.

Lando didn't miss his cue. "Aha, the barricades, the sit-ins, the combats, the chanting! Power to the People!" he enthused. "When I..."

Aldo poured cold water on the fire. "It was all well and good, but where were the factory workers and the peasants while we students chanted?"

A long silver-tipped cigarette leapt to Brada's lips and, keeping the tube in a precarious balance, she suggested a stroll on the beach.

"What a good idea!" Dino exclaimed while clapping her on the shoulder, and he headed for a sandy stretch of coastline, which struck him as a granular body disfigured by nonchalant ramblers. The others followed him.

"It would appear that we're treading on the remains of a summer-long rape," said Aldo.

From the far end of the cove a young woman advanced alongside a darksome young man, waving at regular intervals. "Ciao everybody," she hailed, her golden tresses tumbling over her shoulders, her flowery skirt fluttering in the breeze.

"My goodness, where did you spring from?" Aldo roared with a jaunty wave of the hand.

Dino goggled at the appearance: had Clotho worked herself into a spin while up to the elbows in her stern duty? Or was the fateful goddess a calculating spinster? He tensed up, frowned, relaxed. "Where's Tesorino?" he enquired flatly, and Ange – for it was none other than she – widened her milk-white arms while shadows of regret formed in her sloe-shaped eyes. "This is Medo," she announced, pointing at her companion; "a civil servant, lucky him!" Her forefinger prodded the fortunate fellow in the ribs, and he responded by giving a faint smile and a slight nod. "I was told of your whereabouts, folks. The bush telegraph is not a preserve of the Hottentots, you know," she added.

"I say, it's been donkey's years since Uncle Raf's days," Dino remarked while extending his arms as though in an attempt to keep the phantom of a shady past at bay.

"Oh, *that* man!" she cried. "He came unstuck, didn't he? Well, I suppose that you and I have finally cottoned on: your big uncle had got a score to settle with a few young men fighting from the hills, and he threw his boomerang: it came full circle, of course, but then it was a vicious circle."

"All of us had got a score to settle," Brada barged in. "A place in the sun and all that bloody palaver. Bollocks, nothing but bollocks! Little though I was when the shenanigans went on, I felt pretty bad about them. I kept quiet for years and years, biding my time. Now that I'm a woman I feel more strongly than ever about what's been taking place in our country since the bloody war, and it's my belief that the opportunity I've been waiting for has come. You can say whatever you like, folks; nothing will make me change my mind." There was more anger than sorrow in the elevated pitch of her voice.

Ange turned away and tripped to the sea edge, her hair bobbing up and down as it had regularly done at the farm, her skirt dancing the old country dance; Aldo sprang up and loped to her, followed by Lando who trotted and flapped his arms in a horse rider's fashion; Medo waddled to the houseboat, whereas Brada sank into her settee and lit another stylish cigarette. Dino stayed put, gaping at Lando's pearly bike and experiencing an uncalled-for pang of jealousy.

In the evening, Ange was introduced by Lando to the intricacies of quantum mechanics. Dino overheard his cousin expand on the novel theory that dealt with the baffling behaviour of elementary particles and atoms, and he found himself declining sotto voce "*quantum, quanti, quanto*" without too much of an effort. Latin aside, Isaac Newton's established laws of gravitation made lot of sense to him since, like the celebrated physicist, he had seen an apple drop from his garden tree and for good measure had felt the force of the impact of the fruit on his head. He cocked his ear, but Lando had now shunted the conversation onto the less demanding subject of his moonlighting as a huckster of purses and handbags at college. Then a quantum leap did occur, and it led to a magical casement opening onto a vista of knights, damsels, love and war in an exotic land. At the end of it all, Ange was heard to declaim, "It's a bit of an old hat, my dear Lando."

A short while later, they were all sitting in a circle on a dilapidated carpet, their eyes fixed on Brada as she lit up, hinted again at the "them-and-us" topic, and revealed her long-standing itch to give the system a wallop. "It's just to find out if it has the lives of a cat," she explained.

Medo's beaver face clouded over, but it cleared whilst he pointed at a tawny hawk in a poster. "I have a penchant for the b-bird," he disclosed while negotiating a minor difficulty in his vocal cords. "A bit of a hunter for sure, but a hunter blessed with first-rate eyesight." He gave a short cough. "Besides, he doesn't shrink from fighting for space when another hunter comes too close for c-comfort."

Lando recognised that it was a perceptive assessment, definitely worthy of a thought after the revolution, and he stared at the grin on the phiz of the clown still settled in his rocking chair.

Brada hummed a worker protest song before concentrating on her sizeable portion of spaghetti submerged in blood-red sauce. The fork she'd been twirling adroitly straightened when Aldo argued that labourers were mere components of an industrial machine oiled to a tee, but the serviceable tool went askew again as soon as Medo made a reference to students setting up barricades and then pulling them down swift as lightning.

Lando grasped the opportunity. "Students are in an endless state of flux, and it would take a quantum jump to measure their position and momentum. But then, there's something called the uncertainty principle to be reckoned with," he asserted.

Brada's fork regained its uprightness. "Comrades, how do

you feel about launching an attack on Power Fort?" she asked. "We can do that; we *must* do that."

Medo coughed again and cleared his throat before retorting that the fort holders had a knack for survival. "Just like the fellow hanging th-there," he commented while anchoring sympathetic eyes on the predator on the wall. The notion gave the others pause for thought: they lowered their eyes and concentrated on the succulent victuals waiting to be consumed.

After supper, Brada lolled again on the smelly sofa and a dog-eared copy of the Red Book made contact with her reasonably large breast. One red-and-white-socked leg suddenly raised into the air suggested a reverie about ghastly establishment figures. Instead, she said, "Now's the time to make you privy to my simple plan, comrades," and it transpired forthwith that her simple plan was to get Medo soused and then have him, properly tied up, sitting close to a decent amount of food and wine. Admittedly, it would be something like the Tantalus ordeal all over again, but it was for a worthy cause this time. "If our friend is resilient like the big shots ensconced in their palaces, he'll pass the test without too much bother," she averred with a little yawn.

Ange would have none of it. "My old friend Medo is a respectable employee of the government and I wouldn't like to see him turned into a guinea pig," she rejoined with overtones of resentment.

"What if he's come to us for a bit of low-down?" Aldo put forth. "In your shoes, I would delete the word 'guinea' from the sentence, darling."

Brada produced a fully assenting nod. "I'm sure the character in the poster will have the last laugh," she predicted even though the hawk did not seem to be grinning for the moment: as a matter of fact, the bird of prey had the grave countenance of a pallbearer.

Dino got to his feet and trudged up to the deck. A moon slightly short of fullness put him in a melancholy mood and he cast more than one rueful look at the quasi-complete celestial body while walking with slow paces to and fro. The abrupt perception that he wasn't the only one up there brought him to a halt. At a short distance, Ange and Aldo were murmuring about things such as an angelic beauty, an evil dream and, after an uncanny pause, throes of love. The interchange evoked utterances recorded in a romantic epic, and the eavesdropper was all ears when the voice of the quondam Nut Farm girl reached him like the silvery echo of a mother's lullaby: "There is an island in the midst of the sea, and a king's daughter holds sway over it," she was recounting in a strange singsong voice.

"And every swain that lands there, pays his toll and kisses her fair," was Aldo's counterpoint in a similarly rising-and-falling rhythm. A brief silence occurred before he tagged on, "I can see a comely damsel standing close to me."

"Why not a butterfly?" came as a rejoinder.

In the stillness of the late-night hour their voices wafted along as reverberations of sounds wafting from a remote region where soft lullabies and chivalric speech would meet and uncannily blend.

The uncertain light of the early morning allowed a hazy view of Brada looking in earnest as she strode in front of her guest now trussed to the rocking chair from which the legitimate occupier had been finally dislodged. She sounded adamant when, putting on a taut face, she stated, "One class succumbs and another survives," and in the next breath, "history is in the making, and the working class is on the road to victory."

Medo appeared lost in thoughts of his own until he muttered, "You and your fellow travellers have a long way to g-go."

Her sickle-shaped lighter rasped and snicked before she asserted, "Revolution Road is long and hard. Where there is fight, there is sacrifice." Gently, very gently, the chair squeaked. Her skirt swished as she walked away.

A veil of thin murk hung over the lounge and, oh marvel, the houseboat was now a corsair ship, and an executioner was emerging from the mist and bearing down on a man condemned to walk the plank. Step by step, the sinister figure took on the less ominous features of Aldo, who was soon leaning over Medo and relating how, as an altar boy, he had on a drowsy afternoon sneaked into the parish church sacristy, snatched a wafer and swallowed it. Needless to add, he had promptly gone to confession. "The ways of the Lord are numberless, my child," the priest had murmured in a suitably hieratic tone, and he had glimpsed a seraphic smile pervading the confessor's liturgical features. As expected, he had been granted absolution, and the only proviso was that he should recite the Lord's Prayer and the Hail Mary(in Latin, needless to say, and fifty times over) – both supplications being absolutely essential for a cleansing of the soul and a rout of the fiend from hell. Less arcane had been the priest's request that he should abstain for three weeks from indulging in the lollipop on which he had a habit of spending a modest portion of his pocket money: it would be a salutary act of mortification. Admittedly, the man of God had got a point there, but the fact that he had placed himself as a mediator between him and a tasty toffee still stuck in his gullet.

Dino was in no position to ascertain the effect of Aldo's disclosure, and it came to him as an unholy stroke which added to the doubtfully orthodox quality of the whole picture. The aftertaste lingered on for the remainder of the long, tense day.

The evening sky was embellished with a full-blown moon. Familiar voices reached Dino through mother-of-pearl beams.

"Are you a virgin or a mother?"

"A virgin may be banished in order to make room for the mother."

"Must it be so? Must the victim be cast into the wilderness so that a new birth may occur and the soul be saved? The soul is a stranger on earth and meanders alone just as butterfly does."

"I have dreamt of butterflies more than once. Long time ago I was told that I would never grow into one."

A stray beam exposed Lando in the act of eagerly getting hold of Ange's hand and clutching it.

"How icy," she wailed.

"And just as icy is the hand that is gripping my heart," he uttered likewise. "I... I." Wet eyes glistened in the overwhelming light from above. "I am no longer the Lando of yore," he owned.

She freed her hand and sashayed down the deck.

On the morrow, a rainy spell kept everybody indoors. Confined to the hull, Dino squinted at huge drops lashing down the porthole and glowered at the display of breakers arching and riding roughshod over the fluid body to which they belonged. Behind him the reincarnate Tantalus was sedately going through the hoop, and it made sense to wonder how long he would endure it: Brada had promised only a mock, but her approach appeared to be going beyond the limits of a playful trick. However, the whey-faced civil servant looked increasingly like the joker in the pack: would his resilience impinge on the effectiveness of the mock? It also made sense to take Ange and her close relationship with the captive into proper account; it was no cinch to get rid of a suspicion that further mischief was brewing behind the scenes. As if on cue, Aldo sneaked up to him and asked calmly, "How much do you know about Ange, old boy?" The question cropped up as a turn-up for the book, and Dino scratched his head: Ange had been a frequent companion of his at Nut Farm, yet how much had he gathered about her? She was a girl, and to what extent can a boy really know a girl, he wondered? Still, Aldo was waiting for an answer and he replied, "Ange? She and I played games together at my uncle's farm, and that's all I can say."

A smirk pervaded the other's features. "Please, Dino! Don't come the faux-naïve with your ex-classmate," he snarled.

Dino squirmed, but by a fortunate coincidence Lando emerged like a knight errant keen to save a fellow traveller in dire straits. "Maybe Lando can tell you more about Ange," he blurted out, only to see his cousin shake his head. His back now to the wall, he tried a desperate sortie. "Why not pump Medo for a bit of info? A mouthful of pasta and a glass of wine on the quiet may well do the trick," he suggested.

Aldo smacked his lips. "Thanks a million for the thought. A little bit of squealing would be music to my ears," he replied in the manner of a boy scout vowing to do the prescribed daily good deed for the rest of his life.

When night came, the vault of heaven was cloudless again and the sea had the evenness of a millpond. Standing in a corner of the deck, Dino ruminated on quantum leaps until he was distracted by the renewed presence of Lando and Ange. Now Lando was telling her how he had dreamt of standing close to a stream and feeling at ease until a gust of wind had hit his face. "I heard a voice in the wind, and it was your voice," he was expressing in a murmur. "But your face was not in it, and I... I was afraid."

The secret listener's eyes homed in on the girl gracefully holding two goblets and urging his cousin to partake of a little Burgundy; then, her long eyelashes in a flutter, she was inquiring whether he believed that they were doing the right thing.

"You'd better ask the quaint creature on the wall about that. Hawks have the reputation of being politically correct creatures, haven't they?" the other replied, but a noise like a stamping of feet made both dash into the lounge.

Keeping his distance, Dino tiptoed on their trail. A conversation between Brada and Medo was in full swing.

"You don't fancy this houseboat much, I suspect," she was saying. "The frayed curtains, I bet. Or is it the light? It's like that of candles in a church, eh?"

Medo's answer came through a tentative smile, but Ange

showed up and chipped in, "Our guest's starved. I see a man fighting for survival." She sounded genuinely concerned.

"Shush, comrade; we, too, were starved – of dignity and freedom, among other things – and we, too, fought for survival," Brada thundered, her fawn eyes twinkling with a reddish hue. "You remember, comrades? We came together, we roared, we sang: 'The Egg of the World, the Egg of the World!'" Staring into the heroic, resonant past, she waved the woman sign.

The captive dropped his head and kept it down; his arms rested flabbily on his legs, and the overall picture was that of a dejected alter ego of the clown still grinning stoically from the allotted corner. His guard embarked on a to-and-fro strut, her arms intertwined behind her back in the posture of a schoolteacher confronting a wayward pupil. "You're playing with fire, my friend – the fire of truth, I mean, and you know that you can't put it out because your foam is made of lies, a whole mountain of lies," she put to him while staring at the floor carpet.

Would Medo, fastened to his chair as the sorcerer Brunello had once been to a big fir, finally give vent to his chagrin and woes? A laconic "Grrr" signalled that he would not. Then his head jerked, his tongue stuck out, and his entire body went into convulsions. Brada squared up to the spectacle like someone who had seen it all before. If in possession of a horn she probably would have blown her defiance on it as Roland had done in the good old days of chivalry; lacking the instrument, "Calm down, brother, please," she urged with a softer sound. "Fake hysterics are not in a dobber's stock of magic tricks; because you *are* a dobber, aren't you?" Her tone evoked a bygone youth which was still a spring of beauty. Then, confronted with the prisoner's head swaying in denial, "Come on!" she shrieked. "Just let me hear that your decrepit establishment has the lifespan of a cockroach, and all shall be well." Medo's shakes eased; his head swayed up and down; his eyes glazed over and disappeared behind his closed eyelids; a jelly-like blob trickled out of his nostril.

Oh hell! What was going on? Dino stood transfixed to the spot in utter disbelief. Was Ange rushing to the trussed-up man with an apple in one hand and a knife in the other? Also, was she really dabbing at the blob on Medo's face and then scuttling off in a flash, apparently unaware of the tool still on the chair? The onlooker wiped his lenses: knife in hand, Medo was now making frantic efforts to cut the Gordian knot, and a trickle of blood was followed by Aldo's leap to the chair only to be beaten to it by Ange who had buckled down to taking care of the injured civil servant. Dino's eyes narrowed on Aldo's ashen face and widened on Brada standing seemingly unconcerned and letting bluish rings of thick smoke – her militant idea in the midst of them – spiral into the void. Close to both, Medo lay helpless as a babe, his eyes and mouth open to a slit, his features filled with the smile of a sulky child finally at peace with himself and the whole world. Leaning over him, Ange was heard to say in a low murmur, "Do not desert me, dear Medo. I shall be with thee and all shall be well, I swear." The lingering presence of a spent force seemed to be hovering all over the place, but a loud 'aha-a-a-a!' tore into the silence. Amazingly in the buff, Lando was bellowing as he galumphed around the lounge at full tilt, smashing crockery in the way, tearing the bird from the wall and ripping open the mesmerised clown, but before too long he came to a standstill and flashed a seraphic smile around followed by, "Requite Rogero's love, Bradamante. And thou, Angelica, don't yield to fear – the furious Orlando will be restored to sanity!" Then, quick as a flash, he was out of sight.

Groping through the haze, Dino reached the young woman who'd been his playmate at a sun-baked farm. "Do you remember the railway station on that September night?" he asked; "the crowd surging up like rollers, and you and I in the middle of them? I waved like crazy. Did you see me?"

"Yes, I saw you," she let him know while carefully carrying Medo out of the room.

What Dino said next followed her like a shadow. "My mother took me away from Nut Farm, but I didn't want to go. Do you want me to leave me now?" he asked.

Her dark, slanted eyes alighted on him; eerily subdued, her voice sounded as if emanating from the heroine in the epic poem he had read at the Palladian shrine of Minerva. *Love and war are naught but frenzied rage*, it quoth. Then she and her darling were gone.

He scuffed to the nearby porthole and contemplated banks of clouds drifting at ease. A fleck peeped out from a silky envelope and a butterfly glided along, dancing in a speck of blue. Seizing the blissful moment, the iridescent creature spread out her flaxen-speckled wings before losing herself in the virginal expanse.

5

LEAVING BRUNNHILDE

Once upon a time there was a farm, and a man wearing a black shirt owned it. A bridled heifer would graze in the fields and a neighbouring little girl would often pay a visit to the boy who'd been taken there as to a place well away from a hideous war. At a later time, there was a classroom, and a latter-day Tiresias padded within its walls, offering a vision of the Spirit Absolute to short-sighted hopefuls. Subsequently, there was a houseboat where knights and damsels acted out their heroics and a butterfly made her nest until she took wing and vanished into the sky. What next? Aha, Father Time was holding out a finger in the direction of a perfect *O*…

Glued to the window of the train on which he had hopped early in the morning in the company of his father, Dino felt that there was no way back to his beautiful garden, or up to the blush-pink wall from whose top he had gazed at his cherished persimmon tree or stuck his neck out for a peep at a man with a wolf's soul. The day he had come out of the oasis the tree was covered in blossom, but the chunk of brick was falling into decay as though it, too, had been hit by the warhead that had deprived the local Lilli Marlene of the limelight under her customary lamppost. He had been offered a few crumbs of comfort at Nut Farm and then entered a Palladian storehouse for proper nourishment, but not even an eyeless far-seeing champion of idealism had been able to provide him with the bread that is the staff of life, and he was still hungry. To cap it all, Father Time appeared to be loath to put the clock back so that he might re-enter the garden of old... Heaving a sigh, Dino returned to the present and what went with it: the train he was on, for instance, was so much faster than the string of caffèllatte carriages that had taken him away from the farm at the end of a long, sundried summer! He poked his head outwards and let it become enveloped in floating wisps of steam as the train whizzed past a small rural station where a guard stood upright, duly responding with a wave of the flag to the unstoppable progress of the wagons. With a complacent smile, the lad pivoted and faced his parent seated at ease and holding tight the lavishly illustrated guidebook he had purchased before departure; it appeared to demand his undivided attention and allow communication only by means of a short arm waving in circles, which intimated a thorough appreciation of the contents. He came away from his vantage point and regained his place close to the man until a succession of emphatic whistles signalled the train's entry into Termini Station. He adjusted his thick glasses and crinkled his nose. How happily would he have stayed a little longer on the velvety cloth that had replaced the wartime hard timber! He shot a pleading look at his companion and was rewarded a stentorian "Out! Out". Clinging to his sizeable suitcase, he complied.

While they moved abreast along the platform, Dino set his eyes on the terminal and it looked fresh and grandiose, definitely a far cry from the modest, war-scarred façade of the railway station at his little town! Goggling at the display, he let his spectacles rest on shafts of sunlight mingling on the imperial portal. His mobile face signalled a question, but his father was taken up with a scrutiny of the slender and slightly crooked hands of his Omega Grand Prix 1900, an heirloom as well as a survivor of a couple of national upheavals. The close study was followed by, "The aircraft is scheduled to take off at 6pm, if I remember it right."

He concurred: "Yes, you remember it right."

"Excellent. It means that we have a few hours in hand for a look at our capital city. I'm taking you to a church I'm very fond of." He pocketed the venerable nugget and moved on with short decided steps. Dino tripped laboriously by his side.

About an hour later, father and son emerged from the smother of a trundling bus to the breathing space of a square and an elaborate church façade. "It's an exemplar of the Renaissance baroque," the lad still fresh from high school remarked, and a whirl of the other's head corroborated the recollection. Trotting through the dark-panelled portal, they made a beeline for a statue which stood against the wall in the midst of lapis lazuli pillars.

"You're looking at Loyola," the man said while making his arm go up in gyres. "There he is, the great soldier of the militant church." His plump forefinger singled out a female figure holding a cross above prone figures. "That woman stands for the triumph of true faith over heresy." He made a brief pause. "Never forget this when you are in the country you're about to visit, son." His telescoped body seemed to reach for the ceiling where an overwhelming Christ looked poised to take off heavenwards. "There he is, our Liberator!" he announced with some emphasis. "Have you noticed the illusory effects?"

Dino's short-range eyes stretched to the limit. "Yes, yes, I can see them now, Pa."

"And are they not the signs of a noble art form?"

"They are indeed. Perspective gives an extra dimension to the realism of the work."

The cicerone's features twitched at an angle; flickers of candlelight materialised in his pale blue eyes. "You speak like a book, son," he commented. "Line by line, gen by gen, you may well be a know-all, but never a man." The smile that accompanied the distich bespoke paternal concern. "Famished?" he enquired.

Not half, Dino's spirited nod conveyed.

"Very good. A desire for nourishing food is as healthy as an appetite for the fine arts. Let's go!"

In a matter of minutes, they were sitting comfortably inside a colourful trattoria ennobled by rows of straw bottles hanging from artistic wooden beams. When a grizzled waiter danced his way to their rustic table, balancing two tricolour beef pizzas on his arms and solicitously placing his load on the chequered top, both expressed their deep-rooted appreciation of the delivery by rubbing their hands. The delicacy was briskly taken care of. A squat bottle of red wine, which promptly revealed a quality of robustness equal to the local castle featuring on its rustic label, proved a perfect complement to the pizza as well as, come to think of it, to the church frescoes. After a brief respite, the table companions attacked a pastry highly recommended by the waiter for being Emperor *Vitellius'* favourite dessert and crowned their wholesome effort with a tiny yet mighty cup of pitch-black coffee. The family heirloom suddenly reappeared. "We have enough time for a view of another remarkable exhibit of our precious heritage," the man announced. Both hands moved to his belly and gently kneaded it.

Within the hour, the father's arms were extended aloft and aiming at a white façade while he ejaculated, "Here! The Palace of Labour Civilisation! And it does look as majestic as ever. Feast your eyes, son!"

Dino felt drawn to a gracefully symmetrical stone-and-iron building and a row of lofty arches: the ensemble exuded self-reliance and an awareness of grandeur. "Beautiful!" he burbled.

"Aha, you're being offered the spectacle of something that took my breath away when I was about your age." There was a dash of inspired awe in his father's tone of voice while his fingers leapt to his head and ran across the brownish-grey hair scantily topping it.

Marble figures standing in a silent watch could be descried through huge portholes. "Pity it's empty of living people," the youth complained in an undertone.

"Ah, but there was an ocean of them the day our national leader was around. It seems like yesterday! Our ruler marched along, his right arm stretched up, his jaws set forward; and, yes, he came very close to me, so close in fact that I could have touched him!" A succession of slow, quasi-ceremonial nods brought back to the listener the image of the chief's head flicking up and down in the newsreel Padre Orsino had been in the habit of screening at the end of the regular Sunday school session at his parish hall. "I felt an urge to stretch my hand and reach his shoulder, but I checked the impulse," the narrator was now recounting. "What I did instead was to lift my right arm and call out, 'You are a man of the people. Yes, you are all of us!' I could sense that *il Duce* had heard me, for a fleeting smile materialised on his face." The reminiscing man's jaws tightened, his lips jutted out, and his eyes closed as if to lock in the sheen from the palace designed to pay homage to the civilising influence of labour. Was he being thrown back to a time when youth had been the spring of beauty and the sun had risen free and merry above the imperial city? Was he savouring twenty-odd years in the history of a country fallen under the spell of a charismatic daredevil sent by the Divine Providence in the very eyes of the Holy Father? Hold on! Wasn't this alleged agent of God a shrewd tactician, a political adventurer and a clever opportunist wallowing in a myth sprung up from the muddy soil of his Po valley? Hadn't this father of his country paid tribute to a 'great proletariat finally on the move', as he had put it, while at heart of hearts he had a rather moderate faith in the capabilities of a social class struggling for survival? This much Dino had read in a book written by a supposedly impartial post-war observer.

As an adolescent, he had scrutinised the features of this captain of political industry on the book cover and done so without the awe inspired in him by the same face hanging on the wall of his primary school room. He had lingered on the fierceness in the fellow's countenance and seen it as the icon of a tamer who had cracked his whip at anyone who would dare question the unquestionable truth that living one day as a lion was preferable to one hundred days of sheepishness. Were they the traits of a modern Mercury born to fly on the ivory wings of Victory? If they were, how come the people, his own people, had stood their inspiring leader's body on its head in a grey square at the dawn of a foggy day and made it hang alongside that of the woman who had been his loyal though unsanctioned companion? Could the scene be seen as the epilogue of a lengthy tragedy, a piece of the action performed by the great proletariat finally on the move? "Listen, Father," he burst out, but the man was consulting his Grand Prix relic and saying ruefully, "We must hurry up if you want to make sure you'll be flying this evening. Because you still want to fly away, don't you?" Within seconds he was moving ahead with the spring stubbornly ingrained in his step until he halted to lift his forefinger towards a bird slowly circling in the sky. "Looks like an owl from here; still, owls fly solely at dusk, don't they?" he remarked.

Dino adjusted his specs hazardously aslant on his remarkable nose bridge. "Ah, that's what Hegel, the idealist thinker, noticed as well, according to my old philosophy teacher," he disclosed and then, spurred by his father's quizzical look, hastened to add, "Aunt Hilde once told me that the great Hegel was prone to confusion."

"Aren't we all?" his interlocutor muttered, and in the next breath, "Poor Hilde," he sighed while the look of a grown-up man abruptly deserted by the inner child pervaded his bony face.

"Aunt Hilde also said that her beloved Siegfried understood the language of the birds," Dino added, but no word came in

72

response to the ornithological detail. On looking up again he saw that the winged creature had landed on one of the dummy-like figures standing behind the facade: it was, he confidently surmised, a rock dove.

On the way to the bus stop they passed by a funfair. A man was standing on the pavement and pulling faces at onlookers. The mimic actor's mouth, fully open to let out an inaudible laughter, reminded Dino of the mirth of the ancient inhabitants of the city on the Tiber: on the occasion of the winter festival in honour of Saturn, clowns would impersonate the emperor and their parodic mimicry would equip the spectators with a cutting weapon against the high-flown, humourless rhetoric of their supremo. On impulse Dino turned to his parent and the latter's arching eyebrows made him wonder whether he, too, was thinking that rhetoric and mime had been integral to the national ruler's performances up on the balcony in Piazza Venezia, but no support of his conjecture came through his companion's full lips.

A few minutes later, they were standing inside a ram-packed bus and clinging to straps that looked pretty ornamental under the circumstances. Breathing laboriously, Dino glanced with envy at a mature couple seated at ease in the rear. His eyes blinked, closed, and reopened to a sight of Aunt Hilde and Uncle Carlo inside a silver-framed, black-and-white photo lying on a mahogany writing desk.

She is leaning against a car, he sitting at the wheel, and both have fresh smiling faces. A book is up for grabs at the edge of the polished table, and he makes a dash for it, but he's brought to a standstill by a soprano voice languorously warbling, "Siegfried, Siegfried"; then the door opens and his aunt swishes through, looking her lathy old self. She lets out a deep-throated "Ciao!" and apologises for allowing an old friend of hers to keep a young nephew waiting, but a smile comes onto her cheeks when he says that the singer has kept him good company and asks if Siegfried was young. "Definitely not so young as Brunnhilde was," she lets him know with a furrowed brow and a pointed face, which alluringly conjure up the image of a weasel from her native Black Forest. "A drop of *apfel-wein*?' she suggests with a tinge of Saxon civility, and his head moves vigorously up and down. The bittersweet, earthy taste of the apple wine is one good as well as secret reason behind his frequent visits. "*Gut*," she says, and hands him a goblet; then she shares her long soft divan, crosses her skinny legs and embarks on a native tale. "Siegfried offered Queen Brunnhilde to his friend Gunther, but the former, not the latter, who was the man she was in love with," she begins at a pitch that gives him a strong intimation of how the queen must have been feeling about the offer. "Are you drinking?" she asks. "*Gut*. Siegfried was inclined to return Brunnhilde's feelings, but, *ach*, he was a married man." A moment's silence is followed by, "why did he take her talisman from her? *Warum*?" Lines of unease criss-cross her face; waves of regret flood her saxe-blue eyes; a discreet sigh makes her unobtrusive breast rise and fall. "Hagen the Dane proffered a potion to Siegfried. He imbibed it and forgot all about Brunnhilde."

"What kind of potion was it, Auntie?" he blurts out.

She brushes the question aside with a wry smile. "As if by magic, an additional dose of the drink made Siegfried remember the rock where Brunnhilde had been lying asleep, the fire surrounding it, and the ardent kiss that had awakened her." A pause for another taste of the *apfel-wein* is followed by details about Gunther's jealousy, two ravens flying overhead, and Siegfried looking upward and being speared by Hagen. "*Ach*, the stab in the back!" The lament sounds permeated by Brunnhilde's elegiac quality, and then the poignant finale is revealed in a softened timbre: "Siegfried died with his beloved's name on his lips, and it wasn't long before the bride-that-never-was had a pyre built on the spot, mounted on her beloved Grane, and rode into the flames." The narrator's metallic eyes gleam. "*Leuchtend feuer liegt Siegfried, mein seliger held,*" she strikes up. "In glowing fire lies Siegfried, my blessed hero," she clarifies in a voice that betrays a melancholy mood. "Oh! It's about time you took a bite out of my *torte,*" she adds. Regaining her full stature, she pads away to fetch the cake and – how pleasant – her silk skirt rustles softly on the carpet.

He smacks his lips, darts to the book on the desk, and riffles through it. *Betrayal, betrayal is the heart of the matter,* he reads before replacing the volume quick as a flash because his hostess is already back, holding a silver tray in her scrawny hands and saying, "I dearly hope you will enjoy my cream cake."

The exotic dough melts gently in his mouth. "Go-o-o-d," he gushes.

"*Naturlich.* It's homemade; one of the best-kept secrets of my Black Forest," she lets him know in a conspiratorial tone while pouring dark tea out of an austere pot. He points towards the picture of a densely-wooded region hanging on the wall. "Aha, that was my little world, my paradise on earth," she explains. "It came to an end at about the same time as the *Nibelungenlied* did." She looks and sounds dusky and distant, but reinstates herself when she says, "At times I think of Heidegger, the Black Forest philosopher, and of how he urged mankind to gaze at and listen to a starry sky and a darksome forest. There are one or two things I'd like to say about it, but you've come for Hegel, haven't you?"

His head bends and stays down while he murmurs, "For Hegel, too."

The umber smile she gives in return looks pregnant with humus from her thick, dusky areas of woodland. "Let's have a word about my other visionary fellow countryman, then," *Tante* Hilde says.

Through the glossy leaves of symmetrically arranged pines the terminal leapt into view as a rectangular compound of concrete and glass standing stationary against the busy to-and-fro of human bodies. While father and son moved to the main entrance, a long maroon car pulled up; corded luggage was lifted out of its cavernous boot, and men, women and children – a vastly extended family, at a fair guess – could be seen to exchange kisses and bear hugs. When the affectionate display came to an end, a squat fellow took to the wheel and drove off, pursued by a host of waving hands.

"You see, they're leaving the land that gave them birth, son. And they may never return," Dino was told, and he rubbed his head: never return from where? From a far-away rolling country where cowboys were sold on rodeos, Johnny was regularly plucking his guitar (although the guy didn't seem to be doing anything of the kind in the Western he had recently seen), Sitting Bull was still ensconced in some secluded reservation, and Buffalo Bill was touring with his Wild West show? (Apropos, was Ron, too, on the move and chewing one of his fabulous green bubble gums?) Yes, they'd been going west since day one, those adventurous guys, and of late travelling eastwards with the old unflagging enthusiasm and a miniature icon of liberty inside their new-fangled wagons. His father might well have something to say on the subject, the lad suspected, but all he heard was, "Let's have a beautiful espresso, young man."

En route to the bar, Dino's eye fell on Aunt Hilde's lifelong guru sporting his quaint moustache and filling the front cover of a book on display in a shop window. Had his father spotted him? He asked the question as soon as both were seated at a table.

"Unfortunately, I missed the opportunity," the man owned while staring at hazel streaks afloat in his cup and disregarding, as he unfailingly would, the sugar bowl.

"That man was an evil genius."

"How do you know that?"

"Aunt Hilde told me. People up and down the country were kept in the dark about whatever was taking place at one or other special camp. Nevertheless, there were rumours of ongoing atrocities, but they often fell on deaf ears. And yet, when the worse came to the worst, the Führer gave every sign of having little time for his long-suffering folk and even tightened the screws on the comrades in the eastern region by running them in to the earth like badgers."

"Ah, our dear Hilde," the hearer sighed. "Dying in a fire while she was at home... imagine that! Horrible, truly horrible." His eyes flared. "Also, think of the accident occurring just when my brother was miles away!" A dormant tic awoke while he took a long slug. "You see, after the war Carlo hit the bottle, and your mother and I have subsequently learned that there was another woman in his life when the war was still with us." He sniffed sonorously. "One day an anonymous letter reached the supreme command headquarters. All I can say is that it was not my brother's finest hour. His career came to an untimely end and he was given his marching orders – he, the colonel who, at the front of his young men, had fought like a lion in the Western Desert and was about to be promoted to the rank of Major General! You know, it had been a dream of his since he and I played at soldiers in our garden."

The disclosure cut Dino to the quick. "I saw a book sitting on his desk once," he related. "Written by a marquis who had been a field marshal in the war. As far as I know, the author and the book are not very popular these days."

The other's forehead creased up as though in a bid to recover a deep-seated memory, but it smoothened as soon as he suggested with brio, "What d'you say to another espresso?" The lad shook his head. "Are you sure, but really sure? It may well be your last chance of enjoying the real thing." The head swayed again and a forefinger indicated a half-full cup. With a resigned nod, his father rose and stepped to the bar.

"*Ach*, the stab in the back!" The cry came back as a distant echo. The vast majority of the people in the country did not suspect any evildoing in the newly established ghettoes; this much Aunt Hilde had maintained, and he was inclined to take her at her word. Still, if her compatriots had known the full facts, would the *Dammerung* have never materialised? Also, would she have been passionately drawn to Siegfried? Well, she had told him that Brunnhilde had never forgiven her untruthful lover. He waited for his father to provide him with an answer, but when the man reappeared clutching a steaming little cup, his face signalled news rather pertinent to the moment. "Your plane is taking off in half an hour. The gates are going to be closed pretty soon," he said.

"I have heard the announcement, Father. But please tell me. Why the fire at Aunt Hilde's place?"

An awkward cough rolled out while the man seemed to be striving to come up with an explanation, which came as "Good God! Was it a combination of an overheated stove and a gas leak? You see, your aunt was fast asleep after taking a massive overdose of a painkiller to soothe her arthritis." An explosion of tics enhanced the mobile features of the reminiscing man. "Dear, dear Hilde! If she, too, had understood the language of the birds, she would have never come out of her Black Forest, I suspect. Carlo found her wedding ring hidden inside her favourite hut on the shore of a lake in the woods." The tiny cup he was holding darted to his lips. "My poor sister in-law did not escape the press vultures, I'm sorry to add; one of them had even the cheek to suggest that she'd been a double agent during the war: 'a Mata Hari on a small scale', he wrote."

Aha, Mata Hari! What a lovely name for a spy! Uncle Raf had mentioned her in passing just the once, and was he aware that the woman destined for the firing squad was not much of a spy? All of a sudden, Dino felt sure that, while speaking to him, *Tante* Hilde had been a listener herself, and one taken up with the music from her star-studded sky; a humble listener led by what was reaching her ears to believe in a *weltanschauung* that would give a face to faceless masses and make them think of death as the revelation of the Spirit Absolute. The people of her country had found no way out of the enchanted dark forest inside which the wind of an ill-conceived idealism had mingled with the harsh voice of a moustached zealot, until Chronos the Avenger had caught up with them all. Her own response to the razzmatazz had been a firm refusal at first, and then, at the end of a long dramatic day, a return to the freedom of her exclusive Eden. Dino was suddenly parched and glowered at the absence of hazel streaks in his empty cup.

"Hilde's death came as a shock to me," the man went on to say. "I got separated from her and Carlo soon after the war broke out and..."

The lad's toes twitched, and he clicked his tongue. "You were also away from Mamma and me," he cut in. "I waited for you to come back and I worried a lot, but Mamma said that you were pretty safe at your hidden place."

The other's body slewed in the chair. "The place was certainly safer than a pit in some field or other, son."

"'A pit is a place for the wicked', Don Orsino once said. You know, I still remember the priest at the village where..."

"Only the Lord can keep us safe from pitfalls," his father put in. "An angel tied the dragon up and threw him into the pit, but after a thousand years the beast has been let loose and allowed to ensnare nations. Wartime is a magnificent time for a dragon, son. By the grace of God, fire has come down from heaven and the beast has finally been thrown into a burning lake. The end vindicates my faith in the visionary revelation of old."

Time, history, an ancient prophecy, and a beastly creature appeared to be the topics, each of them claiming to put forward a fact of life, and it seemed to the youngster that he and his begetter were, in divergent ways, fleeing from them all. He saw him produce the smile of a student who has detected the subtext in a fairy tale. "We'd better make a move now. I'm sure you don't want to miss your flying machine," he heard him say, and expected his valuable watch to put in an appearance for the umpteenth time, but the family heirloom failed to do so.

On the way to the gate, the man stopped. "One last thing before you and I part," he said, "you're leaving home and the reasons behind your decision are still beyond my ken; I'm unhappy about the whole caboodle, but resigned to it. Your mother isn't, and I feel sorry for her." He fell silent for a moment before adding, "just as I felt sorry for both of you when the war was still on and I was hidden away." He slid two fingers inside his shirt collar. "I had a bit of know-how and was detained because of it. Can you understand what I'm saying, son?"

An assertive nod, a tight embrace, a long smile and an ample motion of partly raised hands followed in rapid succession, and then the son was past the gate.

As the plane soared into the sky, the Palace of Labour Civilisation made itself visible through the clouds, and it called up a mouth-watering nougat. Little objects were lying on its roof: were they bits of cuttlefish bones and sharp splinters of broken bottles, essential components of life in the eyes of a celebrated symbolist poet? A dark bird was circling above the building and could it be the owl of Minerva? The twilight had sure as hell turned to dusk,

"Action is the name of the game, my friend," a gruff-voiced man was saying to a fellow passenger, and soon afterwards, in a quasi-lyrical tone, "A school teacher I know has conveyed the idea that we belong to a race of bards, saints and navigators. Well, it seems to me that in this day and age a few of us seem content with a pew in a church and a safe nook within domestic walls, ha-ha."

Dino pursed up his lips and went searching for his Walkman, but the silver-grey chain he saw gleaming in his rucksack led to the round face of the Grand Prix 1900 watch. He gaped at the tarnished token of a recent sleight of hand. "Pa, oh Pa!" he murmured while struggling with an uncalled-for lump in his throat, and he turned his attention to the banks of clouds sailing beneath. Within the space of a few seconds, a break in the dense mass allowed the countryside to emerge as a compact shape. A bonfire was vividly distinguishable and, not far from it, a woman was riding a white horse at a gallop. His head twirled aside, but soon it was bent over the scene anew: the quadruped was now well-nigh the blaze and the amazon appeared to be making a beeline for the flames. "Fire, fire, little fire," Aunt Hilde had chanted while his little nephew scoured the fuggy kitchen for an elusive ring. *No-o-o!* he shrieked inwardly, but the scream was superseded by a quiet yet forceful, *Yes!* The steed had reached the burning heap, leapt over the quavering tongues in style, and now it was majestically charging towards the wine-dark line that was the sea.

PART II

6

ANDREUCCIO AT WALKER'S COURT

'Glimmering and vast, out in the tranquil bay'. The verse line extolling a stretch of white cliffs had rated a mention in the holiday brochure Dino had purchased before leaving home. He looked intently at the whale-backed expanse unfolding against a grey-green backdrop and – yes! – the castle he'd been waiting to see showed itself atop the hill, but where was the Pharos? His mighty glasses searched in vain for a trace of the noble reminder of his native country until the island gate gave way to what his *Blue Guide* described as a chequered pattern of farms, orchards, hop fields, and the conical roofs of oast houses. 'Oast?' Surely the valuable vade mecum ought to have shown more consideration for someone not altogether conversant with the lingo! Wrinkles filled his large forehead, but they were dispelled by a pleasant display of soft-looking heaths and woodlands.

Minutes later, the abrupt bending at an angle of a wing made the contours of the island rush towards him and his hand move to his belly while he took a deep breath. The slender beak of the metallic bird was decidedly diving and the rural ground drawing closer by the second. The visual perception caused turmoil in his brain as well as in his guts. In a fluster, he threw a sidelong glance at the adjacent passenger and saw him seated quite at ease like everybody else. Was the flying machine still under control, then? Was it not going into a bit of a spin? His ears tensed up in the event of a "Brace, brace" announcement through the intercom, but all he heard was a finely modulated, "Any rubbish?" issuing from the gracefully rounded lips of the stewardess as she sauntered down the aisle, her platinum blonde hairdo unruffled and an official smile creeping over her rouged cheeks. The repeated question added insult to injury: was the well-trained crew member feigning unawareness of an impending catastrophe in compliance with official instructions? Or was she stoically assuming that a split-second catastrophic impact would be preferable to a headlong descent into disintegration? Aha! *From here to eternity!* The sudden memory made Dino cross himself (he hadn't done so for ages!).

"Good to be flying with a fellow believer," the traveller next to him let him know with a benevolent smile, and his half-smile in response came up in harmony with the demand of his safety-minded self, but seconds later his face clouded over anew: was he getting his just deserts for leaving home sweet home or, if not that, for choosing to be a high-flier instead of braving the waves as the ancient mariners from the Tiber had done? A deep rumble from his bowels put paid to his assumptions. He closed his eyes and said to himself in a very quiet voice, "Brace, brace." When he blinked again, the lavender high-flier was gliding as light as a feather on the runway, and his belly was still as a pond. He asked himself whether he'd been offered a welcoming showcase for the talents of Merlin's country. Feeling completely at ease again, he confidently set foot on *terra firma* and moved with a bouncy step away from the cruel steel bird while darting a bold glance at the rogue pilot he saw sitting nonchalantly in the cockpit. Soon after, 'Let bygones be bygones', he mouthed off. *Survival, that's the name of the game*, he considered and felt in the frame of mind typical of a survivor. He brought out the writing pad that would be a constant companion in his travels. 'Dear Julius,' he jotted down, 'Like you, I have reached the intended outpost. Unlike you, I intend to stay.' In the next breath, "Londinium, here I come!" he whooped, his arms flailing up to a pale blue sky.

Before long, niggling border formalities were negotiated without a hitch and, happily reunited with his accoutrements, he marched on, unleashing the confident smile of a stout-hearted legionary.

A lukewarm sun had disappeared below the horizon when, propped up by a large cup of tepid tea and a couple of alien-tasting pies, Dino went in search of a roof over his head. Within an hour of his landing, a scrap of mauve paper in a shop window took him to a bedsitter in the innermost part of an obviously cosmopolitan quarter. He soon found himself standing in the middle of an ordinary room with a peculiar view and in front of a straggly-haired, bespectacled youth staring at him from a lacklustre mirror. It occurred to him that if you start well you are halfway there. "I wish, I wish," he murmured as his left hand pressed the button on the bedside lamp that evoked Arabian nights. No genie, alas, appeared, but his face did light up. "I've come to a free country," he said to the lad in the framed sheet of glass, "and surely love in some form or other is integral to it." He produced a big wink, and the smile lingering on the faces of both the speaker and the listener was enhanced by the thought that love is the fulfilling of the Law. The apostle Paul had said something of the kind, had he not, and it sounded true. It sounded beautiful, too, for *truth is beauty, beauty truth*, as the ill-starred young Keats had lyrically told the world. He let his fingers go across his head with a round-and-round movement before removing bits of

87

fluff from the tip of the nose of the wooden boy adorning his cream-and-pink T-shirt. Now he was ready. Walking tall, he stepped through the threshold.

Out in the open, the voluptuous feel of the spring evening air made the newcomer feel a sense of occasion and experience a strong affinity for the numberless artists, political exiles and displaced persons who had preceded him in the metropolis on the Tamesis. His lenses converged on the tower of an old Gothic church, and it looked surprisingly attractive by virtue of the tapering spire that thrust at the hazy sky. The sacred building was certainly deserving of more than a cursory glance, but equally worthy of a peep were the glitzy shops, clip joints and near-beer clubs gaining his attention in quick succession. "*Honi soit qui mal y pens*," he muttered on the off-chance of a suspicious passer-by. Yes, "Shame on anyone who thinks evil of it!"; King Edward III's burst of temper deserved to be echoed. A few steps later, he halted to gape at a female form smiling at him, and him only, from a large poster in a shop window. Striking up *Donna Non Vidi Mai* in tune with the gentle musical giant Luciano would undoubtedly be a most appropriate vocal exercise. A sidelong glance revealed the proximity of a willowy, fair-haired, mini-skirted young woman leaning against a brick wall, her cap crushed down over one ear and a bunch of flowers balancing in her arms. A pair of sea-green eyes played havoc with his soul, not to mention his body. Yielding to impulse, he edged to her and said in the staccato manner of an alien visitor, "Excuse me, miss, but I'm lost. Can you help me?"

The presumably native female specimen produced a friendly smile while replying, "Care for a little posy, darling? I'm sure your sweetheart will be chuffed."

"Ahem, there's something I'd like to see very much. You help me, yes?"

The hoped-for helper cocked one eye. "Something like what?"

"Something like… a show."

Her bright face clouded over. "Look here, mate. You've come to a flower girl. No beating about the bush with me, and that's that."

A conflict between boldness and self-effacement got a hold of Dino's countenance, but balance was quickly restored. "I'm a visitor, and I'd like to see what you can show. It's a question of money. Am I right?"

"Well, then. Try and find the show you like without accosting flower girls. I wish you the best of luck."

The visitor's cheeks glowed. "Listen. I buy your flowers, and you help me. Ok?" He gave a little wink. "I'm sure you know every street around here."

She pondered briefly. "I do, and no mistake. Okeydokey, mate; follow me." Elfin lines crossed her pretty features.

Holding tight the cluster of dahlias he had picked out for no particular reason, he followed his newfound companion through a maze of noisy, garish lanes until she stopped in front of a nankeen house. The remnants of the upturned corners of his mouth drooped, and he snatched his guide's little hand. It felt smooth and at odds with the semi-curt voice that was telling him, "I'm well acquainted with the madam upstairs, and I'm sure that she'll be only too glad to give you the hand you want for the show you seem to be so keen on."

Peering through the door he descried an arabesque carpet and purple walls. The love nest of some pasha of bygone days sprang to mind and he stepped back.

"No cause for fidgets," said the girl with a smile which speedily pervaded every nook and cranny in her features. "The thing you want to see is a piece of cake. Not all that cheap, I promise you, but then, in for a penny, in for a pound. How does it strike you, matey?" A wink that hinted at a tit for tat enhanced the quality of her assertion.

His response came through an appreciative nod and then, "Please, what's your name, miss?"

"Amanda, if you like."

What an endearing name! In Cicero's tongue it had meant, 'Commanding love'. "Amanda, would you like to have a cup of coffee with me? There's a bar near here," he said on impulse.

Her long eyelashes flickered. "I wouldn't mind one. A little later though."

"But I need an espresso, and I need it now." He grabbed her hand again, and this time it felt as if grains of sand were in it.

"I know that kind of feeling like the back of my hand." She gave him a congenial look.

"Right, you settle it with me pronto, and I'll sort you out with a little help from the madam upstairs. I'll catch up with you at your coffee place, right?" Awash with relief, he named a nearby bar as a venue, and, "Smashing!" she whooped while graciously accepting some considerably higher-than-bargained-for cash as a prerequisite of securing a ticket for the show that was his top priority. A glance at the church clock opposite them was followed by, "see you in an hour, ducky", and a most reassuring smile.

"You are a bijou, Amanda," he gushed out, and skipped away on cloud nine.

When he entered the felicitously chosen bar, a young man sporting a kinky velvet jacket welcomed him with a sun-drenched smile accompanied by words like, "What nice flowers you're holding, my friend! Been seeing groovy sights?"

"I can't honestly say I have."

"Be on your toes around here. You've come to a funny quarter."

"Actually, I've come here for a serious coffee."

Soon enough a tiny cup lay close to him on the ledge, and it looked disappointingly devoid of hazel streaks. Indeed, the few sips he took lacked the virile tang that was an essential component of an espresso in the region he called his Deep South. He hinted at a pressing engagement and walked out.

A scrutiny of the narrow street revealed no sign of the young lady he was to meet, but his capacious nostrils sniffed a scent of rich sauce and luscious wine. Buoyed up by the aroma to which his grandma had introduced him when he was a nipper, he slung his hands into his pockets and launched into some variously pitched whistling. His eyes drifted to the shop window he had previously peered at and his specs settled on the showgirl's plum-like lips stirring in the floodlight. An old tune about siren charms surged to his lips and he hummed it nostalgically until a peek at his reliable watch made him aware that the rendezvous time had gone by. Girls in plenty were milling about, but where was his flower girl? His spirits sank. What if she had failed to secure the ticket he was after? Would she take him back to the exotic pasha's abode? He snorted. Honest to God, nothing less than his personal integrity was at stake and he would be hanged if he let the wench, for all her classical name, defy his manhood. He frowned. Hanged?! Barely a cheering prospect. He lowered his eyes towards the wooden boy impishly smiling at him from his shirt and wondered whether he would be swinging as the puppet had done under the murderous scrutiny of a cat and a fox. Ah, but the wayward child had been rescued by a nice little fairy whereas only the travesty of an espresso was standing by him! No sooner had the thought crossed his mind than the maligned potion began working wonders. His spirits rose again. 'A man is a man for all that', a poet of note had stated, and his left hand went up and sideways as if to doff a hat to whoever had made the virile statement. He mulled over it, and suddenly his position in that unfamiliar nook of the Latin quarter looked like a matter of sink or swim. So be it, then: he would swim. Chairman Mao had done so across a long yellow river come to that, and it had been quite a feat, not least because the talented swimmer was past his prime. Grinningly from ear to ear, he bent his steps towards the pasha's dwelling.

Inside the nankeen house a plump, crop-haired receptionist seemingly past her prime informed him that to her knowledge no flower girl was frequenting that establishment. His best bet, she kindly suggested, was to take a seat and wait: if the girl he was anxious to see happened to be in some room or other, she would show up before too long. On the spur of the moment he handed her his dahlias with a half-smile and a low bow, slouched to a furry ottoman and, sitting tight like a hound on a hunt, started waiting. At some stage in the silent interval his mind filled with a couple of lines from the Classics textbook he had pored over in his schooldays: 'I am held as a prisoner, fettered by a lovely girl, and take my post as a keeper at her cruel door'.

Half an hour had ticked past when, weary of twiddling his thumbs, he sprang up and stomped back to the woman. Much to his chagrin, cogent arguments failed to win her over. She yawned without even decorously covering her mouth while her heart-shaped specs pinned him down with a withering stare which culminated in her nicely rounded body getting up with a jerk and deserting the allotted desk; her podgy arms showed him the door and pushed him through it by way of an adieu.

Back in the animated street, Dino leant against a wall and gawped at the bright lights surrounding him. They seemed to wink at him mockingly, and he wriggled like a hangdog rejected by his darling little bitch. "I will seek you no more, and you'll be sorry for it," he recited, borrowing again from the textbook of old and soon after, "More fool me!" he cried while turning his eyes back to the door of the greyish-yellow house: it looked firmly shut. "The night is slipping past. Unbar the door," he begged the woman presumably still squatting at her post, and in a flash he saw her as Cerberus guarding the entrance to the nether regions of the flower girl. Staring blankly at nothing, he waited until he sensed that he had been ensnared by the toil of fortune and his borrowed elegiac utterances had been of little use in the shameful circumstances. "I'd better shut my trap," he summed up in case the ancient elegist had heard him and his cacophonous cribbing was making him turn in his grave. "Why did I come? Oh, why?" he moaned as despair loomed up, but the sudden vision of another and hopefully decent espresso gave him hope of recovery and, God willing, salvation.

In a matter of minutes the smartly clad barman was lending an ear to his sob story and nodding between gulps of clam-spiced spaghetti and ruby red wine. As soon as the tale of misfortune came to an end he said, "You've been visiting Walker's Court, man. I say, were you expecting a lie-down on a bed of roses?"

In the grip of disappointment, the visitor gave undivided attention to the street, and – praise be! – the eagerly awaited companion was in it. "I can see my girl, my flower girl!" he shrieked as he pointed to the familiar shape he had spotted standing against a wall and clutching a little posy in her dainty arms.

"Leave it to me. I know how to deal with little minxes," the barman said before dashing out.

Rooted to the spot and imbibing an adequate yet hardly elating coffee, Dino saw the young man and Amanda engage in a verbal exchange which grew vigorous by the minute; then he was on his way back and failing to see two fingers held up behind his back. "The miss says that she was around inside the hour, but you were nowhere to be seen," he reported. "She also says that there were no indications of any great change in the situation, and that some of the wenches hanging about had a knack of ensnaring gentlemen in their nets. 'But I am a good girl, I am, and all I want is a little kindness', she has told me. And you know what? She sounded very much like a well-educated miss, and I know what I'm talking about: you see, there's a duchess who every now and then honours me by her noble presence, and your flower girl spoke just like the duchess does. Quite a situation, I must say," the barman concluded.

"But I waited for a full hour!" Dino retorted with a growl of anger while bringing out the Grand Prix heirloom in a bid to reinforce his claim – and damn! – on checking the time as against that shown by the clock on the wall he realised that the valuable relic was still showing the continental time – which was his father's time and consequently ahead of the girl's as well as of his own on the island he had come to. His ball-shaped face fell, and he racked his brains for a face-saving clarification.

"Come, come. No sulks please, my friend," the other pleaded, making inroads into his mental effort. "At Walker's Court there's more than one show like the one you want to see." He gave a knowing wink, stirred his clams and pitched in again, but within seconds his fork was up once more. "You remind me of Andreuccio da Perugia!" he exclaimed.

Andreuccio da Perugia?! Dino thought quick and hard. "The name rings a bell. Do you mean the character in The Decameron?"

"Bravo! That Andreuccio and no other. He went to Naples for a bit of good business, didn't he? In that city, everybody said, horses went for a song. And so did women. You want me to carry on with the story?" Dino signalled a measured yes. "Ok, then. The ill-advised Andreuccio sang the wrong tune to the musical natives, with the result that his *argent* dropped straight into a nag's breast while he was asleep after... well, you can guess what I mean." The narrator winked again amiably and was rewarded with a midget smile from the listener. "When the young chap woke up the nag had gone, and his wad had gone with her. Desperate for the dough, he went here and there and everywhere, and stopped only when, more by accident than design, he fell into a bog – and a stinking one at that, ha-ha. 'Jesus, how soon have I lost a wench and a purse!' he lamented; yet, stubborn as a

94

mule, he resumed the treasure hunt, only pausing now and then for a sniff at his smelly clothes. And where did his search end? In a tomb, my dear friend – an amazingly beautiful tomb, mind you – and it came to pass that Andreuccio found himself inside it, and with a heavy lid on his head to boot!"

Dino shifted in his seat, managed a smile full of sympathy, and made his left hand go into a circling motion in the air. The other paused, quaffed a totally deserved slug of his gorgeous-looking wine, and added with a beatific smile, "Have no fear, chief. Life can be a rewarding business for those who dare. Tomb thieves arrived in the nick of time and the young man came out of the grave – white as a sheet, but still alive and kicking. Besides, he had a ruby in his hands, straight from the finger of the most reverend archbishop who was waiting in the tomb for the Day of Judgement, ha-ha-ha." The laughter sounded somewhat heretical albeit not unbecoming as the finale of a by-and-large barely orthodox tale. "Didn't you read the tale about Andreuccio at school?" the narrator asked.

"Maybe I did," was the listener's embarrassed reply.

On the way home the significance of Walker's Court sank in, and the newcomer asked himself if he had finally met Delia, the demimondaine who had sometimes come into his dreams when he was an adolescent boy. Or had he bumped into a flower girl transmogrified by a magic-prone phonetician into a duchess? The madam and her assistant at the outlandish house pointed one way, the raconteur at the posh bar another. "Fortune's fickle wheel quickly turns, and I'd better give in. Balance makes a burden light," he declaimed, and if the elegist whose line he had borrowed was finally turning in his grave, well, tough on him. He looked up, saw a solitary star twinkle, and felt that the celestial entity was on his side.

A bookshop window displaying literary items meant for serious-minded readers made him stop and take a peek; through the shimmering glass, a bespectacled Andreuccio stared at him with a glum countenance. He sniffled, stuck his tongue out, and squinted at his ring finger: regrettably, no venerable red jewel was on it. With an unhurried movement, he pulled the Omega watch out of his waistcoat pocket. "I'm sure His Excellency wouldn't have minded a nugget like this, he-he," he sniggered while studiously adjusting the hour in accordance with Greenwich Father Time, mean as he might seem. A subsequent look at the goods on display settled on *The Return of the Native*. "I believe I know where I'll be going next," he whispered and jogged on, inclining his head at regular intervals just in case of a treacherous hole in the paving.

7

THE MOORGREEN PIT MERRY MEN

It was breakfast time. Dino was having a bite out of a re-heated brioche when his overnight dream flashed through his mind: a centaur sporting red travel gear and riding a navy-blue motorbike equipped with yellow wheels, with hands clutching dark handlebars and horn-rimmed specs riveted to the leafy road beneath a sky fleeced with wispy clouds. All in all, a scene proving that oneiric images may well be polychromatic. Chewing the matter over for a little while, the lad acknowledged that a monochrome route master and Shanks's pale pony had been the day-in-day-out reality in his life on the island that was now part of his world. Sighing deeply, he shuffled downstairs.

A striped letter was waiting to be picked up off the floor. The familiar stamp and sender's name made the addressee tear the flap fast and run an equally quick forefinger along it. The blue sheet that came out of the envelope was filled to capacity with slanting handwriting: Aldo's idiosyncratic style at first blush. A galloping perusal disclosed that his former classmate was now working as a reporter for a regional newspaper – a right-wing one, naturally – and an investigative visit to a coalmine somewhere in the Midlands was in the pipeline. Could his unforgettable schoolmate be kind enough to travel to the place in question and organise a meeting with one or two colliers there? A thousand thanks in advance. A P.S. read: 'God save the Queen from pinkies transplanted to her green and pleasant land.'

Oh, yes, it was Aldo all right. He turned the letter over and over. He could certainly be kind enough to make the trip, but then again, was he not being invited to do a favour to someone who had constantly placed himself well away from him on the political spectrum? The bottom line was that it looked very much like a case of a self-avowed pinkie versus a former blackie now travelling incognito. End of story, then? Not quite. What about the string of years the two of them had spent sitting shoulder to shoulder in a cramped classroom? He wagged his head in sync with a couple of sniffs and made for his coat.

The luminous name of the Midlands town on the pastel-blue coach front brightened the sombre morning and bucked up the early bird. Within minutes he was off and his beady eyes were scrutinising graceful half-timbered houses coming into sight like clips of a picture being shown in slow motion before giving way to images of thatched cottages and fox-coloured barns. Down in the fields, packhorses and trucks showed themselves close to farmhouses. Marsh Farm, he knew, had been one of them, under the care of folk who were privy to the intercourse between heaven and earth and felt the pulse and body of the soil. His mental forefinger turned the pages of the novel written by a member of the local community until it came to the passage where a fair-haired young woman had stood in front of the rainbow and seen the world 'fitting to the over-arching heaven in the bow-shaped display'. He turned his attention to the parade of battlemented towers and short spires of churches peeping from behind dense foliage: were they a testimony to a laboriously achieved compromise? His mind was on the verge of further congruous reflections when, after an exceedingly narrow bend in the road, the mining village that was his destination swung into view.

In the space of a few minutes he felt the touch of drizzle as he strode along the Bottoms, marvelling at the absence of a unique motif in the back-to-back dwellings and by contrast the monotonous presence of carnation heads stuck in tiny patches of earth. Furthermore, the human faces under scrutiny exhibited barely any sign of the distinctive character he had anticipated and when he walked into a food store, canned and pre-packed items on display confronted him as a showcase for the villagers' ability to manipulate nature the way city dwellers were famed for. His head swayed in tune with his carrier bag while he returned to the open air and bore into a side street. He came to a halt in front of a plaque which resembled a mammal emerging from a moult. A barred window in the wall of an unassuming little house afforded a meagre view of what looked like an array of mahogany furniture.

"It will be open to the public tomorrow," a tinny voice informed him from a little distance. He pivoted to face the dungarees of a man leaning against the wall, his hands inside his pockets and one leg bent in the shape of a U. "Yet the housekeeper may let you in for a gander if you twist his arm a bit," the bloke went on to say. The way he looked at the visitor conjured up an image of the guard who had scrutinised Alice through a telescope, then a microscope, and finally an opera glass. In addition to that, the hazel-eyed, long-haired girls who trotted out of the house casting a stealthy glance and bearing a coy smile on their cherry faces could easily have been Alice's sisters. "My little ones," the man disclosed at once, "schoolgirls, you know."

It was too good an opportunity to give it a miss. Dino promptly asked them if they were enjoying school. 'Not much' and 'Not always', he heard by turns without the slightest trace of an indigenous lilt. There you are! The effect of hard schooling in all likelihood, but then, why did their dad – a factory worker by looks and self-proclamation – sound a far cry from, say, Joe and Luther, the colliers in DH's 'The Daughter-in-Law' ? Sure enough, folks of that type might well be his next-door neighbours, as David Herbert once had been. He asked for an explanation, and it came as, "It's all a fake, young man. Done for the stage." He produced an acquiescent nod, waved goodbye, and stepped away.

Along the high street, heads of chrysanthemums innocent of the connotations of death they had in Dino's native country made a parade of their showiness, and he lowered his head this side and the other at regular intervals until the rustic and brown-as-a-walnut frontage of a public house made him go full erect through the opaquely glazed main entrance. He hurried to the bar, secured a pint of stout and headed for a rhomboid table in the garden at the rear. After a couple of tentative sips, "Blow me!" he muttered while assessing the taste of the brew he was imbibing. He looked intently at the coaly stuff and found it at odds with the slab beneath him, but on a par with the cock that seemed poised to fly off his perch at the back of a leafy glade.

"Set thine eyes on the bird?" Unexpected, raucous, the inquiring voice had come from an elderly woman staring at him from behind a nearby table; her russet, care-worn face nestled in a ribbon-tied bonnet. His bowing head met her bland smile. "That bird was a peasant's slave. Fettered body and soul, poor thing," she drawled out. "Then a lad purchased him for a piece of silver. He had been taken down from a cross and conquered death, but any feeling for life was dead inside him." A note of sadness rang in her rhythmically stressed tone of voice. "The youth and the fowl trod the roads. He looked on the world of men and saw how dour it was. He looked at the sun and saw it as still smiling at the earth, but where he and the bird were, it was all shadow. He saw death was on him once more." The narrator took a large swig of a drink that looked like cider and, keeping her eyes glued to the stuff, clucked. "A lass sees the wounds on the man's hands and feet and holds her hand to his face.

'Touch me not,' says he.

'Let me anoint thee with a bit of my oil,' she pleads, and sees the fear in the youth's big dark eyes.

'It would be worse than death,' he moans. She empties him of his cloak. He closes his eyes and his wounds cry again. 'How canst thou take death out of me, woman?' he axes. She takes no heed. Softly, her hands touch the gore in his side while she looks at him with eyes like white flowers. The next moment she is off on the quiet. The young man looks up and sees the stars rain down to the sea. He has been anointed forever, he feels, and is now free. 'The cock, too, will be free,' he says and goes to the tree to which he has tied the bird, but all he sees is a cord that has snapped. 'It has been accomplished,' he declares, merry as a grig. Then he walks away, and as he goes he espies a serpent asleep at the root of the tree." The storyteller nodded once, twice, raised her bulgy tankard and deeply, sonorously, drank. "Such is the tale as was told by the son of a pitman. He was no pitman himself," she said, unleashing a deprecatory smile. "Like my son was. He went down the pit ivery day, my son. The lad niver escaped like the cock," she added raising her bushy eyebrows. "There's no knowing how it was, but some stuff fell on him an' cut him off. He'd been rods o' trouble before, dear o' me, but that was because he had something on his side an' he wanted love but none was given to him an' he went pear-shaped. May the good Lord have mercy on his soul!" She heaved a sigh which sounded like a moaning waft of wind; then, her liquid eyes homed in on her vessel.

There! Charles' grandma confronting Mrs Holroyd, the listener thought. Same look, same talk; it was no fake, and David Herbert's neighbour would do well to recognise that. He turned to face the cock again: a cord encircled his leg, and it looked as though it was on the brink of rupture. He wheeled about again; nobody was sitting at the roughly made square table.

The tavern was miles behind when Dino walked across a big sheaf-studded field dominated by an igloo-shaped haystack. The environs had a mellowish tinge, the vast space ahead felt liberating, and the bicycle lying against an elm tree looked inviting. The passer-by paused and remembered how he and a bunch of schoolmates had cycled through a scorched farmland and en route chirped about a foreign novel which was largely about the passionate affair between an upper-class lady and her gamekeeper. The risqué book had gone the rounds under the nose of their strict teachers and with the tacit connivance of elder brothers who saw themselves as men of the world… but a wheel at a short distance in the shape of a large dark daisy made the lad speed off to a little gate. It was open at an angle and he squeezed through. A rough shed showed itself, and he forged into it: a middle-aged, average-sized and moderately rough-faced man stood bolt upright, holding a hose against a whitewashed wall offset by a heap of pitch-black stuff. Leaving aside the boiler suit he was wearing, he might reasonably pass as a bus conductor or a postman or even an accountant in spite of the lack of dark glasses. "What is it?" Dino heard him ask in a thin voice. "On an errand for the NUM, are we?"

"Sorry to disappoint you, sir. I'm only visiting. Would it be possible to have a look at the mine?"

"Be my guest, young man, but you've unwittingly mistimed your visit. The pit's shut for the day, and you may find what you're going to see a bit dull. Incidentally, you're talking to Herbie." Truly enough, no trucks were rolling on their habitual tracks and the lift cage lay stock-still and empty; no men with jet-black faces were being taken into the bowels of the earth like gnomes on their way to a buried treasure. "I don't go down any more," the man added. "I stick to the surface these days – after two score and ten in the pit."

Two score and ten in the pit! With the stars looking down on his green valley all the time! "You will remember the good old days, then," said the visitor.

"Well, I went through good and bad days, squire. Days of hard-boiled bosses and dogged colliers." Particulars followed in an impressive sequence: a long and increasingly lonely struggle had brought in a Black Friday, then a Red one, and finally a general strike. "Not a penny off the pay, not a minute on the day," Herbie chanted in an undertone. Unfortunately, 'Peace in Industry' was Labour's motto. And peace had come in the wake of the miners' final battle and ultimate defeat.

There was silence for a moment and then, "How are things now?" the listener inquired.

The collier snapped his fingers and declared that it was not all doom and gloom at that point in time: better pay, shorter working hours, and safer work to boot. His smile grew broader, his tone chirpier, and both looked one up on the trickle running out of a nearby tap and into a rather modest stream flowing sluggishly and seemingly getting nowhere.

"It seems to me that power is still the name of the game," Dino argued while tapping on his glasses.

"Power?" ejaculated the other. "Some of our governors have got stuck in it like flies in sticky paper. Maybe a fly would come off the trap sooner, ha-ha." His face had the compact, dusty colour of a lump from the pit. "The way I see it, a manager belongs in a colliery like a binnacle does in a ship."

Thrown by the simile onto an ice floe, the probing guest found a sheet anchor in the generation gap. "Perhaps the youngsters can manage better these days," he ventured.

"Aha, the youngsters!" his collocutor croaked. "I see them go down like snails and come up scurrying away like hunted hares. Say what you like, they ought to be fighting their little corner, these lads, just like their fathers did." He let go of the hose. "Maybe this is where the road to Wigan Pier comes to an end," he added at a lower pitch. "Maybe the new road takes to sources of a different kind – I don't really know about that. Renewable energy, as they call it? Or nuclear energy if need be? All I can do is to keep my fingers crossed." His set face twitched before smoothing down into a pale smile. "Come back, Robin. Thy merry men are waiting for thee." A slow, deep sigh pierced the soporific air and expired in it.

Tea was offered, but the brightness of the day was already sliding into dusk and immediate departure was a must in order to catch the last bus of the day. Apologies were duly expressed with a rueful smile and the rider that a second call and another chat over a cup of tea were a distinct possibility.

"It'll be down the pit next time around, lad. Sure as a gun," the collier stated while returning the smile with knobs on.

"Oh, I nearly forgot!" said the leave-taker, mopping and mowing as if in the clutches of an awkward splinter of memory. "A friend of mine is planning to come over for a piece on behalf of his newspaper. Would a kind of interview be all right with you?"

Herbie was nothing loath. "I'll be at your mate's disposal," came his reply, accompanied by a little and slightly droll bow.

Host and guest shook hands in front of a dark cage, agape like the voracious mouth of a beast of prey. At dawn, merry men would come and enter its jaws for a propitiatory rite; at sundown, the mouth would spit them out and turn to fresh victims; without delay, the rite would recommence, ineluctable like the undertow – world without end.

Soon enough Dino found himself a quasi-solitary upper-deck passenger on the pastel blue coach he had boarded again, and he endeavoured to keep solitude at bay by musing over the greenness and the blackness he was leaving behind. The cock at the inn had tipped the balance, but a merry man had restored it. Besides, there was this thing about Aldo: surely Herbie was the person his old friend ought to see. Well, well, well, it looked a most thrilling prospect, in a manner of speaking. As he watched the countryside undulate and unfold, it seemed to him that the greenness and the blackness were blending with each other into a harmonious picture, and that he and his classmate were in it on their bare knees, and engrossed in a fierce game of marbles.

8

MARBLES

"The Ides of March have been and gone, and shades of my ancestor! Julius has been bloodily divested of his imperial robe for the umpteenth time!" The recollection of the historic event materialised in a sharply whispered utterance while Dino was having an early morning wet shave. Then, "Spring comes dancing; comes dancing to my door," he recited in close succession, cribbing the line off a poem he had learnt by heart as a child. He was dabbing a few drops of imperial aftershave on his face when a repeated knock on the front door made him dash to the hinged panel and open the door to the regular milkman, dressed in a barely vernal overall, a notepad in his hand, a biro behind one ear, and a broad smile on his chalky face while he mentioned the weekly bill.

A couple of hours later, Julius's descendant was wearing a caretaker-assistant uniform and scanning the courtyard from a dusty classroom, his forefinger under his nostril and game for an inroad into it. There was no hint of the springtime he had savoured in his pristine garden and all he was able to inhale was a whiff of timidity floating through the open door. He raised his arms skywards, but the limbs were brought down by a dulcet female voice thanking him for his cheerful greeting in the discreet manner of a member of an educational establishment; her sylphlike body conjured up the shape of the fairy tale princess who had felt the prick of a pea beneath her royal mattress. "Gracious me! The dear old thing sounds as if in the throes of death," the young teacher remarked while pointing at the scuffed clock on the wall. Then, with a shrug of her angular shoulders, she glided out.

It was assembly time and everything was in order. Well, it was to be expected from a C of E school, but then again, would a Roman Catholic or any other religious institute look less tidy? Dino let his finger reach his nostril again. Yes, everything appeared to be under control at All Saints primary school – even the streaky marbles with which the mischievous kids very likely toyed when their mentors were not looking lay tidily on the desk tops. He bent his steps among the dark-brown midget tables, carefully depriving the upper surfaces of tidily arranged chewing blobs, and his cleansing came to a pause only when he spotted a marble bob along of its own accord. He promptly picked the little ball up and restored it to its proper place, but soon enough the wayward puny thing was happily bouncing again. He goggled at the antics, recaptured the fugitive and, flashing a partial smile prompted by a sudden memory of the courtyard at his Christian Brothers school, went in search of a hole, but not even a chink seemed to have been given the right to exist in the hardly brand-new classroom. Saddened by the shameful lack, he put the captive marble safely inside a desk.

Within a short space of time a squeak from a corner made the cleaner halt again and hearken, but the place was now as silent as the grave. The job in hand restarted, and it progressed at a brisk pace up to the moment when a second squeak made him jib again, shake his head and resume his task with renewed energy until a fresh little cry froze him to the spot, the duster he had put to good use dangling from his fist. Not for long though: the rag went swinging again, and it did so with the required oomph until a portentously longer shrill cry made it abate. He smelled a rat – alas, not a metaphorical one – and, bravely resisting a deeply ingrained impulse to leap onto a desk, he sprinted to a highly suspicious corner. There was no sign of a mouse in it and he moved from corner to corner, but none of them appeared to be harbouring the furry little creature. Prodded by laudable anxiety to unearth the core of the matter, he went on all fours and, methodical as a combing detective, crawled along searching every nook and cranny. To his chagrin, the weaving and the worming ended in a depressing blank. He sat on a chair and, hanging his head, considered his next move: the diminutive brute must be lurking somewhere and leering in its mousy way. Oh yes, it must!

It proved a well-founded conjecture on the strength of a fresh and finely tuned sound issuing from the self-same corner where the hullabaloo had begun, and it threw the hearer into a hole of his own making, but he came promptly out of it and followed a line of thought that lengthened until cut short by the full impact of squeaks seemingly emanating from each and every angle. The lad felt hopelessly encircled by a furry army and his eyes rolled like those of a skilfully manipulated marionette while his ears were taken up with what sounded like the singing of a mischievous choir. He made for the cleaning box only to stop dead in his tracks as soon as *Mazzamauriello* leapt out at him from a world rife with outlandish characters: the little fellow had acquired a reputation by virtue of getting a kick out of tossing things all over the place in a house and making a hell of a noise in the process. His performance was only too often a raving success: sooner or later his unappreciative audience would feel no longer in the mood to face the music and the sheer force of the feeling would prompt a whole family to desert the auditorium. There was also the *monaciello*, the murderous monk who... but a puff of hot air blew straight onto the reminiscing youngster's face on the spot before breathing down his tense body. In a stupor and heavily dripping in perspiration, he gawked at the sprinkling of goose bumps on his arms; then he darted out and made a beeline for the caretaker's lodge.

The spectacle of the man and his wife having a most placid cuppa took Dino unawares. There and then he saw an instance of the X Factor that makes some people go through a most traumatic experience while it helps other people indulge in a relaxing break. The couple's cocky freedom from unease would doubtfully have been grist to *Mazzamauriello*'s mill – let alone that of the devilish little monk.

"Hullo, hullo," the janitor ejaculated with a winsome smile on his furrowed face. An intense look at Dino's choppy features was followed by, "Anything untoward? You look deathly pale, old chap."

"Holy Mother of God, have you bumped into a ghost by any chance?" the woman echoed with shades of concern on her rosy visage. "A mighty cup of tea, that's what you want straightaway, son," she added and on the strength of her maternal instincts promptly handed him the sorely needed drink.

"I... I don't believe in ghosts, but a funny thing has just happened in the classroom," he hissed and in between swallows of the most refreshing potion, proceeded to relate the shenanigans.

The lady looked duly impressed. "Sure, sure, Dino. I must tell you that an ancient graveyard lies right under the school," she disclosed while her corkscrew ashen curls wagged up and down.

Her consort raised his bushy eyebrows and repeatedly stroked his thin beard. "That will do, woman. No need to bring in Annemarie and the Connemara poltergeist as a matter of record," he growled, and then, turning to his assistant, "Nothing to write home about, to be honest," he added. "The little sods come and go as they choose around here, mate." His grooved facial lines produced an elfin grin as he got up to his feet. "And there's another thing: one or two radiators have been playing up lately. High time we had an engineer in, I'd say."

Dino's eyes stayed stubbornly on his emptied cup. "Could I have some more tea please?" was his hangdog request. Thankfully, the response was less insouciant than the one evoked by the little Oliver when he had dared ask for more in his disciplinary day and age.

The urgently needed engineer was on his way out when Dino re-entered the haunted classroom and set about his stint, whistling in tune with his swaying head. An uneventful hour had passed when he found himself blinking at a marble lying quietly in a corner. He shrugged an insidious thought aside, picked up the stray pellet and with a hearty laughter put it back to where it belonged. His serviceable left hand must have failed abysmally, or why was the puny ball repeating itself by nonchalantly frolicking on the floor? Spluttering a four-letter word which had recently taken pride of place in his vocabulary, he grabbed the joker in the pack and laid it to rest. Immediate recovery was the next thing: another peek at the indecently streaked piece of glass revealed that it was sitting on the desk, as composed as a serious marble is supposed to be. He jumped in glee and shot an oblique shufti at the clock to make sure that his prescribed time was up: the fatigued hands of the austere relic, he perceived, were motionless just as the ludicrously variegated ball now was inside its nook. "And to think that I took the mistress for a latter-day Cassandra," he muttered while mustering all his latent energy for a release of another wondrous f-word. No joy this time: the hands on the wall kept as stationary as gnomons designed to cast a shadow and tell the time. He lumbered away, weighed down with an ego sinking to the bottom of a desiccated id.

9

MARIA, MARIA, QUITE CONTRARIA

Poltergeists do come and go as they choose; there seemed to be no particular reason to dispute the All Saints caretaker's statement, and Dino soldiered on, occasionally glancing at the marbles as they rested in their allotted places and at the clock now methodically ticking away as if no supernatural breakdown had occurred. Time kept flowing along a quiet stream, and more than once the young fellow thought enviously about the quality of life of restless adventurers: if only he could have one of the eighty days Phileas Fogg had spent touring the world, or even one hour full of the thrill enriching the days on earth of Moll Flanders! Alas, no. Dusted-off small tables were making a continuum in his life history. Sitting at his wonky kitchen table he felt that variety, by common consent the spice of life, was a bare necessity, and he took a low dose of the spice by jotting down a couple of lines to Aldo, of all people: had he visited the coalmine yet? If that was the case, had he met Herbie? The beneficial effect of a chat with the miner was beyond reasonable doubt, and an update would be greatly appreciated. Best wishes, of course.

That will do nicely, he said to himself while rubbing his hands with glee, and hurried to the nearest pillar box. As he came back, it dawned on him that he had better prepare for a spicy reply.

The best part of the following day was spent in a search for 'marks of weakness and marks of woe'. From behind his serviceable lenses he peered through the hazy light that appeared to be an ingrained quality of the place that was now a surrogate for his home town, but his painstaking scrutiny didn't bear fruit. A lesser man would have called it a day, but he, Dino Puppi, played it cool and hit upon a solution to his problem: the pitiful marks he was looking for had been left in socially conflictive times; furthermore, William Blake, the poetic observer who had detected them was a bit of a visionary, wasn't he?

A few monotonous weeks slipped by before the reappearance of the regular cleaner made his presence at the school redundant and he found himself a job-seeker again, but taking the bull by the horns, he availed himself of the first available opportunity and ended up sitting in front of a modicum of bacon, tomatoes and Norse-style mash inside the scullery of a hostel.

The Chestnuts, a three-storey house at the forefront of a centuries-old heath, had looked, primarily in virtue of its half-timbered frame and ridged roof, rather attractive to him when, weaving his way through a maze of quaint back streets in the posh, time-honoured village on the north side of the river, he had reached the dwelling and, captivated by its bucolic name, had stepped in.

A sequence of below-deck workdays kept his hands in quick motion and one early morning he clapped eyes on the Norse cook Volsung waddling downstairs in the stillness of dawn and asking, "How are my darlings this morn?" in the semi-dulcet tone of an old-variety artiste – a day-in-day out greeting, almost an incantation.

"Every dog has his day, hasn't he?" he hissed under his breath in response and felt like barking in anticipation, but his glasses homed in on a young woman coming down on the chef's side: hardly an intimation of Venus (or Vesper had she appeared in the evening), yet her pitch-black burning eyes made up for her shortage of divine attributes.

"You've joined a happy crew, Maria," Volsung was heard warble with a hard-boiled grin.

Shortly afterwards and while dexterously dealing with a few rows of frothy plates, the recruit introduced herself as a National Coal Board typist in her native Lisboa, momentarily enticed away from her work by the presence in town of the fabulous Bolshoi ballet.

In the afternoon, Maria and Dino strolled on the grassy blades of the awesome heath. In the middle of the stroll she confided in her sonorous Galician voice that to be a ballerina was her primary aim in life. His eyes roved about the plants in quest of 'white-plum'd lilies and the first hedge-grown primrose' (aha, the romantic heath-stroller John Keats had a fondness for the flowers at issue!), but he failed to spot any. His forefinger aimed at the village patchily visible through gaps between the trees. "It was a spa once," he let his companion know. "People flocked in for its medicinal water. Karl Marx and his family, too, were in the habit of coming for a picnic and a donkey ride."

She let out a brief yet assertive laugh and lifted her arms as if on the verge of embarking on an aerial workout. "Sounds a trifle bourgeois to me," she countered.

"Ah, but Marx was poor. He was on the dole most of the time."

"Scrounging off the system, your Karl, eh?"

"He was only fighting for survival in the name of the class that holds the future in its hands. His words, not mine, to be honest."

"Not bad as the excuse of a well-bred fellow who was unfortunate enough to be thrown out of every educational establishment in his country!" Her eyes glared with a hue of resentment.

He saw fit to shunt the conversation onto a less contentious topic. "Did you come up the hill on tiptoe last night, Mary?"

"Maria, if you don't mind. However, I walked up in a pretty normal manner. Dancing on cobbles makes your soles cry for an end of the show."

"Sure, but haven't you read the fairy story about the little mermaid who would dance on a stone floor? It was hard on her toes, my dear."

An outburst of laughter, which sounded as if issuing from the stream of history that links Aranjuez with Lisboa, came rolling over him. In self-defence, he concentrated his mind on her pointed breasts as they sprang forward and receded like fencing foils, and then he shifted his stare to the ebony hair tumbling down in a cascade of threads. Of their own accord, his far-from-long arms encircled her angular shoulders. "Please don't," she pleaded. His limbs fell back and rose towards the sky for an improbable touch.

A discontenting wintertime of frost, oatmeal, and sausages Norse-fashion was drawing to a close when Maria announced that she would be leaving the hostel soon after paying a visit to her beloved fellow dancer Pavlova resting at the local crematorium.

Dino's hands repeated themselves by going forward and landing on hers whilst he proposed a sniff of poetry at a little house on the other side of the heath. "Adieu! The fancy cannot cheat so well as she is famed to do, deceiving elf," he warbled by way of a prelude to a farewell. Her arms engaged in a repeat performance, too, by gently pushing back his intruding fingers. There was little promise of a joint pilgrimage in the opaque smile that accompanied the gesture, yet, early in the afternoon, they entered together the little house where wafts of romantic poetry could still be inhaled by devotees.

"This is the very place where the young poet I've mentioned lived for a couple of years and got in touch with his cherished Fanny," he said in a confidential undertone while they sauntered across a spacious room. She cast a wondering look. "Fade far away, dissolve, and quite forget," he burst out in front of a painting showing the bard in question hearkening to a nightingale. Her eyebrows flicked upwards. Seconds later, and close to a cabinet topped with a pane, he leant over a wealth of memorabilia – a hank of female hair visibly in the midst of them. "I wonder," he struck up to the accompaniment of a knowing smile, but he abandoned the rest of the sentence on perceiving that she was slipping towards the exit. Both walked across the cosy house garden and reached a plum tree. "It's right here that the 'Ode to a Nightingale' was composed," he revealed. "John was still a stripling, and yet not long for this world."

Woebegone lines formed on Maria's narrow visage, and they were surely signs of a sensitive soul. "What about a nice cup of coffee now?" she suggested. He knit his brows while producing an unfinished smile and widening his arms sideways: it was his innate manner of conveying his assent to something that would be welcome a little later. On their way out, his arms landed once more on her shoulders – not without success this time. "Was it a vision or a waking dream?" he whispered, and was rewarded with the smile of Mona Lisa transplanted to the Tagus estuary.

On reaching the core of the village the pair sat inside an elegant but not unquestionably poetic café. A few drops of a stylish cappuccino were crowned with the revelation that he had recently entered the enchanted realm of romantic poesy at college.

"I hope you will soon be dealing with a less unfortunate poet," was her response enhanced by a grateful appreciation of the potion she was being treated to in compliance with a strict and not always affordable rule of etiquette, and a sustained visual contact.

One day later, the two of them sat in front of an uninspiring dollop of mash surrounded by indecorously warped sausages. The quality of Volsung's menu was scarcely improved by a reminder of her imminent departure. "Would you like to join me on a final visit to the heath?" he suggested. Needless to add, it was an impromptu invitation. "This nature reserve is a credit to the metropolis," he remarked. She had no quarrels with that, and off they went.

In the depths of the wold the air was scented with spring flowers, and he inhaled deeply while relishing the image of Flora dancing on soil pregnant with the semen of the sun god. Agog with expectations, he turned to his companion, only to see her move with an undeniably mortal gait, her thin hands inside her anorak pockets, and her rounded head straight as a ramrod, until she halted and took her coat off. The T-shirt that came into sight bore a familiar *A* logo on it. "I can see a large capital letter," he said forthwith.

"Don't read too much in it. I gladly leave politics to men," she rejoined.

"Wrong. Men and women are political animals by nature," he stated.

"Carramba! We are social animals by nature, but there's nothing natural about our political institutions," said she.

He breathed in and out. "Aren't you forgetting that there's been a revolution for *liberté*, *égalité*, and *fraternité* more recently?"

"Certainly not! The thing is, it brought about the market economy of the capitalist system. The truth is that we came out of the garden long time ago."

"And, once out of the place, we gained a mind of our own. Good and evil are in our grasp now."

A brief silence fell and then, "I've had a strange dream recently," she disclosed. "A revolution was going on in my country, and I was putting a white rose inside a cannon's mouth.

Fancy that!" Her arms moved in a dancing fashion and came to a standstill in mid-air.

He shot a knowing look. "We all have strange dreams now and then. 'Delusional' is the word for them, if you don't mind the jargon."

"Bah," was her exhaustive comment.

He steered the conversation away from the realm of dreams. "I'll tell you what. Let's take a red rose to Karl. He's resting in a cemetery not far from here, and I believe that we ought to pay a visit to the great man." An appreciative nod from her put both on the road leading to Karl.

Not much later, Maria and Dino reached the cemetery and the man they had come for. A few minutes went by in silent scrutiny and then words came.

"My grandfather had a face like him, you know," said he. "He was a great storyteller, my grandpa. Once he told me a tale about men who reached a land blest with milk and honey, and found that it was exclusive private property. The few who were allowed access to it as labourers in the fields – for a pittance, mind you – soon felt that they didn't belong there and saw the landowners as their enemies. There were riots, but order was promptly restored." He ran a hand across his loosely spread out hair. "There you are. Capitalism versus proletariat, and the very beginning of class struggle!" The last sentence had the strong beat of a musical lecture in economics. "To be frank, my grandpa never talked of class struggle. Nor did he ever mention Marx. Not once did I see him reading his manifesto; what I saw instead was a book he kept on his bedside table for a long time, and it was about a man called Cagliostro – Count Cagliostro, for the record – a charlatan by common knowledge."

Economic production, surplus value, estrangement, alienation and revolution of the masses – you name it. Dino was quite willing to expand on the lot with a little help from his old-time Hegelian teacher, but it crossed his mind that those very concepts had stood Hegel on his head: there was no spiritual labour, and the Spirit Absolute over which his classmate Aldo had got into a state was no longer everything; in fact, it had been superseded by commodity, money, and capital – fetishistic forms of value, all of them. Creases came and went on Dino's forehead. "Ideas belong to the land of dreams," he asserted with a flourish – "dreams like yours, for instance."

Maria sniffed. "Ideas are real. Any philosophy of freedom depends on them."

He shook his head. "If liberation ever comes, it will be thanks to a proper use of material and social conditions rather than because of the beliefs of a philosopher of freedom. Philosophers can only interpret the world. The point is to change it."

"Am I hearing again the voice of the man installed in front of us?"

He made no comment. Slowly, they moved away from the monument.

On regaining the heath, he produced one of his choice half-smiles, removed his glasses, and pecked her on the cheek. "Thou still unravish'd bride of quietness," he whispered, but the last word proved barely appropriate, for, quick as a flash, she was holding him with encircling arms. He felt as if sinking into the secret whirlpools of a ribeira from her Serra de Sintra, but he resurfaced in the twinkling of an eye. "Heard melodies are sweet, but those unheard are sweeter," he recited.

The musical line borrowed from his pet poet fell flat. "What's wrong with you?" she inquired placidly and followed up her question with a kiss on his cheeks.

He received the titillating touch as something forced on a vulnerable young male. "Nothing is wrong with me. It's only that even a man is not always in the proper mood for..." he mumbled.

"A mood for what, *caro bambino*?"

She sounded kind of maternal, and there was very little he could do about it because he was under the sway of lips that tasted like a bittersweet pomegranate from his childhood garden. Upon recovery, "*Viva Lisboa antiga!*" he blurted out.

She gave a light bow and with quasi-dancing steps moved out of the grove.

"Some men will never be in a proper mood," he heard her mutter in communion with herself and tiptoed to her.

"What are you taken with these days?" she asked. "Apart from the special relationship between a young poet and a singing bird, I mean."

Caught off balance, he hastened to put a finger on his inner keyboard. "Poltergeists," a single note rang.

"I say, have you been reading about ghosts as well as about nightingales?"

"If you want to know, I have seen a poltergeist. Well, at least I've heard one and…"

She pointed at a nearby hut. "Hope you don't mind if I make a comfort stop," she said with a wry smile, and scampered away.

His eyes converged on a tree: a beech, to go by his smattering of botany. It looked worthy of its ancient lineage and yet sadly deserted by Tityrus, the young scapegrace who had piped away under its canopy. He moved to the tree and sat against its bole. On spotting a short stick he grabbed it, placed it against his lips and was on the verge of a trill when a caw from the foliage made him look up. A rook, by the sound of it, was announcing in its corvine fashion the return of spring, and it occurred to him that in his native country Julius's children would keep crows as pets and when in a tantrum pluck the feathers of another child's pet. "They did the right thing, those kids," he growled and, discarding the pastoral exercise, leapt up and moved towards the ladies' lodge just in time to see his fellow stroller stride away. "Maria! Hey, Maria!" he called out, but she was skittering on like a frolicsome gazelle and was soon beyond reach. Hands in his pockets, he stumped back to the Chestnuts, fitfully swaying his head.

The ballerina was conspicuously absent at the bucolic hostel and nobody seemed to have a clue as to her whereabouts. Downhearted, Dino repaired to his cell and attacked an essay on his cherished young poet's address to the light-winged Dryad of the trees. The piece was rather long and ponderous, and when he made the last line it was already time for supper. Balancing an immortal bird against a transient dancer, he descended into the canteen. Still, no Galician face was in sight, and with a sigh of regret he sat down to a chunk of mutton which tasted surprisingly luscious, a batch of far from desiccated vegetables, and a cup of warm tea. The meal buoyed him up and he dashed to the counter to pay compliments to Volsung, but the deserving fellow was having his night off. A well-timed break indeed. He took his cue from the chef.

Before long he was treading wearily on the heath and heading for the inn known to Joe Public for its Iberian connections and to the chosen few as the venue where the lyric John would often indulge in a pint or two of the hop-flavoured stuff. His head jerked up and caught sight of the Queen of Heaven, her crud-spattered virgin body approaching fullness, and her ghastly visage encircled by a dark brim, as if by a nightcap. "What art thou doing up in the welkin, Diana? Pray let me know," he whispered, but the slightly adjusted poetical fragment from his high school days tasted well past its sell-by date and he felt kind of lost in translation. He resumed his walk at a quick pace, but he halted anew on recalling suddenly the raptures of the star-crossed versifier so close to his heart when, standing on tiptoe upon a little hill – that self-same hill in all likelihood – he had raised his eyes to the queen of the wide air. He joined his hands and lifted them towards the shiny goddess.

The mystical contact was disrupted by a rustle of leaves. He stared at a light shimmering from behind a bush, pushed his glasses up his nose and peered into the spot: a young woman was moving her little feet and lean body at a measured tempo in the light of a torch; a T-shirt with a big 'A' on its front gleamed in the odd spotlight. Mary, Mary, quite contrary, was dancing. At long last! He saw her hand touch her straightened hair sensuously and the dark shock fall down her skinny shoulders while her eyes expanded like ink blobs on a blotting paper. In the whorl of the Terpsichorean ritual she looked beautiful; she *was* beautiful.

Leisurely, flawlessly, the dance came to a close. The performer stood on tiptoe, crossed her arms, and made a curtsy. "Bravo, bravo!" the only spectator, a man squatting on his haunches, whooped with a gentle clap. The voice was quasi-dulcet. "I can't sing, but I'll do anything for you. What's your wish, my little bud?" it added. The accent was unmistakably Norse.

The little bud stretched out her stems and lifted upwards a visage that seemed to mirror the flickering globe in the sky. "I wouldn't mind the nose of Dino the lefty on a platter," she let her adoring fan know, her ethereal lineaments embellished by a seraphic smile. Then there was a burst of laughter – the ballerina's silvery rings merging with the chef's mellifluous, sexually borderline chortle. Gingerly, the onlooker took himself away from the artistic scene.

He was close to the inn on the hill when he sensed that he'd been blessed with enough Iberia for one night, and the abrupt consciousness made him bend round. His nose crinkled as he fixed the heavenly sovereign with an icy stare. "I wish thy nose torn off, and thee in pain like Clytemnestra aslant on the palatial steps, thou fey, deceptive queen," he called out, scanning for good measure, and marched back to the Chestnuts, propped up and at the same time burdened with the feeling that he had got something off his chest and left with tough nuts.

As he stomped up the stairway, the force of facts as bare as Mussorgsky's Bald Mountain gained momentum: obviously led by the heavenly guide, Salome had found her way to the heath:

a queen in league with a ballerina – women, both of them. The uncalled-for notion made his left hand clutch the rail and slide along it while the remainder of his far from long body forged, round-shouldered, towards the upper regions. Women, he resumed, were creatures one moment willing to nurture a sensitive wooer with Beatrice's gaze, the next ready to devour the sacrificial lamb with Cleopatra's eyes; and weren't the one as well as the other creature facets of a primordial womb and a constantly elusive mind? He stroked his chin. Come to that, how did he stand on the issue? It would appear that he had so far paid lip service to a naked truth which is also beauty, of course, and at the end of the day it's *all we know on earth and all we need to know*. On the other hand, had not the young poet he'd been quoting for the umpteenth time maintained that one ought to be *capable of being in uncertainties, mysteries, doubts*? He suddenly felt that it was quite possible to give an upbeat meaning to the plaintive anthem of the nightingale. When his arching fingers grasped the door handle, he stepped in and groped about for the light switch: exposed by the meagre bulb hanging from the ceiling, a plate displaying a courgette-shaped item made itself hazily visible. For some reason, his left-hand forefinger leapt to his nose.

10

THE JARNDYCE FILE

Several weeks after Maria's leave-taking a letter from Lisboa landed inside the hostel pigeonhole. "Oh no, not the ballerina again," Dino croaked, but the sender was none other than Aldo. He read, 'I have to inform you that I paid a visit to the Midlands coalmine not long ago, and it came a cropper. I did meet Herbie and he proved an amiable host. We had a lively chat, but what he told me was not exactly what my editor and I wanted to hear from a down-to-earth miner. Have I been sent on a fool's errand by any chance? If I have, I can hardly cry, 'Mission accomplished!' and, to rub salt into the wound, a good deal of dough has gone down the drain.'

Dino grimaced, breathed out a 'he-he' and read on with growing interest.

'I was subsequently despatched to Lisboa to make contact with the local coal board, and things went swimmingly there. In the course of the assignment I chanced upon a typist called Maria and took her out. Over a repast (palatable, but not a patch on our home-made pasta and sauce) I was told of her coming over to Londinium in hopes of seeing a Bolshoi ballet show close to her heart, and I suggested the Chestnuts as a nice place for accommodation; besides, the hostel would give her a golden opportunity to meet you. I trust her presence has given you a big fillip. Yours affectionately, Aldo.'

The reader let out a deep breath and considered the eventuality that the dancing girl would reappear (the universally acclaimed troupe, if still in town, certainly was worth a second attendance) and take Aldo with her. He stepped down into the scullery with a leaden heart.

Not much later, visual memories of Maria's coquettish performance up to her finest hour on the heath for the exclusive gratification of a suave concoctor made his still heavy heart sink under the weight of a suspicion that Aldo was associated with the mischiefs he had been the butt of, but his submerged organ floated again when on one of his regular visits to the job centre (he had come to feel that he'd got to move with the times) he spotted a card advertising a part-time time position as a filing clerk at a chartered accountants firm. Among other things, landing the job would allow him to aspire to new, self-contained lodgings and he was ready for a move in the teeth of the name of the hostel and the charm of the heath.

On the morrow – and what a luminous early summer day it was! – he walked with short but decided steps (Julius would be pleased to see him on a march!) to a Georgian house in a corner of Grosvenor Gardens and came out of it as a filing clerk. In the wake of his employment he moved to a one-bedroom basement flat equipped with a chequered kitchenette and a pink lav which the tubby landlord showed to him with a grin and words like, '*Et voila, la toilette pour votre plaisir, mon ami*'. Granted, the toilet could give him pleasure: thank heaven he would no longer have to queue for it. More importantly, he wouldn't be bound to have a regular taste of dubious Norse-style mash.

A couple of uneventful months in his newfound occupation allowed the novice clerical assistant to become conversant with a thriving breed of satellites orbiting around the Old Lady in Threadneedle Street. On an uncharacteristically hot day he emerged from behind a stack of files with not much of a spring left in his step (good job Julius was not around!), but a desire to be on the go surged up when, back home, he set about preparing tomato sauce as the perfect companion to butterfly-shaped pasta. While waiting for the chopped garlic to take on a nicely brown colour in the yellow-green olive oil bubbling at the bottom of the frying pan (a metamorphosis crucial for a decent sauce, his cuisine-wise granny had told him), he mulled upon the young accountant Gavin's failure to reappear at the end of his fortnight's hols, and it struck him that it would make sense to examine his unexplained absence with the help of one or two flashbacks. A proper assessment of recent events in reverse would probably allow him to come up with a plausible conjecture about the disappearance as well as to make for a clear-cut pattern in the crisscross. Moreover, joining the bits and pieces in the plot would keep the narrative in perspective and enhance his insight. Very well, then: the story about his recently obtained colleague would contain an end, a middle, and a beginning.

A glance at the garlic made him aware that the little cloves were imbued with the prescribed yellowish-brown tinge, and he carefully poured a can full of nicely chopped tomatoes into the pan; a generous sprinkle of oregano and parsley was a *sine qua non*, too, and he obliged; the next move was some slow stirring of the concoction before leaving it to simmer towards consistency. "Be a hut, my belly!" he roared and rubbed his hands just as his gourmet grandfather had been in the habit of doing while fixing a plate of lasagne with an intense stare. As to his grandmother, she would undoubtedly be proud of her grandchild... as a *cuisinier*, at least. He imbibed a large draught of full-bodied red wine hailing from the Etrurian Hills, got hold of his big armchair and took possession of it. "Sitting at ease?" he asked himself. Well, then, on with the investigation!

***

In the sultry afternoon before the Bank Holiday weekend, the spacious Georgian rooms resemble cabins on a becalmed ship. Gavin emerges from the senior partner Leo's office holding tight the purplish-brown file that has been causing him some concern and seems to have grown into an appendage of his slender body. His China-blue eyes are glued to the arabesque flowers forming a neat pattern on the carpet and he has the bearing of a sailor inured to a lull in the storm.

"Thank goodness it's Friday. It's going to be a long, hot weekend for us and a considerably longer sunny spell out in the country for you, Gavin," Stella, the thirty-odd-year-old secretary, is heard to say with a sense of glowing anticipation. "I'm positive that you'll have a whale of a time wherever you're going to be with your gorgeous sports car."

Gavin's response is a mutter about sticks and stones breaking his bones but words failing to hurt him. He springs into his room at the pace of a creature of the wild scuttling into a waterhole, re-emerges at the close of the workday and makes for the exit, but on reaching the door he performs an about-turn and says, "See you all in a couple of weeks, guys." Scant traces of his ingrained buoyant smile are the only variations in the monotony of his glassy features.

When the break comes to an end, he fails to keep his word. An out-of-the-blue phone call from the local police station informs the senior partner that the young man's sports car has been found abandoned at an archway and there are no vital clues. In accordance with the company ethos, the show goes on and business is attended to as coolly as possible, but things hot up in league with the weather. A chit crops up in the absentee's desk drawer, and it contains a reference to one Sir Gavin who, as Leo has reminded the missing writer of the note, in chivalric times had displeased a knight dressed in green by hoarding a girdle belonging to the lady of the castle where he was staying as a guest.

"Never mind the knight and the thingummy he failed to pass on; it doesn't sound fair on our Gavin, but then he, too, seems to have got the wrong end of the stick." Such is Stella's hushed comment.

Dino's eyes run through a copy of the memo: 'Michael has come to me like a solicitous father, but I wanted a mate, someone with whom I could be in touch man to man, heart and soul. At college, I learnt that we see only copies of beautiful ideas and hanker after a whole of which we are a half. Michael has come to me with a copy of a copy, and I've knocked him a little for that. Now, I'm feeling bad about it, very bad indeed. On the other hand we are demons, a Greek philosopher stated, and what shall I say?'

The piece of paper returns to Stella and she looks at it with widening eyes. "It's all Greek to me," she says, "but then the whole business looks a bit of a hotchpotch." She pauses before adding, "Oh, it nearly slipped my mind. The boss requires your presence, Dino."

When he enters his superior's room, Leo is sitting without a stir, and Michael is facing him across the desk, twiddling his thumbs. With a steady wave of the hand, the senior partner motions him on. "It goes without saying that Gavin's absence is quite an inconvenience," he begins in a hoarse voice. "Well, that's life, I suppose, and I'm confident that my valuable assistant will be with us all again pretty soon." A twitch intrudes upon the calm that pervades his spotty features, and he slews around in his comfortable seat. "Gavin has proved a bit of a comedown lately, I'm bound to say, and when I spoke with him last I didn't mince my words. Yet, I find it difficult to justify his staying away for longer than anticipated – and without the courtesy of an explanatory message at that. As to the note in his desk, to my mind it does not provide a satisfactory reason for vanishing into thin air, and I'm taking his lines with a pinch of salt. Wouldn't you?" There's a silent gap, and a twitch of the junior partner's bushy eyebrows fills it. As for Dino, his reply is a couple of slow nods. Leo shifts in his seat anew. "Please bear with my fidgeting," he resumes. "I see fit to put the blame on my gammy leg as well as on a distant wet day." His eyelids converge to a slit. "I was at the wheel of my sports car, you see, and my little boy was with me. He was no longer breathing when he came out of the damned thing. I still was." His eyes reopen, and a tungsten filament is lighting up in the pupils. He rises and hobbles to the window through which the sun has caught the large room in a gauzy net. Fully erect, he slowly turns round and adds, "Mind you, I, too, had my college days, and in the course of one Shakespearean evening I heard a character – the Earl of Gloucester I believe he was – declaim that we are to the divinities what flies are to wanton boys. 'The gods kill us for their sport,' the noble fellow stated – or something to that effect." His long arm juts out, and he clenches his fist as though in an effort to capture a stray beam. "I daresay the good earl hit the nail on the head," he comments.

Dino is abruptly put in mind of a high school lecture on reverent tutors of old initiating young and vulnerable male pupils into the virtues of a close rapport between men. Giton, the gilt boy from the Aegean Sea, is coming through the door on cue, and two deep folds can be seen ploughing through his high cheeks.

"Our Jarndyce case ought to be closed for keeps," Leo goes on to say, his mouth in line with the open one of a young man crossing a bridge in a poster on the wall. Hey presto, the bridge is a barn and inside it a little boy is on his knees close to a heifer; a shriek comes out, and it's couched in an awkwardly broken voice. Dino looks again at the lips of the passer-by in the poster, and they are still wide apart for a cry. Thankfully, none of them are able to hear it. Or are they?

***

Oh dear! Something was burning! The cook rushed to the pan and – damn! – the blood-red sauce had turned into a lump which looked a miniature replica of the stuff that had confronted him during his visit to the Nottinghamshire coalmine. He frantically turned the gas off, stared in horror at the monstrous dollop and on recovery flopped down in his armchair. "Why me-e," he bewailed. Mercifully, his grandma had been spared the sight! Soon after, another 'why' shunted his thoughts back to the track he'd been following up to the discovery of his culinary botch. Averting his stare from the doomed sauce, he waved a dismissive hand and returned to the abandoned track. What had been going on at the firm before the Bank Holiday weekend? It was a key question, and a satisfactory answer could solely be provided by a careful arrangement of people and incidents. Well then, let the story unfold.

***

Summer had re-established itself when a letter concerning the Jarndyce file lands on Leo's desk. Gavin is requested to go to his office. Walls may well have ears, but they are deaf as gateposts on this occasion. When he, Dino, gains admittance to the senior partner's enclosed space, the gentleman is standing upright with his wonted dignity and dwarfing his assistant from his six-foot height. His towering head is at a rakish angle and his spacious brow looks wavy with traces of the *terribilita*' Michelangelo had detected in Moses' gaze. Gavin's pale features summon up the image of David being rebuked by Michal for leaping and dancing in the buff before the Lord, yet looking game for an encore.

Later in the muggy afternoon, the account-keeper can be seen pegging away at abstruse figures with renewed alacrity, and it does look like a fine feather in the youth's cap. Equally cheering is the little laughter he gives in the kitchen while saying, "I see the whole shoot as a storm in a teacup," and it's most unfortunate that the cup he is handling slips out of his hand, drops into the basin, and breaks in half on impact.

Business progresses in line with the mercurial liquid suspended on the wall beneath a print showing a snowy slope of Kilimanjaro and in the middle of another sizzler he, Dino, fixes his clammy lenses on the mercilessly rising bar while Stella's pleasantly cool voice chuckles, "The heat is on with a vengeance," before bringing up the latest meeting between Leo and Gavin behind closed doors, and relating that the latter has been holding himself incommunicado since then. "I had a word with him the other day, and he wore his heart on his sleeve," he rejoins. "I told him that I was very happy about his new sports car, and he smiled and said that he was soon going to put the pretty model to the touch."

Would now Michael re-enter the scene and, in the manner of an Epicurean tutor of old, look after his fledgling ward? A couple of days later he, Dino, raises the topic, and "Don't worry, our Michael is a real gent," says Stella, her slim body bent on gaining control of keys moisturised by the exceedingly balmy day. He regains his room and worms his way through files which give him a feeling that they're biding their time in their drowsy corner.

Michael does return onto the stage. A providential gap in the door allows a glimpse of his ruddy lips stirring at a short distance from Gavin's delicate features poised between hope and fear. Then a reedy "Ouch!" is heard, and Giton, the gilt boy, is seen leaping from a dog-eared book and dealing gently with a cut on his mentor's forehead. The steady clack of Stella's typewriter restores the place and the time. "God, let news come," he, Dino, prays, and on the assumption that a bit of tactical quizzing may prove fruitful he lingers on the threshold, hoping to catch the typist-cum-secretary's eye. Unfortunately, her pupils stay steadfastly on a sheet of paper presumably crammed with details about a shark hopelessly flailing in a quicksand of his own making. As he trudges back to his cage, furry thoughts sneer at him with the impudence of the baboon who has recently stared at him from behind zoo bars at Regent's Park.

***

The smell of burning was almost gone, and Dino rose to his feet in order to do something about the mishap, but persistent whys and wherefores made him regain his seat and recapture one or two significant most recent moments in his office life.

***

"You know what? I haven't been able to find any cheap sacks in Soho," he is letting Stella know with a hangdog face on returning from his lunch break.

"Cheap what?" is her question prior to convulsions of laughter, but she regains her balance quickly and adds, "Don't be downbeat, Dino. Leave it all behind when you go home. I'm dead certain that you'll have more than forty winks tonight." She's playing her part deadpan, but he suspects the imminence of another bout of mirth. Not for the world. "On a more serious note, the case Gavin is handling is no cinch," she suggests while her Nile-blue fingers dance on the keys with a syncopated rhythm. "It's a good show Michael is lending him a hand."

Her words find him in agreement. "I'm sure Gavin has a guardian angel by his side."

The young lady's neatly combed curls waggle like dancing honeybees. "He and Michael seem to be good buddies, and that's quite nice if you want my opinion. You see, Gavin lost his dad when he was only a kid – sadly, the man died of heart failure not long after making a cock-up of his firm accounts – and soon enough he was in the doldrums. The story goes that he was taken into care as an emotionally disturbed child with an irregular pulse, but he recovered and went to college. He came out of it with two A-levels – one in philosophy, mind you – and decided to follow in his dad's footsteps." The narrator's hairdo stirs again, and a blend of confidence and concern shows up in her doll-like features. "Gavin's made himself strong now, but when things hot up he still seems to want the support of a cool older man," she adds. Her purple-varnished nails come off the keyboard. "Don't mature blokes take care of unsure youngsters in your country?" she inquires while flashing an impish smile. Back in his room, he gives another thought to boys initiated into the joys and sorrows of manhood by salted tutors. Then, he mulls over Gavin and the shades of concern on his face: amazingly, they seem to melt away whenever Michael approaches him with a soft hue in his sepia eyes. There may well be some truth in Stella's appreciation of the mores of his compatriots.

When he takes another and equally discreet peek into Gavin's room, the youth is bent over his massive file, and Michael is seated adjacent to him. The passer-by overhears the one say in an undertone, "This thing is proving rather tricky," and the other echo, "There's no denying that it's a bit of a challenge. I myself came across more than one facer of the sort when I was a young administrator." Soon afterwards, the junior partner is proposing a quickie at the public house round the corner and then a perilous journey to his own little place on the river, file and all. "We could have a proper look at the knot and end by having a bite into a decent measure of spaghetti bolognaise," he's saying. "Or is chop suey your kind of deli?" A smile flowing down the corners of Gavin's reddish-orange lips appears to settle the matter – for the evening at least.

Had that been a significant moment in the élan vital of two worthy accountants? Dino pondered over it while staring at

132

the pasticcio still on the cooker top. A niggling sense of guilt was soothed by the awareness that he had gone a long way in retracing his narrative steps and, yes, the beginning of it all was in sight.

**

A couple of weeks inside the walls of the Georgian dwelling have made him suspect that he has swapped masses of unwashed plates for loads of pages crammed with inky blots on the escutcheon of entrepreneurs, but a rather warm morning in the early summer ushers in a fresh start. After the regular mid-morning cup of tea, he goes into Leo's office and to the increasingly appreciated sight of plush armchairs, two large glass-fronted bookcases and up on the wall the striped male figure moving close to a bridge rail, his hands on both sides of his oval face, his mouth forming an O which intimates a scream. Installed in his writing desk, Leo is talking to Gavin and saying in the cultivated fashion of a consummate manager: "It looks as though we have a striking case in our hands. It's fraudulent bankruptcy of the first magnitude, I'm afraid, but also a feather in our cap, I make bold to assert, and I want you to size the case up for us. Dino is kindly going to bring the pertinent file to me, and then it will be all yours."

"I shall put my best foot forward," the young fellow returns before padding out of the room with his loose-limbed gait.

"Having your baptism of fire, old boy?" Michael inquiries from his paper-strewn place in the distinctive tone of an executive on the up and up.

"Something of the kind," comes as a reply, and it sounds bullish.

Stella's curly-haired auburn head pokes through the door of the typing room. "I can see heaps of pages dropping onto my little table," she moans in her la-di-da manner.

On re-entering his room, he, Dino, senses an aura of

honourable partnership in the firm while he gazes at a couple of dolphins and sees them glide over coral reefs in a mauve expanse on the poster that appears to be the pièce de résistance in the cramped enclosure. He tiptoes to the print and puts his left hand behind his earlobe in case the sensitive sea-dwellers are singing, but no sound can be heard. At a closer look the dolphins seem to be frowning above their beaklike snouts. "In a bad mood, are we?" he puts to them before returning to Leo's room, the case at issue under an arm.

"You can bet your boots, if you have a pair of them in your cupboard, that our Gavin is the right man for the job," the senior partner tells him, and he, abruptly assailed by the recollection of a reckless bet on the edge of the fountain in his native town public gardens when he was younger and naïve, pushes out the under lip and puts aside the prospect of a wager. "You know, Gavin is about the age my boy would be now," Leo goes on to say while casting a look at him and Michael ensconced in an armchair. Then he limps with a dignified gait to the window through which an increasingly warm sun is filtering in. "I had hopes that my only son would be giving me a helping hand. Heavens above, he never would." He moves to the wall, and his slightly spotted face overlaps that of the slim figure moving along the bridge rail and voicelessly screaming. "It's a bit of a conundrum, don't you think? I mean our Jarndyce case, of course."

"There seems to be at least one clear spot in the brainteaser though," his partner observes. "No more sumptuous villas and obliging senoritas in Almeria for the fop at issue. Gavin is sipping the mélange, as far as I can see."

"O for a draught of vintage!" Leo exclaims, and he, Dino, welcomes the echo of the yearning of the fine young poet close to his heart as an exquisite change from the gentleman's fondness for a sobering cup of tea.

***

134

It did seem to be the end of a new beginning. His eyes still closed, Dino sensed that he had managed to untangle the plot and come up with a smooth pattern. For all that, had he found the answer he badly wanted? He was not sure yet. One eye sprang open and the partial sight proved broad enough to empty him of any extant doubts. He had better dispose of the hideous lump still sitting on the cooker, and have another go at the delicious dish he had shamefully mad a botch-up of. He owed his grandma one.

On the following day, an early phone call brought him Stella's voice along with the tidings that Gavin had been tracked down inside a bush underneath the bridge where his sports car had first been spotted. "He seemed to be looking at the water and smiling at it," the caller reported, "but he was dead as a doornail. A small bottle and a couple of white pills for the benefit of his heart lay at his side, and a tiny piece of paper was in his hand." She had not been told about its content. The office would be closed for the day as a matter of course, and the funeral service would take place on the morrow.

As he went slowly downstairs, Dino had a vision of Gavin's family and friends huddled together within sight of a crematory fire similar to that, it flashed on him, had made Mila, a wench from the Abruzzi Mountains in D'Annunzio's drama, cry at the stake, 'The flame is beautiful! The flame is beautiful!" In the next sequence the mourners were filing quietly into a nearby room and swapping anecdotes about the loved one while having tea and cakes. Everything was as it ought to be, but was Gavin's nonattendance part of the 'ought'? As to himself, now he knew how the story had ended, and the only remaining question was whether, had he been aware of the denouement the night before, he would have started reliving the events from the final moment in the story.

A few days elapsed before a vital clue was provided by a couple of lines in the scrap of paper Gavin had been holding in his

135

hand while smiling at the water. 'Another philosopher has come to mind', he had recorded. 'I've been thinking of Socrates, the chap who was blamed for the corruption of young men in his native Athens and dispelled the charge with the help of a bit of hemlock. It's a funny thing, but this bloke has helped me catch up with the idea behind the copy. I feel quite happy about it; and that's for sure, folks.'

Late in the evening, Dino felt pleased about his elaborate reconstruction of the case. A managerial voice saying, 'A feather in our cap, I make bold to assert' prompted him to conclude that the metaphorical statement had been the prime cause of the whole affair. The whys and wherefores had been given an answer at last, and it lay at the very beginning of the story. "Eureka!" he squawked, but in the next breath, "Come to think of it, does it really matter?" he put to himself. A postmodern poet had told the world that the beginning invariably points to the end, and surely the lyricist could be taken at his word while he was envisaging a Second Coming. Regrettably, there would be no Second Coming for Gavin, the fledgling fellow who had come to see friendship as the love of man for man conducive to a marriage of true minds. He swayed his head and headed for the kitchenette. The Jarndyce file was now closed, yet wasn't it was worth another thought over a mug of piping hot pitch-black coffee?

11

A DUMMY RUN

Had Fame, daughter of Earth, come to his door? Well, sort of. The status-enhancing novelty was in fact a grant by courtesy of the local council, and the letter conveying the heartening news made his arms reach for the not too distant ceiling. The monies would afford him more time for the utterances of romantic bards as well as help him out of the Grosvenor Gardens dwelling where an unfortunate young accountant had sadly succumbed to the niceties of the Jarndyce file. Moreover, the income, modest though it was going to be, would allow him to put a few coins in his piggybank regularly with a view to buying a bike on the never-never; just think of the bliss of riding in the country as his cousin Lando had done on his shiny motorcycle at Nut Farm! The limbs he had elatedly raised came down on the sobering thought that finding somewhere else to live was a top priority. Honest to God, he'd had enough of a restrictive basement in spite of the pleasurable toilette! High time for a move, he said to himself and dashed to the nearest newsagent's for a copy of the local weekly. Back indoors, he set his eyes in motion until they paused on an advert concerning a spacious room in a flat with all mod cons. It did look a matter of now or never, and it would be 'now'! He got to his feet, threw out his chest and made his body move up and down in the exacting rhythm of a gymnast having an invigorating workout. A two-minute exercise made him feel proud of himself and put his charming Gallic landlord to shame. He kept up the beneficial contortions until he felt that he'd better see to the room on offer. A hopeful half-smile (it still made sense to him to save the other half for a rainy day) accompanied him to the telephone.

At first blush the flat into which he marched twenty-four hours later did not reach the height of sophistication, yet the room allocated to him was ennobled by pretty posters on the walls, including one showing Salome holding the head of John the Baptist on a platter: a remarkable picture, he acknowledged and then, swallowing hard under pressure from an uncalled-for Galician memory, he hung next to Herodias' daughter's picture a rather old print displaying a Roman legionary duly equipped with Claudius' eagle. A hazily coloured poster displaying Boudicca, Queen of the Iceni, went up in close succession, and the lady could be seen riding on her lofty chariot, her arms bravely ignoring the reins. In a pleasant mood, he set about pacing the fauve carpeted floor and felt that he had come to the right place.

His inchoate feeling of satisfaction was corroborated by the timely appearance of his fellow lodger, a lean, medium-sized, ginger-haired lad from the South Downs, who introduced himself as Bernie and welcomed him with a smile suggestive of his native chalky hills. Within days, their coming together did look like the outset of a success story. Arguably, Cicero's recommendations on the subject of friendship were being implemented, also with the aid of a sequence of teas and digestive biscuits, and when the kind request to do something about the mammoth cassette player sitting suspiciously behind Bernie's door provoked the retort, "What's the big deal, mate?" in a stubbornly adolescent voice, Dino shrugged off a sense of unease; it was only because of persistent rhythmic sounds piercing the silence that he turned the music lover into a negative number while murmuring, "But yet the pity of it, Bernie" with a felicitous adjustment of the doomed Moor of Venice's sad remark.

Not long after that, it was a case of 'but yet the cheek of it, mate', for Bernie was heard to assert with a knowing smile, "What these digs want is good tiles. See my point?" Still, Dino felt duty-bound to see his point because it was being made by a tile-fitter and he'd been under the spell of clean-cut, lean-shaped tiles since childhood; apropos of that, he had a vivid recollection of how on one occasion he had let a little piece of baked clay drop bang on a corpulent rat and seen the dark creature drag her presumably pregnant body along an unevenly cobbled courtyard, squeaking no end.

In all honesty, there was not a shadow of a doubt about Bernie's ability to do something about the worn-out tiles in the kitchenette and to do it promptly by virtue of the fact that he was provisionally signing on in the aftermath of a tiff with his Teutonic foreman, who had dared dispute the value of the 'mathematical' tiles originating in his quasi-native Lewes. The obverse of the coin was that skilled tile-layers were in demand, and the young labourer was rather high in the chart. "I have nifty hands. No pulp, you see," he had stated once with the unshakable conviction of a Jehovah's Witness, and by all appearances there were no flies on him. Besides, he was his flatmate, and two's a company – it takes three to make a crowd, does it not?

Soon enough a crowd was made by the appearance of Linda, a petite brunette with short hair and a mauve ribbon on it, spirited umber eyes and a doughy visage on top of a cryptically patterned sweater coupled with a hem-frayed miniskirt offset by blush-pink laddered stockings. "My lady friend is in charge of a boutique," her companion disclosed over a cuppa, laying stress on the French word. There you are: women on the up-and-up and men caught in a thickening web! In fact, Linda seemed quite capable of managing her slightly younger sweetheart, and her no-nonsense disposition reached its climax the evening he tapped her for a tenner and she walked out without an aye or nay, leaving her darling at sea – and no, it didn't look like the Sea of Serenity.

Within the space of one week, the jilted lover announced with a winsome smirk on his downy cheeks that he was expecting his lady friend back any moment. "To be quite candid, she's sold on my body," he disclosed.

Spot on. Linda reasserted her presence and as soon as she ran into Dino she said with the help of a couple of taps on her brow, "Don't you think that your flatmate could do with a little help?" Her umber eyes flashed with a maternal tinge.

A couple of weeks had passed without much ado when the phone came alive in the early morning and a well-known voice croaked, "I don't mean no trouble, but I'm laid at the hospital round the corner right now. The sister here says that a change of get-up would do me no harm. Could you bring over my black slacks and pink sweater, mate?"

Dino obliged and a few minutes later found his companion lying in a ward bed and getting to grips with a batch of stones in his gall bladder. The patient's whey-like countenance coloured as soon as he caught sight of his clothes coupled with a small bag of healthy oranges and a packet of not necessarily healthy cigarettes. "You're a regular bloke, you are," he chortled while shoving the cigs inside his chequered pyjamas trousers. "The matron here is not for puffing," he added with a meaningful wink followed by, "I've got plans, Dino" and a bigger wink.

Bernie's big plans were afoot indeed, and they came into full swing the day the youth showed up wearing a snazzy bottle-green suit, a gaudy spotted tie and shiny black shoes topped by a golden buckle. "Don't you see a toff?" he asked while swinging this way and that with the satisfied grin of an about-town, or about-village, fop. "Most of my bleeding pay has gone on what you're looking at," he owned, without sounding too sorry for the financial hurt. "But the shoes are a freebie, courtesy of Linda, of course," he added with a beam of appreciation before revealing that the two of them were about to tie the knot.

"Good to hear this. You'll be making your parents happy, I'm sure," Dino was pleased to remark.

The beam faded. "My parents, did you say? Mum and dad have separated, you know. Dad's living with his ladybird at this moment in time. Tough on my mum, but I've lot of time for my old man."

"Your trousers sure look fine," the other acknowledged on a different tack.

"Boy, it's because of your ironing gadget, pal!" The grey-green colour of his military jacket looked equally nice, and the pleasing display was duly recognised. "You've put your finger on it," said the clay virtuoso while bringing a photo out of a crumpled wallet: a slightly younger Bernie was in it, a rifle in hand, a glow of pride in his eyes, and an air of insouciance on his face. The ensemble impressed the watcher as a black-and-white illustration of the insolent, devil-may-care countenance of youth. Within seconds it transpired that there was less than an ounce of love lost between the former private and the army, and a justification of the feeling emerged from a couple of details about his superiors' idiosyncratic ways. "To give you a coincidence, the sarge comes to me and says, 'In 'ere you do like you are told, boyo.' And if I get a little pissed, the psycho sneaks up and snarls, 'It'll be the cooler for a couple of days, man. Com-pre-hen-ded?'" A snigger was accompanied by, "I got cheesed off, Dino, sure as a gun. Any road, I picked up one or two things about tiles in the god-awful barracks, and after discharging myself I got work on a site without too much of a knocking about."

There was no denying that Bernie had a knack of securing a job, yet he seemed to find matters relating to a sweetheart in a managerial position somewhat perplexing. A significant episode occurred when a mighty sound replaced the giggles, sighs and suchlike that, late in the evening, would offset the occasional silence of the ogre sitting behind the door. Keeping one ear glued to his door panel, Dino heard his flatmate strike up, "I say, if you woz in my shoes" and Linda blast out, "Your shoes? You just see what I can do with mine!" A thud suggested footwear flying across the room and landing on a hapless male body. "Feeling better now, darling?" she was then asking in a tone that would have made a mythical Fury blush. Some impressive stomping followed the question, and then there was the dull sound of furniture in motion. Soon after, a shrill cry against a manageress that knew how to 'bite like a bitch' pervaded the air, and it was enriched by a string of ominous gasps. As soon as the storm subsided, the discreet eavesdropper slumped in his armchair and, doubled up in it, embarked on one of his profound meditations on the perks of female companionship; then a sudden impulse made him thumb through his bilingual dictionary until 'absolute shambles' arrested his attention. He rose to his feet and said to himself, "Thanks, folks, and now for a cup of char"; he liked the term for the drink used by the ex-private Bernie. While waiting for the prescribed five-minute infusion to materialise, out of the corner of his eye he espied the very lad sneak to the fridge and seize a bottle of the *XXXX* malt-and-hops kind of tisane he appeared to be extremely fond of; then he heard him mutter, between longer-than-usual slugs, "Something is not proper in here, chief. To give you a coincidence, there's bugs in me bed." A slow turnabout brought out the spectacle of a face drawn with discomfort and rendered almost grotesque by a weal on a cheek. Golden buckles were versatile devices, and no mistake. "I'm going to look for a decent bunk at some other digs," the face's owner added out before lumping away.

The infested bed did not stay vacant for too long. At a most becoming early morning hour an easily recognisable voice wheezed through the phone, "Don't mean no bother, mate, but I'm coming out of hospital right now; it's the old bleeding thing, damn it. See you in a minute."

No sooner said than done. The bug-and-gallstone-ridden youth came to the door, looking at loggerheads with his golden-buckled shoes. Following request, a cup of char was gladly offered. "You are a brick, Dino," he ejaculated with a laboured attempt at a smile, and, on being asked about Linda's whereabouts, disclosed that his lady friend was after a better position. "She knows all the tricks of the trade, my Linda," he pointed out. As to his position, "I'm out of work right now, but no cause for alarm – the bosses are crying out for tilers," he disclosed, while producing a poor sample of the bounce he'd been blessed with in his army spell.

No cause for alarm indeed: the job seeker was soon given another chance, jumped at it, and soldiered on without a trace of hoity-toity, Teutonic or other, foremen in the way. For a good while there was no trace of Linda either, and it did look a baffling coincidence: was this stripling from the chalky downs devoid of any chivalric streak in his veins? A knight of old would have set off on a perilous quest for an elusive damsel, whereas his quest seemed to be primarily motivated by a proclivity towards off-the-peg garments; however, it would be unfair to gainsay his success on that score, considering that whenever a pleat looked out of shape he was only too glad to borrow Dino's valuable steam iron and then make an appearance in his glad rags. "This nugget of yours is just the ticket," he had recognised more than once on returning the precious tool, and yet his sartorial finesse did not seem to be the lethal weapon of a man with a passionate interest in 'birds': only one swallow had landed on his roof so far, and she had barely nested in it; it stood to reason to suspect that no Valentino was lurking inside the youngster's cuirass. The lack made for a rather bland state of affairs, which in the long run took him down a peg or two in his flatmate's eyes. When all's said and done, his lackadaisical attitude was making the shared life somewhat wanting the flavour he had bargained for and going down like a lead balloon. The descent went on ceaselessly until a bolt from the blue (or rather the grey of the tenement) made the balloon float anew. It happened when, at a late hour, Dino found himself espying a gallant escort a damsel from the top-floor flat to the basement and then up again in the wheezy lift. He hastened to inform Bernie of the transfers and was confronted with a most edifying reaction: "I see no reason for losing our marbles, mate. I've noticed the coincidence and poked my nose into it. The word in the block is that the bleeding bloke is a fashionista. He and his dolls are in the habit of travelling up and down, I reckon." It sounded well-thought-out, and how sad it was to see such a sensitive as well as judicious youth cling to a nest now devoid of punk rock reverberations.

For all that, recovery was in the pipeline, and it came about when, on another late night, the figure of the fashionista materialised again inside the cage, inordinately close to a female body. The watcher gaped at the show and scratched his head before bursting into Bernie's room. "I've just seen the man, in the lift… in the lift again! A young female form was at his side – and it seemed to be breathing!" he blurted out.

The recluse removed his eyes from the strip cartoons in his beloved *Beano* and unleashed a benevolent smile. "Don't be a puppy, Dino. Dummies don't breathe, do they?" he remarked.

Within a minute, the impressionable witness was making ready to indulge in a few mouthfuls of his cherished Montello grappa as a matter of great urgency when his chum's voice hit him: "Next time you see the pillock squeeze a doll in the blooming ridiculous cage take a gander at her boobs, will you?" A glassful of the tipple rushed down the hearer's throat.

A few days after the happening, the newcomer found himself ambling amidst waxworks. A close look at life-size figures ennobled his mind's eye with the image of amorphous matter moulded into a meaningful shape. Was mimesis been put to good account? He bestowed an undivided smile on masks of death pleasingly arranged in a chamber of horrors and intimating the survival of creation in the shape of a phoenix rising from the ashes, thanks to the magic wand of a demiurgic madame. He emerged from the celebrated museum in a relaxed frame of mind. "Death does not exist; it's only a matter of change and novelty; dying is but to cease to be the same," he told a portentously overcast sky. Whoever had been the source of the aphorism had put a fine point on it. Hunched up under his telescopic brolly, he hummed 'Singing in the Rain' while braving a sudden downpour and keeping his beady eyes peeled in case a scarlet double-decker should jog down his way. Fairly wet, he made his block of flats and mounted the uneven stairs, whistling 'Nessun Dorma' to arguably dormant tenants. When a rumble of thunder presaged more water, he produced a forceful shrug and jerked up two fingers: he was beyond the reach of crotchety Uranus, ha-ha-ha. In a split second, the divine grumble was followed by a mundane squeak; he nuzzled his forefinger against his nose and spun round: the lift, probably coeval with the god, was descending to the nether regions. With a kick of his heels, he sprang to a vantage point and stopped there as though the spring implanted in his back had run its full course. *Notorious* swooped into his mind with a vengeance, promptly followed by *The Thirty-Nine Steps* and *The Third Man*; the late hour seemed to provide an excellent backdrop for eerie pictures, and so did the place. "Just wait and see," he whispered to his frozen self.

His self didn't have to wait for an inordinate length of time. A well-known male silhouette passed by in slow motion, clutching what looked a female body even though, to his great disappointment, the bosom was beyond the range of his strained horn-framed eyes. He planted his forefinger beneath his chin and tiptoed downstairs, but the cage suddenly halted, moved upwards and came to another standstill. He frowned, thought hard and quick as a flash went in pursuit. The contraption restarted its sluggish progress and retraced its steps. There was a pause followed by a fresh movement: the lift ascended again with a smother of cacophonous hissing and then, abruptly, the tenement block reverted to its inbuilt silence; the shabby, erratic cage must have made the summit. Weary of the antics, the pursuer darted back to his door, but a new motion of the cables made him slip his glasses off and on and linger at his strategic post. On a course of its own, the erratic apparatus wheezed by on its way down, offering a blurred view of the couturier propping up yet another female figure wrapped in a fluttering shroud: a mannequin at a cool guess. Sniffing, the onlooker waved a hand by way of a farewell, shut the door gingerly, and adopted a posture of utter detachment. Soft strains from Bernie's room soothed him like a balm; he padded along and discreetly knocked on the door. A flimsy "Yeah?" made him enter. Sitting in bed, at one with the total eclipse of the heart experienced by a singing female and articulated for the convenience of hoped-for empathetic listeners, the youngster received the news without a stir. "It's all right, old chap. Come to me again when you have chewed the cud, will you?" he requested with a yawn.

A sudden suspicion of being an undesirable visitor made Dino step away, but on reaching the doorway he did a U-turn and delivered a Parthian shot: "Tell me, have you been in touch with Linda recently?" he inquired.

"Ugh. My lady friend's gone for keeps," was the reply, accompanied by a bigger yawn.

"Oh, has she? A sorry state of affairs, I daresay, but your punk is still with you. Two's company and three's a crowd. Am I right?"

"Now look here, Dino. Punk is buggering middle-class crap. Gimme soul any time," the other retorted before resuming his exclusive communion with the blotted-out heart of the hypersensitive singer.

The intruder moved out, gently closing the door behind him. A card lying on the yellowish-brown cabinet roused his curiosity and in the blink of an eye the postal item was in his hands. 'I'm in a bit of funk at the moment,' he read. 'It's because of the dummies and all that jazz. Back as soon as I'm in the clear again.' There was no signature, but the curling characters signalled Linda's hand.

Snuggled down in bed, he mulled over the youngster let down by his father for the sake of his lady friend, bullied by a bumptious sergeant, and finally deserted by his highly-strung sweetheart. In the next breath, his mind shifted to the commuting fashion designer and his female partners: what if the mannequins were actually breathing? "Much virtue in if," Touchstone had stated, and, like any other jester in Shakespeare's plays, the fellow deserved to be taken seriously. Could it be that there was in it more than met the eye? Say, the *Murder, She Wrote* kind of thing? Hang on. Hadn't the good family doctor warned his mum in days long gone about the suspicious conjectures of a child's fevered imagination? Gradually, he sank into drowsiness and was on the brink of total surrender when a string of squeaks engendered a precipitous recovery. He pricked up his ears and tiptoed to the front door, cautiously opened it, and let his bleary eyes wander across a most tranquil scene. A stealthy backward walk was followed by immobility at the sound of scuttling feet and a stifled cry. The listener stood on tenterhooks and then bounced all the way down to the basement. Standing in front of a closed door, he scanned the dark door facing him. There! There! A hand is jiggling the knob; a voice is whispering, 'Abracadabra' and hissing, 'Open sesame'. The door obliges and a male bespectacled figure squeezes in. Camera-like, a shadowy head pans across a spacious room; a moderately-sized body pussyfoots to a long narrow table which cuts across the place. For a few long instants, the prowler stands face to face with a dusty full-length mirror before padding to books stacked on a big chair and magazines precariously balanced on a stool. A washbasin emerges from a shadowy nook and not far from it a striated bed is sitting against the wall. A sudden thunderbolt discloses female frames quaintly aligned against the opposite wall, and seconds later another burst of light exposes waxen faces and spirited eyes evocative of stylish waxworks; a laddered pink stocking is hanging loosely over a table, and ruddy clots form blotches on the floor.

Unable to tarry any longer, Dino bolted along the landing, dashed past the cage now at a standstill within the shaft, bounded upstairs and, keeping his head down in the posture of an enraged bull, got to his door. His unsteady hand grasped the handle and then let go of it; his throbbing body swerved back to the stairs and climbed up until it reached the top; his dilated pupils settled on a landing that looked empty save for a blush-pink stocking and a mauve ribbon. In the twinkling of an eye he reeled downstairs again with the bearing of a distressed koala bear and hurtled into his flatmate's room: it was in good kilter save for a heap of bed linen which suggested a rather quick exit. He rushed to the blower and dialled 999.

A couple of days later, a succinct piece in the local *Guardian* reported the bizarre tip-off to the police of a tenement tenant who had found himself in a fishy situation and followed the false scent laid by a fashion designer in league with a young shop manageress to the detriment of her moonstruck boyfriend. As to the sudden disappearance of the lady, the incident was not regarded, notwithstanding the stocking and the ribbon found on the spot, as a cause for immediate concern and further investigation. Similarly, the clandestine exit of her presumably distraught fiancé did not look all that suspicious: "It sounds like the toccata and fugue of a Bach aficionado," was the comment of the obviously musical-minded reporter.

The reader adjusted himself to the peculiar shape of his armchair and took in the empty feel of the place. Then, "About time I moved on," he thought aloud and hastened to celebrate the prospect of new digs by imbibing a few drops of his handy Montello elixir. A glance at his baggy trousers made him embark on a search of his badly needed iron, but where on earth was the precious tool? His painstaking rummage was halted by the dropping of a most unwelcome penny. "Oh, damn! Damn! Damn!" he squeaked. "Villain! Jackanapes! Just the ticket, eh?" Disconsolately shaking his head and throwing his arms skywards, he flitted about until he came to the bedside table in Bernie's room. Inspired by *Spes* – the goddess of hope and therefore a heavenly being of last resort in the eyes of the high-flying Cicero – he opened the wooden accessory's little door: no iron showed itself. In lieu, shiny golden-buckled shoes gaped at him. He balanced his specs on the tip of his unhappily planted nose and tried on the ex-private's keepsake: the footwear fitted to a tee. His face sinking in a sea of smirks, his tongue sticking out, he bowed to defeat.

12

PUPPETS ON A STRING

The curtain had fallen on the extravaganza. Dino struggled out of the egg-shell sheet, inside which he had echoed Giacomo Casanova lamenting the passing of youth. Had the audience seen through the emblematic bed cloth and the flickering candle he had precariously held in his hand as a surrogate Venetian candelabrum? What should he make of the fitful laugh and the allegro moderato applause at the end of the soliloquy? The amateur thespian hurried back into his routine pale grey outfit and walked out of his adult education institute.

"Ever thought of going on stage as a pro, Dino?" a female voice asked from behind.

He wheeled around and met the amiable eyes of his fellow student Fiona. "Poor Giacomino. Hope I've not made him turn in his grave," he replied with a melancholy smile.

"I daresay his moan struck the right chord." A twinkle in her eye heightened the mobility of her doll-like features.

He shot a glance at her short, neatly arranged auburn hair, and it looked steady as a rock, but was it in the nature of things? A slight putting to the touch would probably bring out the truth, but he was aware that self-control was a golden rule on the island he had come to and that aliens were expected to comply with it.

"I belong to a race credited with a flair for acting, especially off stage," he stated. "Well, such is the view of one or two foreign observers. Honestly, I don't give a monkey," he added, arching his arms, but the limbs resumed their regular position in the wake of the listener's quizzical glance and crinkling nose.

Twenty-or-so-year-old Fiona had joined a weekly evening course on European modern literature and been a regular presence in it. More than that, on the occasion of the show she had wholeheartedly given a helping hand. On reflection, she could well be a Brownie Guide with a chain of daily good deeds to her credit. "My little van is parked outside, you know. I'd be delighted to give you a lift," she let him know as if to support his assumption.

"That would make a change!" said he.

Both moved to the vehicle and hopped in for a drive. To him the journey came as a pleasurable deviation from getting on and off a route master, not in the least thanks to the set smiles on the papier-mâché faces of a bunch of puppets ensconced at the rear of the van.

Equally pleasant were the rides that took place in the course of the following weeks. It did seem that the twosome was getting a kick out of coming together away from the brick-red walls of the Edwardian establishment they were entering weekly, and it was nice to see that the puppets regularly lying at ease in the back of the conveyance were keeping up their spirits. Moreover, juxtaposition innocent of ulterior motives engendered familiarity without any sign of the proverbial contempt; on the contrary, it provided an outlet for closely-guarded secrets. Dino let the cat out of the bag and told Fiona about Nerino, the pitch-black and sinewy pick of the fourteen-strong bunch of domestic felines that had roamed in the garden of his childhood. Alas, the dainty little fellow had the makings of a bully and he had finally ostracised him, but on a chilly winter night Nerino had sneaked in and broken the neck of four newly born kittens. Had it been a vendetta? A crime of passion, maybe? He had mulled over a possible motive for the slaughter, but then again, were animals capable of feelings? Not really, Descartes had opined, and yet the fact remained that a furry thing from hell had caused havoc and a pussycat had been left licking nasty gashes on the necks of her hapless babies.

"Faithful love will never turn to hate, or so Christopher Marlowe thought," was Fiona's comment and then, off on a fresh tack, "Teaching is my profession, puppetry my vocation. Goodness knows, one fine day I'll tour the country in the company of a batch of cloth creatures. They are pliant friends, you see: they move, they speak, they act just the way I want them to do, and they give me the thrill of being in control on my own stage. Yes, I look forward to my travels." The winsome smile she produced seemed to have been borrowed from one of her merry puppets.

The following week she was a visitor to Rome, and the ride after the vacation was peppered with observations inspired by the City of the Seven Hills. "The past is present down there wherever you go," she declared at one point in her recount, and was she signifying what he hoped she was? Moreover, she had been most impressed by the venerable countess who had hosted her in compliance with Dino's request. "Dear little lady!" she exclaimed. "Ever heard of Betsey Trotwood?" His brow creased as an effect of concentration, but to little avail. "I'm thinking of David Copperfield's eccentric old auntie, naturally," she explained forthwith while upturning the corner of her mouth.

"Last time the lady in question and I were together it crossed my mind that a troubadour had told a countess that life is the shadow of a fleeting dream, and I couldn't help reciting a relevant line," he let her know. "Her response was, 'Life is a canopy, and here I am, walking in the shadow.' The lady admitted that she was not the author of the metaphor, but that's beside the point, I'm still tickled pink with it."

The journeys continued without a break, and so did news and views. It was all hunky-dory in spite of the fact that the driver's gift of the gab appeared to carry the day most of the time. Dino saw their weekly contact as something fostering a growing relationship as well as the conveyer of signs made meaningful by a variety of social tones, suggestions and judgements. There were no ifs and no buts about it unless – dared he entertain the outrageous idea? – Fiona was hoping to drive a hard bargain in due course. He prepared for any eventuality.

One evening she said, "I'm taking you to a nice place you may have not explored yet. Father Thames, here we come." *Ipso facto* they were walking along the dusky river and experiencing the melancholy feel of a wind-blown misty night until both stood behind a parapet, taken by the lap and the swash going on beneath and the shimmer of yellow lights along the banks. Purplish-red bands streaked the vault of heaven, and he pointed at them while saying, "I really thought that a sky like that existed only in the eyes of a Gothic stargazer."

"Oh, that! It's the reflection of the city lights that mainly causes it, of course," she explained.

Perish the thought! There she was, the goddess of wisdom pouring cold water over a warm gush of fancy! Half-smiling, he aimed his forefinger at a grey house across the narrow road.

"That's where the clink used to be. It was a prison, as you probably know," said she. "It accommodated thieves, ruffians and above all, heretics." A quiet laughter rippled through her small lips. "Clink," she reiterated, making the *k* vibrate. "Sounds nice, doesn't it?"

He gave a repeated nod. "It makes me think of men being taken to *I Piombi*, the Venetian prison, glancing at the lagoon from the bridge and sighing. None of them expected a return journey. Remarkably, the great Giacomo Casanova I managed to belittle on the occasion of our social evening, managed to escape from the dungeon."

"How romantic! Well, I'm bound to add that the jail here probably took its name from the piece of iron that kept the captives safely tied to the wall or to the floor." She sounded and looked apologetic.

"Chin up, Fiona. Time is a healer, as everybody knows. Pompei is a case in point: we go to the museum in that unfortunate city, and what do we see? Human forms doubled up on their ledges. As likely as not, we leave the place feeling as cold as the ash that got stuck to the bodies of hapless victims." No signs of horror appeared on the listener's face; a pensive smile did instead. "Or consider the Holocaust if you like," he added for good measure; "the mere thought of it can still send shivers down the spine – yet, for how long? Some people say that it makes sense to forget it all; other people maintain that the eruption was nature's way of keeping its balance. It seems to me that reason is at stake here." His historical statement was rewarded with a twist of her lips.

They came away from the parapet and moved on, taking in the aura of the place. She kept looking ahead, as elusive as a well-educated young lady is expected to be; he waddled along staring at nothing in particular, his hands firmly in his pockets.

The silent stroll came to a halt when an age-old inn came into sight. "I see the Globe. It would be a shame to pass a pub of the kind by," she said, and in they went. He opted for a pint of stout; her choice was cider laced with brandy. "It's on me," he said in a macho voice. Without further ado, she gave her assent. They sat close to a Renaissance replica and took a few sips. Suddenly, her agile fingers went into her large handbag, fumbled in it, and brought out a brown parcel. Smiling broadly, she thrust the item into his hands. Wagging his head, he undid the wrapper. The white cover of a large square book showing an amorous cat and a perplexed female companion emerged. "Oh, no, you shouldn't have taken the trouble," he said.

Her head swayed gently. "It was no trouble at all. I just thought that it might help you get reconciled with your old flame. Now, peek inside. I'd gladly be told of the apple of your eye." A few more drops of cider went inaudibly down her throat.

He moved leisurely from page to page and paused at the drawing of a feline pair caught in the act of discovering that love is a many-splendored thing; then, mopping and mowing, he turned the pages all over again and finally placed his forefinger on a cat who happened to be a slow specimen endeavouring to grasp a simple fact.

She looked at the creature intently, and the laughter that followed made the surface of her trimly-cut hair ripple as if brushed by a soft wind. Keeping her eyes on his favourite type, she said amiably, "Well, I was expecting that you would plump for the circus character secretly rehearsing *Hamlet.*" Her irises looked a shade darker than usual. There and then, a bell rang along with the publican's voice announcing that it was closing time. They downed their drinks and took leave of the premises.

Raindrops were falling with uncharacteristic vehemence, but within seconds the van provided cosy shelter. Dino nudged his specs and said in a murmur, "Oh, I haven't told you about Lulu, the prettiest of the furry bunch roaming in my garden. One day I succumbed to the temptation of tying a tiny Punchinello to her body. The next morning, I saw her lying as stiff as a poker against a tree, and it dawned on me that, in an effort to rid of the puppet, she'd gone round and round the trunk until the noose had become too tight for her little neck. I was ashamed of myself." He turned his head to his companion with the countenance of a sinner yearning for absolution.

"You are something of a character, Dino. It's a funny thing, but I'm getting a kick out of your company," was her reaction while she switched the engine on.

The Easter break entailed a brief hiatus in the continuity of the drives, confabs, and the presence of puppets in the background. At the same time, it provided a golden opportunity to join fellow ramblers in a couple of salubrious country walks and savouring cool soft beer at some picturesque rural pub on the route. In addition, Dino relished sizeable portions of tricolour fusilli and thick tomato sauce sloshed down with glassfuls of deep red nectar from Mediterranean vineyards to the accompaniment of generous doses of Rossini's operatic tale about a thieving magpie. In the course of one of those inspiring as well as nourishing repasts he gave a thought to the tenancy partnership that had made him a term in an 'a + b' expression as well as to a combination of variables opening up the possibility of a soft option: playing it safe was high on the list of his philosophical imperatives.

The summer term brought about renewed proximity to his van-steering classmate and made him put the evening journeys almost on a par with his morning cups of coffee as a contributory cause of his welfare. He immersed himself in a review of the salient moments of their social intercourse.

Week one: Fiona and he are snugly seated, and there's a decent space between them.

Week two: their bodies are sticking to the orthodox posture albeit with a slightly less wide gap in the middle.

Week three: a little fellow in the employment of the GPO fills the void, wearing a blue uniform and sporting a snail on his large cap; round metal-rimmed glasses straddle his impressive nose, and a walleye enhances the peacock blueness in his beady eyes. "Postman Pat transferred to a better van," Fiona explains with a cute smile. "A most conscientious chap, I must say," she goes on to say while hitting the postie's cap lightly. "A pat on Pat," she comments with a chuckle and then, "I'm sorry Jess isn't at his side today, but I can assure you that he is a nice kitten; a far meow from your Nerino, if you don't mind," she asserts melodiously. Soon afterwards, she changes the subject. "How much do you know about the communication between this island and the continent during WWII?" she asks. "Our tutor has mentioned the Enigma Code on one occasion and mentioned Bletchley Park. I'd welcome a comment."

He rubs his nose pensively. "All I know about the park at issue is that it's part of Milton Keynes, and as far as enigmas are concerned I know a little more about Elgar's variations," he replies, but music does not appear to be a topic for the moment, and a voiceless gap in the conversation is filled by a memory of Uncle Raf hinting at a park with a curious name and swearing blind that boffins were shamefully spying on other people's top secrets in there. Should he now let another cat out of the bag and pass it on to Fiona? The thickly-haired creature tosses inside the sack and then goes out like a light; he gathers that it's miles better to leave his uncle and his view of what was going on at the park buried in the past.

At the end of the week-four class, the distance between the two is narrowed by the presence of a Jurassic creature – long neck, an even longer tail, and all the rest of it. "It's a diplodocus, of course," she clarifies. "A dinosaur, in plain English." She pauses, and then, "Dino-sour," she adds deadpan. He cocks his eye and sees the explanation as a symptom of a puppeteer's idiosyncratic brand of humour.

Week five: a hunch-backed, white-clothed clown wearing a pitch-black mask joins them in the vehicle. "Punchinello was lying on his own inside a drawer, and I thought he'd be quite happy to share the rear with his fellow puppets," he says by way of an introduction, and her appreciative smile in response prompts an invitation to a stroll in the park near at hand.

Soon both are seated on a bench in the shade of a venerable

oak. Her eyes laugh while scrutinising Punchinello now comfortably sitting on her lap. "A clown is a mythical figure," he lets her know in the manner of a well-read tutor. "He is expected to swap his life with that of the king when the time for the ritual dispatch of the archetypal monarch comes."

"Quite interesting. Flowers are full of mythological symbolism, too," says she while indicating a pink hyacinth at the edge of a flowerbed. "Pretty, isn't it? Please don't talk piffle if you can, it signifies."

His gaze falls on a stinging nettle close to the flower. "The weed next to it doesn't look all that pretty to me. It means cruelty, as you probably know."

"Now we're quits." Her recurrent laughter runs through her likeable features and rolls out in pleasing rings.

He sniffs. "Good to see you amused."

"Aren't you amused as well?"

"Oh, I'm pleased as Punch." He sets about whistling an old tune emerging from several layers inside him.

"Your trill is music to my ears. Shall we make a move?"

"Where to? May I suggest the old pub by the river as a convenient port of call?"

"Can't make it now, I'm afraid, but there will no doubt be time for a nice drink when we next meet." Her quick-witted eyes grow fully animated, and her curls arranged in well-smoothed, drooping clusters partake of the commotion.

"I've been thinking of your dummies. They shouldn't stay caged in for too long," says he. "You see, sometimes I have a feeling I've got stuck inside my little place, and when I go to the door it's locked and somebody else has got off with the key."

"Couldn't you try and get hold of the golden key, as your Punch did?"

"Why should I? Judy has gone, and I don't think she will ever come back."

She looks at him with deeply sympathetic eyes. "Same boat

for you and me. I've not been having an easy time at school lately: unruly kids and all that jazz, you know." She gives a gentle cough. "There was an advert in the TES the other day about a teaching post Down Under. Owzat as an idea?"

"Sounds great, but wouldn't you be deserting your post?"

"Would I?" A soundless moment is followed by, "What about you? Why have you come over?"

He makes his specs keep in line with her eyes. "You really want to know?" A demure bow of her head signals a quintessentially feminine desire. "All right, then. One good reason could be that a pope is not a king, and a king is not a pope." Her countenance suggests difficulty in decoding and he promptly discloses that such was his grandpa's favourite answer to all his whys when he was a child. More than once the elderly man had lifted him onto his lap, harrumphed, and told him some fairy tale or other, which he had found less mysterious than his rigmarole.

A dark hue of bewilderment appears in her pupils and is soon displaced by a tinge of curiosity. "Could I hear one of them? I'm sure it would please my little mates as well."

He purses his lips. "I'll do my best to remember. Prepare for a good listen next week."

Alas, no good listening took place the following week: on leaving the institute, Fiona joined a tall, square-set, young fellow sporting a pale-yellow mane curbed by a ponytail, and the two of them went to a vehicle which did not appear to be her mauve van. Dino pulled a long face, gave a shrug, and made for the bus stop. On board, *La donna é mobile*, he mouthed in tune with the unhappy Rigoletto while riffling through a novel which was all about a non-existent knight and he would presently be discussing with his classmates as a notable example of contemporary European fiction.

Seven days later, he stood behind a pillar, his cheeks twitching with heebie-jeebies up to the moment when he spotted Fiona following the same youth into his convertible car. The watcher rejected a feeling of déjà vu, flicked his shoulders upwards again and hurried away.

Two more classes came and went without his shapely classmate (he was now willing to go so far in his aesthetic judgement) materialising on her regular seat next to the window. Could she be on a tour with her puppets and exercising her controlling power by pulling handy strings as though they were those of a harp? Even so, what about her newfound companion?

When the vacant seat was reoccupied one long week later, no explanation for the absence was given, nor was it expected. The girl was past the age of compulsory education after all. Time and again his searching eyes met hers fleetingly, and he saw the intensity in them match the colour of her reddish-brown locks.

Out in the open air, he espied her go to her own means of transport and an uncalled-for stimulus prompted him to trot to it. From inside it she wound down the window and darted an inquiring look. "Glad to see you back on your chair," he blurted out. "Hope you haven't been ill."

The grin on her well-moulded face was completely reassuring, and so were her words. "How nice of you to be concerned, Dino, but I'm happy to report that I've been in the pink all the time. It's only that I've been visiting places, and my Postman Pat as well as your Punchinello have kept me good company. Someone I've recently met had arranged the whole kit."

The account vindicated his guesswork. "Super. And could this someone be the owner of a posh convertible car?"

"Bullseye! The young chap happens to be an impresario."

"An impresario?! Good for you. Are you coming to the class next week?"

"I certainly am. I'll be all yours next week."

"Is it a promise?"

"Judy's word."

A sailor's word would have been a better term of comparison. Her renewed absence made him feel acutely uncomfortable. Could she be on yet another tour with the obliging producer of public entertainments? It was a distinct possibility. "The lady's a tramp," he groaned, but the lady gave the lie to his assessment by being present one week later, attentive as usual and putting forth an intriguing interpretation on the nature of the non-existent knight. At the end of the class she approached him with a kind invitation to a quickie, and he readily accepted it.

Sitting inside the nearest pub – not a landmark in the local district – both opted for the usual. "My round," she said forcefully and, repressing his macho self, he concurred. Then, "What about your granddad's story? Please make my evening," she pleaded.

After some token hesitation, he took a piece of paper out of his briefcase. "I've jotted down one of his tales," he said. "Hope I haven't made a mess of it. Unlike my grandpa, I am no born storyteller." A reassuring smile on her face bucked him up. "Are you sitting comfortably, bambina?" he asked. She took a tot of her cider, slightly shifted her posture and flashed a look enriched by a twinkle in her large reddish-brown eyes: the bambina was sitting comfortably. He gave an appreciative smile, took a long pull at his drink, and slowly unfolded the scrap. The prelude was over; he tackled the large score.

***

Once upon a time there was a beautiful seaside town along the Mediterranean coast. Lots of ships laden with splendid merchandise would come to anchor after days and nights enveloped in a silence solely pierced by the cry of a gull or the song of a siren, and sailors would file ashore.

As time went by, the trading town shrank into a quaint village; only fishing boats would now leave the little harbour in the evening and stay overnight in the offing, their lamps shimmering while the fishermen offered old tunes to the heavenly breeze.

Amidst the fishermen there was a young man known to one and all as Masino. His above-average height, ebony hair and eyes and sinewy body darkened by long sun-baked hours of work on his boat made the girls cast furtive glances at him, but he did not seem to notice.

The lad was not well off, and yet he felt content with his lot because he greatly enjoyed staying out all night, his sturdy form stretched out on a plank, his eyes up to the starry sky, and his ears caressed by the lapping of the waves. "In one such night anyone can be a god," he whispered to himself more than once, unknowingly echoing an ancient lyrist.

Masino often went underwater although not for fishing, for he loathed the spectacle of creatures from the deep flapping and writhing in the net, and, like a colt at odds with the bit, he had come to terms with the spectacle solely because compliance for the sake of survival was the name of the game. Beneath the waves, it was another kettle of fish. Aha, the beauty of orange reefs surrounded by slithering silvery shapes, oysters shining as if they were jewel caskets, and shells dazzling like splinters of variegated marble! He would tread on patches of seaweed as if on a soft green meadow, and while doing so he would feel that he had entered his exclusive Promised Land. "Yea," he would say to himself, "I'm walking in the recesses of the deep on the way to the realm of the light; I can discern the paths to its home." Old Job's confident answer to the Lord was grist to his mill.

Blissfully, the world into which he regularly dived was innocent of any other human presence, and it stayed so until, in the middle of one of his balmy swims, he spotted an ivory female form leaning against a reef. He goggled in amazement: was the unbroken body a testimony to some bygone shipwreck? Seasoned fishermen had told him stories of ships gone down to the bottom of the sea only because Poseidon had thrown a tantrum. He took a closer look at the woman, and the sight of her marbled physique as well as of her visage encrusted in seaweed and shells filled him with a novel yearning. He swam away, but as soon as he regained his cottage he felt that the newly discovered creature was his inheritance from the word go and destined to be his forever.

The sun was on the brink of setting when he plunged in once again and joyously met the challenge of the chilly water. Quick as a flash he was close to the mystery woman and working on his task in a collected frenzy: a coil of rope secured her body, and both rose to the surface. With painstaking care, he lifted the precious load and in the dusky light saw her emerge like an ancient sea goddess coming up to strengthen his faith as well as that of other doubting mortals. Glowing, he hoisted the ivory being on board and started rowing at a measured tempo while indulging in uplifting visions: the find would bring a touch of magic into his humdrum life and, yes, the young woman from the sea would be his sweet companion for ever and ever! All that was needed now was a name. A long look at tiny stones forming a chain around her neck made the appellative come to his lips: "Corallina," he breathed.

Late that night the newcomer was afforded pride of place inside his cottage. He switched the lights off in case some passer-by should nose inside; then, holding a torch, he stood in front of his guest and, making no sound, let his dark eyes glide on her. Through a chink in the curtains a moonbeam revealed the woman's milk-white skin in all its chaste nudity. Had an angel been driven underneath the blue waves by a fondness for the flora and fauna of the deep and then made unable by the sudden heaviness of her saltwater-soaked wings to fly back to her heavenly abode? A sudden image of the countenance of the winged messenger of God hovering inside the village church aroused a burning desire to see the angel's features, and the feeling made him gingerly work on the crust hiding it. The painstaking effort prompted the cleansing youth to suspect a fierce resistance to his desecrating hands, but the thick layer finally gave in, and "Aha-a-a!" he whooped. Seconds later, the joyous utterance sank beneath his bewildered look, for the lineaments confronting him made up a grotesque beehive-like mask, an utter stony waste. With increasingly frenzied movements, he slid a sponge all over the creature's face and stopped only when two royal blue little stones sparkled star-like in the moonlight. He gaped at them and teetered back under the sway of a virgin emotion. Corallina kept motionless, bathed in the setting moon.

***

Dino's piece of paper crackled into a fold. The storyteller drank up his tumbler, crossed his arms and waited.

"You've told me one of your grandpa's stories, haven't you" she said.

He gave an easily managed nod and a hardly-won full smile.

"Time to make a move, don't you think?" she suggested, and he agreed. They rose and moved to the door.

Outside, no mauve van was waiting for its legitimate owner. "My four-wheeled mate is undergoing an overhaul," she let him know and walked with him to the nearest bus stop, but an ebony taxi rumbled along, and she flagged it down. "Would the non-existent knight have been prepared to share a cab with a damsel?" she asked with a roguish smile.

"Very much so. Unless his bus was coming along," said he. His fleshy forefinger went up in the direction of a double-decker trundling to a halt.

"Oh, I see a knightly option. Till next week, Dino." With a jaunty wave of the hand she went on board. His face twitched slightly as he stared at the rear lights slowly fading into the night.

It was class day again, but where was Fiona? Dino stared at her unoccupied chair with some irritation, and the unpleasant condition turned into a nasty shock when, soon after the tutoring and the laying to rest of the knightly ghost who had never existed, another fellow student came to him with a sombre face.

"Poor Fiona has fallen victim to assault and abuse," he relayed with bated breath. "The vile misdeed was perpetrated in a black hackney. She's been hospitalised and is slowly but surely recovering." The cabbie, Dino was also informed, had treated the passenger to a few glassfuls of champagne: a lucky lottery ticket called for a celebration, he had happily divulged, and the young lady was quite welcome to it. A dreamt-up windfall, a spiked drink, and a pill forced down her throat had set the scene.

Minutes later Dino was trudging to the bus stop, weighed down with reflections on a male predator's betrayal of trust. He recalled all the journeys Fiona and he had shared, and thought of the one they had not, then he pictured in the same breath wires pulled by a controlling puppeteer and animated marionettes in full swing – among them a fellow clad in white and wearing a black mask which let a full-blown smile creep out of it and spread over his hollow cheeks. The king who was not a pope had been ritually sacrificed, and he had duly taken over: Punchinello at his puppet best.

13

LITTLE LADY CHATTERBOX

It's a small world. Dino sensed the truth in the adage when he was given the telephone number of a lady who claimed to have been a friend of the family when the war was on and now dearly wished to make his acquaintance. What a lark! A mystery woman who'd been in touch with his folk and obviously remembered him as a little boy was keen on catching up with him as a grownup. He thrust out his lips, walked to his local, treated himself to a couple of pints of the refreshing usual, sauntered home, and answered the call. A cracked mature voice made him twitch his ears: would he be kind enough to go and see her at the weekend? The familiar accent gave him a feeling that letting bygones be bygones was not an option. "I can't see why I shouldn't," he replied.

At the weekend, he stood on the threshold of a semidetached house in the suburbs, distinguishable from the other semis in the street by virtue of the number and the lilac tint on its door. The musical sound of a clapper bell endowed with a rural charm made a suspiciously copper-haired head peep through a gap in the panelled surface and a dark-brown face emerge into the autumnal light. The visitor sensed that the gravitational force of destiny had engineered the meeting of two terrestrial bodies orbiting around the focal point that was home sweet home. His mother would undoubtedly regard the event as a manifestation of destiny. Family news were hurriedly exchanged in an increasingly spirited atmosphere. Strong tea, for which both had an acquired taste, was taken in by degrees, and family ties were painstakingly traced. Hadn't a lad called Mario, a cousin of hers, been a bosom friend of his as a Boy Scout? Elena (for such was his host's name) believed that he had, and he was only too happy to confirm her recollection and at the same bound to disclose that the two of them had lost touch after their primary school years. Well, then. Mario was a geologist now, and also a happily married man as well as a respectable member of society, Dino was told, and it occurred to him that the society into which Mario had integrated had survived the ravages of war and restored proper social mores: the fasces as well as Romulus and Remus had been taken down from classroom walls and replaced with a crucifix. Admittedly, it had been tough on the Martian babies, but it made sense to suppose that Don Orsino would have given a blessing to the change on the strength of the fact that the twins had been born out of wedlock.

The next moment Dino's father came under scrutiny: Elena had been fortunate enough to strike up what she described as a solid friendship with him but gradually boiled down to little more than a nodding acquaintance between urbane street neighbours. She vividly remembered his parents' wedding day: as a young woman – "A mere child, actually," she promptly corrected herself – she had sat on a pew in the cathedral and, as an uninvited guest, been a witness of the young couple's solemn entry and stately progress up the nave while the strains of Schubert's 'Ave Maria' wafted along. The bride had looked slightly flushed, the bridegroom profusely so, and a few hankies had discreetly touched moist eyes. Yes, it had been a deeply moving function! "I haven't told this to anybody else," the reminiscing lady revealed with an emphatic squawk. Sometime

167

after the wedding she had moved to a region in the north of the country, and from there to the island overlooking the Channel.

The visit was proving a success: they were already on familiar terms and she had intimated her resolve to comply with the rules of her adopted country's social etiquette while producing sounds that strongly suggested a refusal to give an inch to soft-spoken natives as well as a knack of taking a whole yard and making inroads on their common parlance with results of the first magnitude. The listener felt that he was being given living proof of the theorist Chomsky's belief in everybody's innate knowledge of linguistic phonemics; struggling with out-of-the-way subjects at college could be rewarding after all, he considered with some satisfaction.

"Not everybody is a spoiled child of Fortune," his interlocutor put forward while grabbing a cookie and fixing her guest with hazel eyes tinged with suspicion.

"What d'you mean by that?" he countered.

"Not much, as God is in heaven. It was only a passing thought," she replied. Still, could he in all frankness deny that his father was providing him with a bit of dough for his educational pursuits abroad?

"Well, I am doing my bit to support myself."

"Ah, but my father... no, no, I'll say more about him next time we meet. Let's have a beautiful cappuccino now," said she.

On a second visit, and over an equally decent tea, Elena did make her father the main subject of conversation, and Dino shared a ramble along twisting and turning paths where Ariadne's skein of thread would have certainly been a boon. En route he learned that his fellow countrywoman had come over soon after the end of the war: she'd made the long journey in order to move away from a little world of which she was no longer able to make sense. She'd been long dreaming of the far-away country where, it was bruited, one could find what was hard to find at home, and she had fulfilled her dream by hopping on a northbound train, only to discover that she was not the only passenger travelling in quest of salvation. She had mulled over making tracks after being parted from the dashing young soldier she was in love with. Sadly, a seemingly endless clash of armies had taken him away and left her with a broken heart and a ring. "One day I looked into my chest of drawers, and oh, ah, the token of my engagement was no longer in it!" she related. 'A gypsy has been in,' his father had explained. 'I saw the woman run away, but it was too late for a chase.'" The loss had been a body blow to her, the narrator disclosed before swallowing a mouthful of a pastry redolent of a good *pasticceria* in their quasi-Deep South; still, why had the ring been the sole valuable item nicked by the intruder? Not much later her father had fallen gravely ill, and she had nursed the patient on her own because the war had snatched her only brother.

"What about your mum?" Dino asked; it looked barely in keeping with the family bond that she had made no mention of her other parent so far.

Manifestly caught off balance, Elena shifted in her seat, filled two flowery cups with a strong brew of tea, handed one to her guest and lifted the other to her small lips. The vessel returned to the table with an assertive clink. A king-size cigarette rustled out of a packet, and it looked at odds with the barely royal size of her compact body. A second cig jutted out, kindly offered and accepted for a later smoke. A slightly trembling hand lit the cylinder up, and a leisurely drag ensued. Then, "Mamma was no longer with us. She died a couple of months after the war broke out," she replied. The hue of her brown eyes intensified. "You see, my mother had got the idea that I was not her own flesh and blood. 'Somebody made a blunder at the hospital where you came into the world,' she muttered once. She had a horrible feeling that I was a changeling – a changeling, *capisci*?" The narrator sucked at her cup, drew breath, and took a long puff.

"Ah, but my father never fell in with the idea. 'Bollocks, nothing but bollocks!' he bellowed when, after mamma was gone, I let him know about how she'd felt about me. 'You are my flesh-and-blood daughter, and I'll never let you go now that your dear mother is no longer with us. Never!'"

While Elena's digging into family affairs was in progress, Dino flung a glance at the cabinet from which the man under consideration was smiling inside a silver frame, his pince-nez installed on a small spherical face, which presumably belonged to a small spherical body. *Like father, like daughter*, he silently commented. Moreover, the photograph seemed to chime with the sort of picture that relations of the loved one, following in the footsteps of forebears treasuring protective household gods, would devoutly keep in full view; in fact, the portrait smacked so strongly of the hereafter that he couldn't help having a hunch that, like a marriage, it had been made in heaven before being delivered by angels to the bereaved relations on earth.

The woman's tale unfolded: on a scorching summer afternoon and while her father was having a siesta, she had dashed to the balcony and in no uncertain terms made her presumably equally dozing street neighbours privy to her determination to jump down. The unexpected hold of her father's strong arms had interrupted the performance in the nick of time, she disclosed after taking a rather longer puff at her dramatically shortened cigarette. One year after her aborted attempt she had left home and got on the long train that would eventually take her to the distant island for a 'fresh start and a new hope' – her watchwords since her personal D-Day.

Had the narration come to an end? Not by any stretch of the imagination. After a visit to the toilet she picked up where she had left off. A few years' stay had made her sanguine again. A steady job in a biscuit factory had allowed her to take out a mortgage for a spacious two-storey semi as well as to buy an estate car on the never-never. She'd had her fair share of cares, of course, but then she was no molly coddle, and those who knew her would not hesitate to swear on the Book in respect of that.

This much she stated most emphatically, and any doubts the other might have on that score were promptly dispelled by her mention of a most cogent case in point: a thorny dispute with the gas board concerning the installation of central heating at her house had seen her come out wearing a victor's garland in the contest with a batch of supposedly know-all engineers and inspectors. Doubtlessly it had been a great personal triumph, and the report of it sounded like a climactic passage in a swashbuckling novel. When the tea-for-two party was over, the visitor took leave of the little lady under the impression that Chomsky's tenet had been fully substantiated.

For the record, Elena saw herself as a woman still in her prime. When, standing once more on the doorstep of her abode, Dino greeted her with a sonorous, "Hello, dear Miss Brodie," she responded with the smile of one at a loss for a proper appreciation of the name. Petty details of the kind aside, a penny-wise lifestyle and a strong determination to succeed had helped her to attain to the creature comforts that are the aim in life of any sensible human being. And then there was Bibi, the tabby pussycat she'd spotted meandering devoid of an identification tag in the local common and, yielding to the claims of her sun-warmed heart as well as, arguably, to the demands of a soul yearning for companionship, had taken to her comfy nest and made a sharer of her dinner table and double bed. "Bibi knows about me more than I do about her," she was pleased to admit with a rising intonation, which seemed to issue from her troubled past. It was not difficult to imagine her bosom friend lolling in her lap on a cold winter night and lending a striped ear to one or other of her stories from bygone days. "My darling always listens to me with great attention. She's very civilised, my little baby," she whooped.

To all appearances, the expat had made it, but was the past

really the back number she had sworn it was? The anguished look fitfully showing up on her Hellenic-Iberian face suggested that painful memories stubbornly lingered on. When, as she poured thick coffee out of a huge and tarnished pot that was a reminder of home and all the good things that had gone with it, Dino called attention to her father's face on the cabinet, she let him know with a most becoming sigh that he, too, had passed away: a coronary thrombosis had been the cause of his leaving our vale of tears a few years back. "The news made me rush to the airport; I couldn't help it, you know," she added, sounding kind of apologetic. "Try and see little me crouched in a corner of a jumbo-jet and weighed down with memories," she muttered. And how had the perilous pilgrimage ended? Sadly, home had come to her as scarcely a place for further sharing. Her brother had been hard put to recognise her, and the general welcome had been, to put it mildly, lukewarm. The episode had brought the family saga to an end and extinguished any extant hopes of a tangible reward. The final battle in her private war, certainly longer than the one that had wreaked havoc on her peace-loving country, had been similarly lost, and she had returned to her suburban home and her urbane Bibi determined to forget. No buts about it, but there was something called forgiving to be dealt with. When, after being defeated in the 'Ace Sweeps the Board' card game she and Dino had been playing over some additional coffee she said in a subdued voice, "You've taken it all from me just as my brother did," he found the stress on 'me' and 'my brother' somewhat disconcerting.

A few weeks went by before Elena's voice came again through the phone line. "How about a drive in my brand-new automobile?" it asked, gruff and caressing as usual. They could visit some place of interest, and suggestions would be appreciated.

He hummed and hawed, and then 'Murder in the Cathedral' came to the rescue from a shady nook in his mind. "I wouldn't mind a trip to Canterbury," he said. "It's an overdue visit, you see."

"*Bellissimo*. Let's go cultural for a change."

'Women at the wheel, danger at heel.' Aware though he was of the adage, Dino was far from prescient of a pilgrimage that would provide him with an excellent opportunity to put the male-wisdom exemplar to the test. A couple of miles sufficed for a display of the lady's idiosyncratic style: she would hold the steering wheel tightly in the manner of someone engaged in mortal combat with a foe; she also exhibited the requisite energy for a change of gear combined with a soft spot for the lower toothed wheels even while driving on the flat. In the grip of bemusement, the passenger expected wheel and gear to give in any minute, but it was her hands that time and again shrank from the good fight and opted for a lull motivated by an urge to get an urgent message across. They were minor particulars, to be fair, for in any other respect she was treating the showpiece with laudable concern. Her large eyes would sparkle with self-confidence in the manner of a runner fully convinced that slow and steady wins the race, and only once in a while did she step on the gas as if having sudden doubts about the maxim. In addition, she never failed to signal before changing direction by gently waving her hand as a native driver was expected to do. Occasionally, the hand did not seem to be at one with the actual course, but the discrepancy was dealt with utter composure. Slightly more puzzling was the fact that, while overtaking, she seemed compelled by some mysterious force to cut in; when a male motorist wound down the window and gave her the bird, her reply was, "Please shut up, my friend. I've got plenty of road sense. Could you say the same about yourself?" The felicitous juxtaposition of her emphatically cupped hand and withering stare appeared to put the impercipient road user in his place.

It transpired soon that Elena had one or two more tricks up her sleeve, and a roundabout gave her a golden chance to execute one of them. She did not let it slip, and managed to kill two birds with one stone by getting in everybody else's way and at the same time accomplishing a daring and elaborate U-turn which took her back to the very spot where she had entered the treacherous road junction. Shortly afterwards, her intriguing performance reached its climax in the shape of a sharp reversal when a huge pitch-black cat leapt across the road and came to a stop ominously close to the front wheels. The admirably responsive driver reacted to the uncouth presence by stepping hard on the brake and bringing the vehicle to a screeching halt. Her eyes grew wider in horror while she said in a shrill cracked voice, "I need a strong coffee, Dino, and I'm sure you could do with one as well." Her nicely rounded hands chopped the air.

A short time after the event both sat in front of two large cups of the highly beneficial potion. Keeping her small shoulders at an angle over her drink, she admitted feeling a bit below par. "Good Thomas will forgive us if we don't go and see him today. He is a saint, and saints do forgive," she stated. Her table companion waved a sympathetic yes. Then it was time to drive homewards, and it was a sedate and judicious performance. It was probably through intercession of the saintly archbishop that no more roundabouts showed themselves en route, and the only domestic feline that emerged into the uncertain light of the late afternoon turned out to be Bibi, patiently waiting for her mistress to return to her for mutual comfort.

The ill-starred pilgrimage was a fading memory when a familiar ring brought Dino once more to Elena's door and to the sight of her laborious traipsing along propped by a tiny walking stick.

"Awfully sorry to see you in such a state," he said for want of a less conventional utterance.

"I fell off my stepladder," she explained. "And I nearly broke my legs." Her first and fourth fingers jutted out and her eyes rolled upwards. "Thank you, San Gennaro," she said with a sigh and an upturned face. "I'm on leave at the moment, but it seems like providence that social security is all right in this country," she remarked, a bittersweet smile suffusing her small face. "Nothing like what's going on down there. Would you believe that my brother is still waiting for his war pension? O yea, *campa cavallo!*" Like a horse waiting for the grass to grow, her brother could only hope and pray to be still alive at the time of the provision of the sacrosanct benefit. A blob of dew formed in her eyes while she summed the situation up by crying, "What a farce! What a shameful farce!"

"Oh, I nearly forgot!" said Dino forcefully in a bid to change the subject. "Sophia Loren of all people was in town the other day, and fans flocked to catch a glimpse of her. In the film I've seen at my local cinema club she plays the part of a woman who travels on foot with her daughter while the war is still on. Both come to grief when black-skinned soldiers crop up. She and her daughter get... well, you can guess what they get."

Disgust and horror flooded the listener's fleshy face. "Don't mention the war, please," she rejoined. "Didn't you watch the comedian on the telly the other night? I'm talking of the dark chap with crazy eyes and the long legs he moves like scissors. He is funny, very funny, and so is his Spanish waiter." Her voice crackled with laughter, but the quality of the sound underwent an amazing transformation as soon as her confidante entered the lounge and padded to her: "Bibi, my sweet Bibi," she murmured while taking the kitten up into her arms. Her finely pencilled long lashes grazed the creature's velvety fur while she added in a soft tone offset by nasal strains, "I shall always take good care of you, darling. You'll never end up impaled on a door as your little sister did." A brief silence fell and a long breath followed before she added, "And you know why a dastardly brute did it to her? Only because she happened to be my little pet, and I'd lost my heart to a young man who was guilty of loving his country and doing his duty as a soldier, oh, oh." It looked and sounded as though Bibi was her sole interlocutor and the guest's presence utterly redundant. "Then my fiancé was brought home in a coffin," she continued. "When I went to the mortuary he was lying there, and many other men lay with him. I saw black shirts, red shirts, green army jackets and then the one that belonged to the young man who had been my only love and promised to lead me to the altar, oh, oh, oh."

She was still giving her undivided attention to Bibi, and he decided that it was high time he reasserted his presence. "Elena," he said with a touch of tenderness, "your story has made me feel sick at heart, but it has a silver lining: animals don't suffer in the same way as we do, you know."

She twisted and turned; her well-smoothed curls shook. "Ah, don't they? And who says so?" she asked with a flushed countenance.

"A philosopher said so. Animals have no thoughts or feelings, only instincts." Hadn't he mentioned something of the kind to another, younger, lady? An uncalled-for memory of his childhood companion Lulu flashed through his mind: had not the kitten been visibly in pain because of the murderous Nerino? It did seem that the answer was still blowing in the wind, as the oracular Bob had stated.

An assertive smile found its way across Elena's classical facial folds; her eyebrows flicked up and down in quick succession, and a graceful closing of her eyes gave her the air of a doll flowing in a sluggish stream of thought. An instant later, she was gulping a morsel of cake while her compressed body swung back to her flatmate. "Did you hear him, Bibi?" she said, stroking her and being rewarded with a liquid look and a purr before the tabby thing leapt off and padded away along a straight line and then in a zigzag as if exploring the various possibilities open to her. "You see! You see!" she squeaked, her evenly thick copper hair now in a state. "Bibi recognises me, decides to make a move, and goes wherever she fancies going. She wants a life of her own, my Bibi!

No mind, eh? You can go to hell, you and your philosophers, I say!"

A radically different approach was sorely needed. "You've sure had your share of pain, Elena. No philosopher having a sense of right and wrong would deny that," he acknowledged.

She looked appeased. "I went to the balcony, but my father didn't let me go."

He nodded. "Your father did the right thing, I'm sure."

She slapped her thighs. "Shall we have a good espresso now?"

He concurred: "What a splendid idea!"

They spent the rest of the evening savouring a proper measure of the ritual stuff and chatting on this, that, and the other – about the city they had come to, for instance. "Charming like a mature lady whose still appealing attributes visitors discover at their peril," Dino remarked, and Elena found the simile appealing.

Next, the royal family came up as a topic. "A little expensive to keep, but *simpatici,* she stated.

He admitted that the royals seemed to have some practical as well as ideological value. "Apropos," he went on to say, "you have a noble name." Elena, the mother of Emperor Constantine, he elaborated, was one of her illustrious namesakes, and so was Elena of Troy. The coincidence made the listener let out a grunt of approval, but he couldn't help suspecting that if the ancient beauty had resembled her, Greeks and Trojans might not have been at one another's throats for ten-odd years. Wisely, he skipped over the aesthetic detail, and they went on to talk about their respective plans for the future: would both of them be staying in the country they had come to? She intended very much to stay put, whereas he had no definite plans.

When he took his valuable watch out to check the time, her eyes got wider than ever. "How did you get the nice gadget?" she inquired.

"It was my father's parting present," he replied, "but it doesn't show his time any longer." The remark was rewarded with a short movement which looked like a nervous twitch. He smiled sympathetically, and then it was time to leave. She showed him to the door, and it did not escape his attention that she could afford to walk without the aid of her stick. "Glad to see you can move without any prop-up," he said.

She guffawed. "I say, do you take me for a cripple? However, the council carer is not supposed to be around tonight." The big wink accompanying her words said the unsaid.

Through the window, her back garden loomed up and he pointed to it while saying, "Your patch of green looks beautiful."

"Aha, Francis is helping me with it, and what a nice man he is! Come again some other weekend and I'll introduce you to him," said she.

On a sunny Saturday afternoon Elena did take Dino into the garden, and a lean silver-haired man was seated on a bench, his head bent over a mug he was holding as though it were a flower cup. "There he is, Francis, my *bravissimo* gardener," she announced with a gurgle. "He's Irish." Her tone of voice lowered dramatically when she added, "His wife died in an accident not long ago. Some men were shooting in a street, and she was caught in the crossfire. Go and meet him while I go and make some more tea."

Dino flung a look at the bloke – was he actually Francis? Or was he Biagio, the handyman who would occupy a rough wooden seat in his grandparents' grove and hold a large cup of wartime barley coffee in his huge hands? He went to him. "Hello there. Having a nice break?" he asked.

"Sure I am," the guy replied in a low-pitch tone while raising his head. An amiable smile crossed the intense lines on his weather-beaten face; his pale-blue eyes twinkled in the morning light. No, he was not Biagio: the handyman who had been a fixture in a profusion of oranges and lemons had bushy eyebrows beneath a folded forehead, deep-set eyes, an ancient face, and spoke with an accordion-like sound. "So, you are Francis," said Dino. "And you take care of Elena's garden, don't you?"

"I help a little at weekends. If she wants my fingers, that is."

"Of course I want your green fingers, Francis," Elena warbled as she emerged from the kitchen, carrying the additional drink on a tray. "I see you and my little garden as one thing."

"That's very generous of you, Elena," said the man. "I'm happy to come in handy; besides, it's nice and quiet in here. Not a jot of the troubles we're having at home." Then, turning to Dino, "your friend is an exquisite lady," he added. "She's a bit of a chatterbox, mind you, but I like the way she talks to me." The smile he produced had the breezy quality of the sea he had left behind.

A wicker-work easy chair stood next to the bench, and it took Dino no extraordinary flight of fancy to visualise Elena taking central stage at the core of her green enclosure, surrounded by flowers and trees bowing in the light wind like courtiers in the presence of their royal mistress while Bibi lay sprawled out on a cushion at her side and Francis sat in the allocated chair, holding a mug in his hand like a flower cup and having a quiet word with his weekend employer. It was tempting to think of the little lady offering embers of feminine warmth and receiving petals and stems from her gardener's green fingers; two decent human beings, both casualties of somewhat different wars, who would come together in a cosy orchard and stick by each other for weekends on end.

Sometime later a phone call from Elena conveyed the tidings that her beloved assistant wouldn't come to see her any longer. "He's suddenly gone, poor Francis. The man had a heart attack soon after leaving his regular local last night," she sobbed out. "It should have never happened. Never. My God! Who's going to take care of my little garden now?"

Dino received the dreadful news with a discreet silence, but as soon as the saddening story she'd plunged into came to a much-needed pause on a deep sigh, he expressed his sympathies and added that he was also sorry to have to inform her of his imminent leaving town in order to attend a three-month college course in the north of the country, but he promised to come on a visit soon after his return.

True to his word, a few months later he tried to contact Elena on the phone, and he did so more than once. The monotonously ringing tone brought about a good deal of guesswork and eventually took him one more time to his compatriot's lilac door. A 'for-sale' sign supported by a pole was stuck in the front yard. He grimaced at the sight, pondered, and rang the bell regardless. An oriental-featured young woman welcomed him with a sloe-eyed stare and asked him if he was a potential buyer. The house owner, she added, was detained in her native country for family reasons.

"I've come to say hello to the lady, really. I am an old friend of hers, you see. Thanks for the info," he said in response and stepped away, but a sudden impulse made him turn on his heels and ask if he could have a peek at the garden. The provisional occupier had no objections and he walked inside the green enclosure, feeling glad to see it look as variegated and healthy as ever. A figurine in the middle of a flowerbed caught his attention: a grizzled fellow of the rustic stock was pensively sitting on a bench. By all appearances, the statuette was made of heavy cut stone. "Francis is there to stay," he said to himself and then, standing akimbo on the verdant tiny spot, he felt that he was being given a living proof of the ties that had made a chatterbox little lady and her laconic gardener stick together as if in a surrealist pattern of live-and-breathing decalcomania.

For a good while after the visit, he waited for Elena to get in contact with him. She had decided to part with her comfortable house and gone home for family reasons; presumably, she was still with her kith and kin. He entertained, but promptly rejected, suspicions of a mere material concern; it was comforting to assume that she had travelled back home in the hope of restoring the old link with her brother. Come to think of it, blood was still thicker than water, was it not?

A few months later the reports of an earth tremor in their native region cut Dino to the quick. A frenzied use of the telephone and a finally successful contact with friends assured him that everybody at home was safe and sound; then Elena, who had come to play second fiddle to the pressing engagements of his life as a conscientious student of things literary, swooped on his mind. She had failed to contact him and was probably still staying in her native country. Had she, too, escaped disaster? He had no phone number to hand and resigned himself to wait for a message, which came before too long: Elena's family house had been affected by the vibrations of the earth's surface and rumour had it that during the cataclysmic seconds she had dashed to the balcony for a jump which had not materialised. But there was also good news: she was not known to be one of the mercifully few fatalities. Unavoidably, the affected area was in turmoil and finding out about her whereabouts and state of health was no piece of cake. Still, an update would be passed on as soon as possible. While having a cup of tea within domestic walls which, as far as he knew, were practically immune to telluric upheavals, Dino reflected on the seismically troubled woman returning to the balcony for a jump of a rather different nature from the one she had attempted in days of old, and it occurred to him that her father's arms had not been with her upon such an occasion. Then his mind glided up a boot-shaped peninsula, flew over a silver sea, and came to rest in a verdant little garden where a green-fingered man was still sitting on his homely little throne in expectation of the weekend and a word al fresco with Little Lady Chatterbox.

14

THE MANCUNIAN WAY

"Mancunium. Not a major spot on Albion's map in the eyes of the notable gens from the Tiber. Would you like me to elaborate, old boy?"

"Actually, er, Boadicea, if you don't mind, sir. She was a remarkable queen of the Iceni, was she not? And a rather unfortunate lady, I suppose."

"She was one thing and the other, in the opinion of reputable historians. When all's said and done, the lady was driven to extremes."

"Could you say a little more about her, sir?"

"Nothing loath. The year is 56AD and Boadicea – or should I call her Boudicca? – lodges a vehement complaint against the proconsul Scapula for enforcing the conquerors' law to the letter, but to the governor's ears the woman does protest too much; ergo, she is whipped into line while a soldier enjoys one or two of her virginal daughters. Pandemonium breaks out: the outraged mother goes up in arms; a few towns go up in flames, and I could mention Camulodunum and Verulamium alongside the up-and-coming Londinium; Roman citizens are burnt to death inside a temple for good measure. To add insult to injury, the redoubtable and still unvanquished 9th legion is ambushed and decimated; Monte Aquila is the fateful spot where the Roman eagle that gave the name to it is brought down to earth, and how could such destructive failure occur? It's a mystery, really. Virgil has told us that Anchises urged on his son Aeneas the Roman duty to use imperial strength in order to 'rule earth's people... battle down the proud', but was the big event the dawn of freedom for the Iceni? Good grief! Not for the world. Disaster struck soon enough: the imperial might was unleashed under the command of the ambitious as well as ruthless Pollinus and the natives' big army was routed, battle-axes, helmets, chariots and all, by the disciplined legionaries. It's a tragedy for the freedom fighters and curtains for them. Their passionate leader is fatally knocked off her chariot and vanishes. Did she take poison, historians have asked themselves? Imbibing venom was barely more than a nicety of guerrilla warfare with the wisdom of hindsight, but was an entire race wiped out in the aftermath of the massacre of women and children as an appendage to the saga of a victorious army? It's a moot point and still a bit of an enigma although recent archaeological excavations support the theory that the ancient tribe was in effect annihilated by dint of sophisticated marginalisation. Now then, what was the root cause of Boudicca's revolt? I shall be pleased to go into that some other time if you so wish. Meanwhile, a visit to Mancunium could be well worth the effort. I daresay you'll find it liberating. Vale." The tutor closed his notebook and rose. The lesson in ancient history was over.

The young day vibrates. Sunbeams quiver like wind harp strings plucked by a mischievous Aeolus. An extensive rural dwelling whizzes by, exposing its crib-like beauties through verdurous patches as well as umber spots that conjure up magnified spiders. A midget tree peeping from behind the foliage calls up a crab apple stretching its stumps towards the sky in a bygone garden reeking of November rain. Then a slate townscape looms in the distance: Mancunium, surely; also, Mancenium; or Mamucium, maybe? Whatever the name, the eagle-sporting victors could have done better. Had they come up with three forts and one name, the marauders from Limfjorden would as likely as not have failed to play havoc with the lone relic.

It isn't long before the passenger's lookout and reflections come to an end and he stands, a book in his hand, on a cobbled pavement. 'Cotton industry in decline and transformed into general textile industry; half of the manufacturing base dying, but electrical engineering, rubber dyestuff, clothing, foodstuff and beverage still of note and boding well for the future.' Going by the book, he has entered a city with a mission even if accomplishment is still some distance away. Luckily, Mancunium knows where it wants to go.

A phone booth is within easy reach: oblong, exquisitely chiselled, it's redolent of Euclid and Oldham. He toddles into the box, slaps the handset onto his lobes, hunches his shoulders and dials. "I'm hoping to have a quick word with Jasmine," he says in a tremolo voice as soon as a lady (mother?) is on the line.

"Jasmine is not around for the moment, I'm afraid. Who's calling?"

"Jasmine, er, doesn't know me, but she's been corresponding with a cousin of mine."

"Oh, I see. She's having a stroll the local park, I suppose. Could you call again later – say, in an hour?" A gentle cough ripples through the phone.

He clears his throat discreetly. "No problem. I've some urgent business on my hands, but it won't take long."

"We'll ben touch again anon, then."

"We will indeed."

His urgent business takes him to the town hall; the unmistakably Gothic exemplar is closed to the public for the day – and oh, the shame of it, for he'd have relished taking a close look at the bumblebees dancing on the hall floor. He is well and truly fond of the hairy creatures.

The Royal Exchange is his next port of call – 'A theatre with a spectacular auditorium,' he is informed by his serviceable guidebook – unfortunately, he is rather early for the evening performance. What about a visit to the cutely perpendicular cathedral, then? It's a priority, only second to the neo-classical art gallery. First things first, he reminds himself, and accordingly sails, his hands clasped behind his back, into the temple of the arts. What he sees makes him pause for thought: has he entered the shrine in order to catch a glimpse of the realistic commotion of men labouring under the bemused gaze of bourgeois observers? He almost certainly has. Or has he walked in to capture an image of the pugnacious yet elusive dancers now in front of him? It's a distinct possibility. He moves on with growing self-assurance until he comes to a standstill again, for what should he make of the Cornish intensity in the adjacent surrealist brushwork? Open to debate, but hush! Bar Conte, inscribed upon the windowpane, sounds familiar. A few steps on, a watercolour Medusa puts an end to his soul-searching. Mesmerised by the Gorgon, he gapes at her in an ominous silence, but within seconds he is bravely escaping her green coil of hair as well as the flaxen fixity of her eyeballs and regaining the freedom of the high street. Standing akimbo under a specious sky, he screws his eyes in case a phantom or a glory-ho fellow emerging from the fields should make an appearance. "Ah, Peterloo, Peterloo!" he exclaims just as another and equally stylish call box shows up at close quarters. "Aha, Jasmine!" he cries and in the next instant a scarred receiver is glued to his ears.

"My little girl has just come off her regular patch of green," the lady (her mother, bingo!) is pleased to report. "She is all yours, now."

"Well, in a manner of speaking," he comments inaudibly while his eyes converge on white knights batting and bowling in a nearby field, but the lady's daughter is already on the phone, sounding irremediably young and ineluctably school-girlish. He takes a long breath and gets down to bedrock: the invitation he has sent her on behalf of his cousin to join both at his holiday cottage – does she remember?

She certainly does.

Would she like to go, then?

She would indeed.

Say, in the summer?

Summer would be fine.

It's hunky-dory so far. In a flash, he sees his young relation patting him on the back, and his pumpkin face bursts into an undivided smile. A nanosecond later he asks himself where he ought to go from there: move on to inquire if the girl has blonde hair, cornflower-blue eyes and an upturned nose? No harm in that, naturally, and yet wouldn't it sound a trifle suspicious? Or tongue in cheek to say the least? No, it's far more judicious to hold the tongue in check. He sniffs and is put in mind of the commonly held belief that school is a safe topic, especially when chatting with gals. He opts for it.

"School's great, thanks," Jasmine is happy to let him know, and it feels as if a whiff from the City Gallery Bower Meadow is wafting through the blower.

Is she enjoying the classes? "I want to hear the truth, Jasmine."

"Well, not all of them, to be absolutely frank about it."

He scents the proximity of a cool head on presumably exceedingly warm shoulders, and the sensation makes him blush. "I'm sure my cousin will be delighted to know about your plans to come over," he says.

"Super."

"I say, could we meet somewhere and have a word about your trip?"

"We could indeed."

"In an hour?"

"An hour will do."

"Fantastic! Only that, ugh, my bus is due to come along within the hour, and I can't miss it. Hard luck! I hope you understand."

Jasmine understands pronto. "Cool it," she says.

"Listen, what about a get-together next time I'm around?"

"Smashing!"

"Delighted. See you soon, then. Bye for now, Jasmine," he says with spirito.

"Bye," she echoes with a lilt.

He hangs up with his steady left hand and steps out of the stifling enclosure. *There will be a next time around before long*, he promises to himself as well as to an impassive lapis lazuli sky. For the time being he has an alibi: Jasmine is in her early teens, and he can barely see himself playing a benevolent avuncular role. His massive specs turn up to a hopefully sympathetic sky, but it's hot – too hot, really – for an autumn day, and he's feeling kind of dry inside. "Life's a dried-up well," he moans, dearly hoping that the metaphor has reached the ears of the elderly man who's crossing him as he marches past the gate of a public garden.

The place looks empty but for a girl swaying on a swing. He sees her sable tresses tumble over her shoulders and her skirt flutter in the light breeze, but a boy dressed as a scout comes to her and with a broad smile gives the rope a violent pull which throws the girl down to the ground. Quick as a flash, he throws himself over her, his eyes aglow with anticipation. The captive endeavours to wriggle out and the youngster laughs loud, but a man with a wan face and a monk-like tonsure approaches and yells, "Let the child well alone, you brat!" and the Cub springs to his feet and scampers, flushing with an embarrassed triumph. And then? Then they are all gone through a sudden mist. Aha, the thrill of it! Also, the futility of it.

A basin is standing nearby. The roving young man moves to

it and leans over. No fish are swimming; only a round, twisted face is rippling in the pearly water.

"Who are you?" he asks.

"Are you?" says the face.

"I know. You are the imaginary."

"The Imaginary."

He walks away from the uncalled-for echo and sits on the grass, sipping a tepid cup of tea from his new-fangled gadget; then he lies down and subjects his moderately-sized body to one of his cherished feats of endurance: one leg goes up, the other follows and both pedal in unison. One, two, three, four, five… he isn't going to stop until he has counted up to fifty (the minimum expected by his exacting sometime PE teacher), but he is prevented from reaching the prescribed number by a mature female voice enquiring whether she has chanced on a Territorial Army recruit. Confronted with a lukewarm half-smile and tight lips, the crepuscular passer-by loses interest and plods on, offsetting the lavender sky by her cotton-wool hair. As he resumes his profitable jerks, a gap in his legs reveals the near presence of a solitary big scarecrow in the field adjacent to the gardens. He peers at a worn-out hat falling over a skeletal face and at ungainly arms stretched out cross-like. "A paltry thing. A tattered coat upon a stick," he intones, putting a Gaelic poet's graphic picture to excellent use. Would a crow fly away in terror at the sight of the straw man? Only a fledgling sparrow might – it just might. He regains a vertical posture and trails away, his eyes up to an arched, incongruously churchly, capital letter towering over the fields. M, it reads. M for Mancunium? For Magic? For Moment? For Myth?

It's M for Marna when a young woman's travelling bag knocks against the skirting board of the coach station door. His unsolicited and duly weighed-up offer for assistance is accepted with a blush, and both mosey into the passenger terminal.

"Tea?" he proposes; tea it will be. They sit at an oilcloth-covered table, and his face tightens while he hunts for a meaningful utterance, but it softens into an ice-breaking smile when he asks if she is expecting somebody.

"An old pal of mine should turn up any minute now," she lets him know.

He scrutinises her flaming red hair (could it be a wig?) which enhances eyes that share the hazel tinge up in the sky. Her lavishly rouged face looks at some variance with her immaculate tam o' shanter. He ventures an impromptu conjecture: "Am I talking with a fashion designer?"

She takes a sip of her tea. "A beauty parlour owner, actually." She gives a good-humoured smile. "And a singer in a pub at night."

"Sounds rather interesting."

"Until you get to know that it's mainly housewives that drop in during the week. The chicks show up mostly at the end of their school or working week. They put a finger on some style or other in their glossy mags and say, 'That's the ticket, Marna. Make sure I get it, please.' Kids of that sort are after the Golden Fleece, I guess." Her face veers in the direction of the door and lights up as though welcoming the friend she is to meet; then she stares vacantly at her cup. "On weekdays, my regular customers file in and wait for their turn; there's not a sparkle in their eyes. They just wait."

His eyelashes narrow to a slit and focus on unsmiling wives briefly away from home sweet home and a row of semis each boasting its own heart-stone angel, custodian of the sink, and winder of swaddles. Is she happy with her occupation, he asks? Hopefully he is not being a nosy parker.

Her mascara-darkened eyelashes quiver. "A few years back I gave a serious thought to going on the stage. I had a room of my own... a whole world of my own." Graceful folds form on her snub nose. "It was kind of crazy, a pie in the sky, really. Hairdressing is OK for a country girl like me, I reckon, and I'm quite happy to do the job my way," she sums up.

189

He rolls out an impertinent cough. "This singing of yours at night, I say, is it a hobby or what?"

She straightens her shoulders. "To be perfectly frank with you, it's a way out, yet I'm getting a kick out of it. And so is Rose." As if abruptly aware again of the drink in front of her, she imbibes a modicum of it. "Hmm, it's pretty cold now." She waves a dismissive hand. "Rose is my partner. We were close friends at school, and now we share our little place. We have eyes for each other." Her cheeks crease into an allusive smile. "We care lovingly for each other and make no great fuss of it," she adds with a weird sparkle in her eyes and a twitch of her ruddy lips.

"Will you stick to your housewives?" It's another no-nosey-parker question, naturally."

She homes in on the surrounding empty space. "Who can tell? Will Rose stick with me for as long as I choose?" Her purple-nailed fingers nudge her cup to a tilt. "Oops, that was a close call," she adds in an apologetic undertone and then, "Look here," she snorts. "The magazines, the radio, the beeb, not to mention mum, dad, grandma, and grandpa; full of know-how, the whole lot, and often staring suspiciously at my bonnet in case of a bee inside it. Thanks awfully, folks, I say. I'm bunged up, honest. I fear that one day I'll wake up and find that the balloon I blew when I was a kid has burst." A quaint smile crops up as she turns to survey the door for a second time.

He hears the penny drop; the young woman facing him is equipped with a fitting narrative. "What about your pal?" he asks with a touch of tease which seems to be lost on her.

She peeks at her watch. "Frigging late. Most unusual, I must say."

"Rose, hard Rose. You are caught in the drift," he recites silently on the spur of an imagist moment.

"It helps to have someone on your side, doesn't it?" she asserts while scouring the little world they've entered. "Penned

in a cage, aren't we? The best one can do is to sit and wait…
more or less as the housewives do at my salon. I really…"

"I hope your friend won't keep you waiting for too long,"
he chips in. His cheeks balloon. "I for one wouldn't." A squint
at an indifferent clock on the wall is followed by the sudden
announcement of his having to push off and an uneasy smile.

"Tara," says she, branding him with a flutter of her thick
eyelashes.

Late at night he's up to his eyebrows in thought while undressing
in front of a speckled dusty mirror. *The friend Marna was
waiting for… hmm… was it an alibi for nipping in the bud the
dreaded advances of a perfect stranger, a quintessentially feminine
trick in the art of self-defence?* Come to think of it, she hadn't
even asked for his name. His forefinger moves to the tip of his
respectable nose. But then, nor had Jasmine; only her mater had.
There! The generation gap; a gaping chasm, by the look of it!
He turns his eyes to the wall: a postcard on it shows a pottery
fragment bearing, writ large, the letters NTA. He slaps his brow.
Venta, and that's for sure! *Venta Icenorum*, to name it in full:
the Iceni market town with a Roman layout and inhabited by
a vanquished tribe to whom a new identity had been given as
the civilised equivalent of annihilation. A fine instance of *Pax
Romana* without a shadow of a doubt!

Adjacent to the card, a poster displays the queen of the
tribe at issue dwarfing him from the chariot she's riding in her
unorthodox fashion en route to Camulodunum for a sweet
revenge. Slowly but decidedly, he kneels down, joins his hands
and lifts them. "Ave, Boadicea – or should I call you Boudicca?",
he utters sotto voce; then, back on his feet, he glances at the
moderate size of his bare, hazel-haired body exposed by the full-
length mirror. "There's a time to cast away stones," he declaims
with undertones of gravity. He claps eyes on a pair of scissors
glistening in the orange light of the bedside table lamp. With

a measured movement, he gets hold of the item, lifts it to his crotch and lets it stay there for a few long instants while he screws up his eyes in anticipation of a deed that is going to be – dare he borrow the word? – liberating. Soon after, guided by one fully re-opened eye, he moves the scissors to his fingernails and gingerly sets about trimming them. When the job's done to a tee, he plunges into his vacant double bed with an impish smile and a glowing face, snuggles down, and stares at an indifferent ceiling. "The mission will be accomplished in due course," he vows solemnly. "For everything there is a season, and a time for every matter under the sun. Am I right, Preacher?"

"Midnight," a male voice announces out of the wireless.

"*Kai ego de mona kateudo,*" he tags on quasi-content; "And I lie alone," he adds for the sake of the broadcaster. "Once upon a time there was a woman from Lesbos, you know," he hastens to relate, but a sudden hoarse cry makes him prick up his ears and guides his mind back to a scarecrow stuck in a Mancunian field and acting at his side in a comedy of errors. "If a crow help us in, sirrah, we'll pluck a crow together," he croaks and turns over

15

STONING THE CROWS

Miles away from the stick-and-rags guard clinging to his patch of withered grass, corvine creatures found themselves the target of a scathing attack at a riverside inn. It all began when Dino took a long disconsolate look at his thin wallet and – Gods above! – the grant awarded to him was proving not entirely adequate. With a worried frown, he paced the floor of his room until a few mouthfuls of the generous grappa from the Montello Hills brought the sum of two half smiles onto his rosy cheeks. Heartened by the elixir, he explored a number of options.

Choice number one: communal digs. Namely, a place embellished by a colour after his own heart, even though communards of the Parisian kind seemed to be at a premium in the capital city of a kingdom where a major peasants' revolt had been nipped in the bud, a civil war culminating in the severing of a royal head had been superseded by the installation of yet another royal head, and a couple of revolutions – one peculiarly industrial, the other politically glorious – had been virtually bloodless events.

Choice number two: a second move to a youth hostel. His tongue grazed the roof of his palate, and the lingering taste of a dollop made of sausages and mash Norse-style put the idea to instant flight.

What about a spell of busking in a subway, then? It would be a bohemian experience, no doubt about it, but it smacked of destitution. Besides, he hadn't plucked Ariana, his old guitar, for an unconscionable number of years.

Another copious dose of the medicinal spirit from the Veneto region dropped into the lower regions of his body and stupendously cleared the upper ones: a small amount of moonlighting might well provide a way out of his predicament. Oh yes, that was just the ticket! Startlingly warmed up as a grilled toast, he got hold of the weekly paper conveniently delivered to his place for free, flipped through it and, thank goodness, temporary help was needed at a public house by the river. No relevant experience was required; an enthusiastic novice would be quite welcome. He was in luck, and no mistake! His forefinger circled in the air and landed as expected on his accommodating nose. His blurred eyes slid across his body and down to the shoes that were Bernie's keepsake, and they looked in pretty decent shape. With a slightly unsteady step, he reached the telephone stand.

The enquiries that followed led to arrangements for an interview on the morrow, and he prepared for the event by consulting an old pub guide. How fortunate for him to have spotted the reasonably priced paperback on a bookstall table! He patted himself on the back for picking up an item that might well prove of service on the subject of booze. His slowly sobering up mind paused on quaint names such as *crabbers nip, bishops' finger, old peculiar* and, weirdest of all, *wee willie* (something to do with Kipling's Willie?). "Yes, I am your man," he said to the employer waiting in the wings at his tavern on the river. When he hit the hay, his eyes blinked on the vision of a foamy world about to be discovered and, hopefully, tasted to the full.

While advancing towards his destination at the heart of dockland, the job-seeker scanned the area surrounding him.

What would Marcus Flaccus say about it now? Would the brave legionary be impressed by the double row of docks, wharfs, and buildings bearing marks of their quondam warehouse status? Or by the succession of tower blocks and terraced houses stuck in the soil in the guise of huge slabs hankering after classical harmony and letting straggly foliage peep out through constricting gaps? Would the colourful cruise boats rumbling along make him stare in awe? Last but not least, would the geese nonchalantly floating in the silver-grey water warm the cockles of his soldierly heart? A cluster of honking sisters had saved the Capitol once, hadn't they? A gentleman was seated quietly on a bench, wearing a copper suit topped by a bizarre hat, and waving at a little girl who stood next to the parapet; her smile endearingly played around her lips, but a brown cat crouching on the low wall looked seriously intent on a lunge at a scurrying water vole. Now then, would the scene make Marcus halt on his steady trek to the outposts of the Empire, lay down Caesar's eagle and take steps towards a civil liaison? Dino raised his eyes and the name on the façade of a brick building made him come out of his brown study; also, it loaded him with a dilemma: which way in? Would it be the public bar or the saloon? An easily won broad smile illuminated his round face; he brought a tarnished successor to an imperial coin into the light, tossed it, and marched at full tilt through the saloon door.

His searching eyes quickly take in the aura of the locale. A tall, muscular bloke is standing upright behind the bar, and he is up to the elbows with a batch of customers. A feast of facial pockmarks outranks his sinewy neck, and luxuriant sideboards offset his barren crown. On hearing Dino give his name, he shoots him a spirited glance. "Dino, of course. You were expected," he booms with a congenial smile. "I gather you haven't helped in a similar establishment before. No cause for worry though. I'll show you the ropes." Some lip-pursing in response proves of little consequence to his compact eyebrows. "It's child's play, young man. Get on with it pronto." His voice is imbued with a colour suggestive of a spell in the army. "My given name is Alex but do feel free to call me Al." His smile has now expanded and reached his pistachio eyes. The hand he extends feels in keeping with the voice.

Within minutes the recruit is on duty in front of a spacious hall. The 'Dilly Dally' soft strains flowing from the scuffed teak speaker hanging on a wall sound catchy, and period bric-a-brac sitting on ledges makes an orderly contribution to the nautical feel of the place. Up in a poster a fairy-looking woman can be seen caressing a man with an ass-like head, and the newcomer is keeping an eye on the odd couple when a gentleman nears the bar. Will he ask for a dose of Dirty Sam or a taste of Little John? His guidebook has mentioned both drinks without going into detail, and he shoots Alex an imploring look, but the arrival says in a finely modulated timbre, "Hello, hello. Give us a Bloody Mary, there's a good lad," and the potion made up of tomato juice and vodka strikes the uninitiated lad as a household name by courtesy of the Galician girl who had strolled with him on the Hampstead heath.

He glances at the gent's navy-and-white-striped suit and long, suspiciously sable hair encircling his amiable face; it rings a bell. "I, er, I think I've seen you on TV," he blurts out.

"Oh, have you? Capital. Being recognised is one of life's magic moments, old chap." A swig of the blood-red mixture goes through his wide-open jaws and his lips part for a bout of mirth. "Some time ago a well-known man of the theatre graciously welcomed rapturous rounds of applause from his audience, and I see no reason to quarrel with that," the gentleman states as soon as his Adam's apple reverts to normal. Then he leaves the bar and moves sedately to a table next to the window.

The melody still issuing from the wall mingles with the assertive yelps of a toy spaniel, which can be seen squeezing through the entrance ahead of a petite, golden-haired woman.

Sporting a frayed miniskirt which exposes a couple of strawberry marks on her upper legs, the incoming customer progresses trimly to the counter. "It'll be gin 'n' tonic for me if you'd be so kind, Al," she says in a hoarse colour tone and with a glint in her teal eyes.

"You're quite welcome to it, Pam," is the publican's response. "Only, I'd be obliged if you would refrain from bringing your pet in. The rules of the place, I'm afraid. No savvy, eh?"

The woman looks baffled and a tad disappointed. "I've just been walking me Charlie, guv. A snifter of the booze, and orf we go," she rejoins, and is rewarded with an appreciative nod. Holding her tumbler aloft, she moseys, balancing on her high heels, to a blurred mirror. Her perm waves this way and that while she mouths lyrics belonging to the 'As Time Goes By' tune that has now superseded the 'Dilly Dally' melody. Momentarily let off the leash, Charlie sneaks to the window and sets about sniffing the telly man's trousers, but "Come back to your auntie right now, silly boy!" his mistress calls out before scuttling after him like a whippet springing out of a box. "I say, is 'e giving a spot of bother?" she anxiously inquires while her hands saw the air.

"Not an iota of bother; it was love at first paw, young lady. My heart melts at the sight of a Cavalier King Charles. Take it from Walter," the man replies, a colourful beam weaving through his gelatinous features.

"I think me Charlie wants the street," says Pam. The gin-and-tonic concoction disappears through her puce-coloured lips. "Ah, what a beauty!" she gushes and, jauntily waving a hand, waddles to the exit, pulling at the lead of her Cavalier pet.

Walter steps back to the counter and sits on a stool. "Much of the same if you would, my amiable friend," he orders. The flowery shirt peeping through the gap in his dark blue jacket smells of the stage. "Have you ever been told that the holy monks of Bermondsey ran a tavern on these banks in the good old days? I'm sure they were quite busy, Bloody Mary and whatnot," he adds with a quiet laugh.

"You, too, must be a very busy man," says Dino.

The artiste lifts the glass and gives it an intense look. "Showbiz is a funny business, you know: not a thing for ages, then a hit, a palpable hit, and hey presto you are back in the spotlight." His hand sinks into his pocket and re-emerges holding the fox-papered picture of a young woman displaying a splash of rouge and spirited eyes. "Here! Elaine as the leading lady in *A Sucking Leech*. A roaring success, I'm proud to report." With an actor's well-rehearsed gesture, he helps himself to a sizeable measure of his drink. "The gal and I were together again in *An Awful Blunder* – a farce for a change. We packed people in." He does sound and look a man of the theatre, and Dino is chuffed; it would have been a thrill even for the hard-nosed Marcus Flaccus to come across a reincarnation of Roscius. "Allow me a fleeting break, sire. It's about time I spent a decent penny," the thespian chap declaims before moving to the nearby gents. When he comes out of it and makes his lithe body roll to the bar for an additional taste of Bloody Mary, his long forefinger indicates the fairy on the wall and, "Ha, ha," he chortles with delight. "She reminds me of Elaine and I sharing *A Midsummer Night's Dream* in the West End. Out of the theatre, we walked down to the river, and when I said, *Nay, I can gleek upon occasion,* she returned pat, *Thou art as wise as thou art beautiful.* I shall drink to that." He taps into his tipple with growing relish. "I had a proper crush on the girl, you see. A classy little bird she was, and not a shadow of a doubt about it."

"I think that little birds are easy to catch," his intrigued interlocutor comments.

"A subtle remark, dear fellow." The actor's oval features light up with *joie de vivre*, but they dim as he squints into his empty glass. "I'm about to leave the stage again, but it won't be for too long. Be ready with a decent portion of Tia Maria, lad. Moreover, a devilled cheese tart, if you have one under the counter, would be highly appreciated." He goes the exit, wobbling conspicuously.

On the morrow, Dino hurried in the direction of Alex's inn for another stint, but he couldn't help pausing for a look at wavelets quivering as if in response to the presence of a musical naiad. On the opposite bank, elongated moonbeams flickered along the peeling stucco of a warehouse, and the cheerless fabric was colouring at the touch. His eyes searched about in case breast-plated men should be holding the fort, but the silhouettes that came into view looked devoid of any legionary traits. Verbal shreds hit his ears, as the snooker balls would do when knocked off the table at the tavern. "Dough… cor… git… trouble… more next time," he heard, and saw Pam and Walter emerge with Charlie at their heels. At a short distance from them, a pony-tailed young man was leaning against an orange Vespa, and the sight of it made his mouth water: if only he had a scooter of the kind plus a flaming getup and boots to match the gadget! He let out a long sigh superseded by the heartening recollection that once upon a time an ugly duckling had metamorphosed into a beautiful swan. Were fairy stories solely meant for naive young children, he wondered?

"I'm out of the muck, folks," Walter was heard to announce before moving on with the loose-limbed deportment he had presumably practised on stage. There was a moment's silence, and then the youth was coming away from the motorcycle and saying, "C'mon, pussy, give us a purr."

"I'll scratch your pate, first," was Pam's swift rejoinder.

"You do that, and your yellow perm will be a kinky twist before you can say Jack Robinson," snarled the other. Moans, grunts and a strident, "Gotcha!" from the bloke coalesced with loud yaps, and soon afterwards Pam was seen to incite Charlie to action and her interlocutor to kick the intruder away. The yaps grew sharper, but they were replaced by a whine which soon faded into the dark backdrop.

What happened next brought in an abrupt reversal: the pony-tailed chap was pleading for a song and, "What should I sing for yer?" the woman was asking.

"Your pick, luv. You know that I'm easy as a pie," her partner replied.

Pam struck up a popular tune inspired by the city on the Thames and the folks born within sound of Bow Bells, and the eavesdropper listened in fascination until he was reminded by a peek at his Omega Grand Prix that a small army of thirsty folk was expected to be marching into Alex's stronghold by and by. He reluctantly turned his back on the scene and resumed his fast walk towards the public house.

Sadly, nobody was singing inside the locale. A small number of regulars were sitting at ease and conversing in a barely audible tone of voice. He went to the publican directly. "I've just seen the blonde who was in here last night on the bank of the river," he spluttered.

"Fair enough," his employer countered while holding a goblet overflowing with rum. "The lady in question walks the banks regularly for a constitutional, as I understand it."

"Ah, but she was there with the gentleman who was in here, too, last night. And there was a young man with a ponytail with them. They all said and did strange things."

A sequence of whimpers from the entrance door made both turn around and look at Charlie sneaking in and limping forward. "My word! Not you again!" the landlord roared. "Blow me down, hobbling now? Come to uncle Al, dear," he added soothingly, but the four-legged creature gave the newly gained uncle a wide berth and limped on, pursuing a course of his own. "Do I see insubordination? I'll get at you, little sod," the man thundered and, holding his glass, bore down on the toy spaniel. "Under the table, lily-livered boy, eh?" he groused.

"Charlie was kicked by the young man, Alex," the chance witness hastened to disclose. "He and Pam had a fight. And then she sang a song."

The man took a few deep gulps of his spirit. "Did she? Ah, it's no singing matter, take it from me." He turned to Charlie. "Come out of the shelter, lad; show up a paw and let's see if you have a blighty one," he requested, and he was still holding the pet's forelegs when the woman at issue burst in, herself faltering.

"Giving me boy a leg up?" she asked and then, "Uh-huh, your auntie's back, darling," she called out.

"You, too, hobbling, sweetie?" Alex marvelled. "Was it an accident or what?"

"Just been with me partner. 'E is weird sometimes, me partner. Lor! Sometimes 'e let 'imself into the shit up to 'ere." Her hand darted to her chin.

"It comes of being human, luv. We all muck about at a pinch."

"Crickey! I never reckoned you was a phisolopher," said she.

Alex let go of Charlie's leg and went back to the bar. Another dose of rum filled his vessel to the brim and he raised it aloft. "I have no truck with philosophy, Sally girl, but you stay well away from the ponytail and keep your head screwed on while you can," he suggested in the earnest tone of a zealous Sunday preacher before giving his attention to a customer waiting at the counter.

Pam smiled hazily and clasped her pet tightly. The affectionate hug had a touch of romance in the middle of yet another comedy of errors.

Early in the evening, Walter and Archie were caught by Dino in the act of performing a less sentimental dumb show in the spotlight of a riverside street lamp. The man of the theatre was seen reaching the youth, offering a small wad and being regaled in return with the sight of one long finger stuck up and straight as a rod. What occurred in rapid succession suggested a dummy run show: a swap of blows culminated in Archie slumping to the ground like a marionette dropped by a weary puppeteer, yet leaping up quick as a hare and making a dash for his scooter with Walter hot on his heels. The Vespa jolted and rumbled off while the pursuer bounded to a car parked nearby, hurtled inside, and launched into a chase.

The characters in the open-air show had obviously left the stage and the accidental spectator stepped away. As he trotted towards the pub, it was borne upon his mind that the celebrated Christopher Marlowe had been known as a bit of a brawler, and the final bust-up in his short life had taken place at a riverside tavern. There was no sufficient evidence to substantiate the fatal accident, and yet...

When he re-entered Alex's territory, Pam was sitting on a stool, gin-and-tonic within reach, but no Charlie on her stiletto heels. The spaniel and his mistress appeared to be complying with the rules of the place. "Busy tonight, boss?" she inquired.

"A matter of regulars, as I apprehend it. Listen, love, I think this is an appropriate moment to have a word with you about a slaphappy crony of yours."

The blonde's eyes grew large. "Me mate 'as rough 'ands but a soft 'eart. 'Struth 'e was beat by the other geezer – Walter, I mean – last night."

"You don't say! The bloke hardly looks the belting type to me. Look, as a special favour I could have a little chat with him next time he shows his jolly mug in here." A huge wink heightened the benignity inherent in the idea.

Pam ruminated briefly and then, "Ark, chief," she said. "There *is* a favour you could do for me. The man 'as a wife. I know 'er name and I 'ave 'er blower number. Know what I mean?" Her wink was almost as impressive as Alex's had been.

He knew what she meant. Holding the scrap of paper that she had handed to him, he strode up to the telephone on the wall, dialled a number and moved his lips for speech before coming back, his carbuncular face awash with the gratification pervading the face of a Salvation Army officer who has just saved a soul from perdition.

The woman heard his report, got the message and moved to a table where she stayed for the rest of the evening, imbibing drops of comfort from more than one pink gin. When she swayed back to Dino for her last order, her yellowish-brown eyes conveyed a yearning for communication. "You want to 'ear a nice little story?" she asked, and without delay plunged into narration, making a glazed eye-to-eye contact. "The cherries are in season and I'm picking them in my little orchard when Uncle Terry crops up and pipes gay as a lark, 'Just the sort of thing I'm after. I have a thing about little cherries, darling.' 'E comes closer and paws me body. 'No cause for alarm, little Pam. Uncle Terry wants no trouble, least of all with a sweetie,' he says with a mouth greasy like a frying spoon." The narrator's eyes roll, and her hand dabs her perm. "My 'ead went into a whirl," she continued. "I was going for fourteen, you see. By gosh! When I had a shufty at me tubby uncle again, 'e was strutting away, one 'and on 'is slacks, and squeezing a cherry into 'is big mouth." Glowing with embarrassment, Pam swallowed her last order.

Restoring eye contact, Dino said softly, "Another gin-and-tonic? It would be on me, of course."

"A nice thought, very nice indeed, but no, lovey. All I want now is a leak." Her voice was huskier than usual and her smile was slightly twisted while she moved to the ladies. It wasn't long before she tottered back, arranging her mop. "I say, ever 'ad a funny dream yerself, dea'?" she asked, gazing at him with maternal eyes. Had the blue-haired fairy bestowed a similar look on the misguided wooden boy in the tale he had read when a child, the lad wondered? Her flaxen-haired counterpart pivoted and teetered to the exit, amazingly made the doorway, and with an ample wave of the hand headed for the freedom of the street.

Later in the evening a chart-topping singer was reminding the transient patrons about the way of all the flesh when Walter charged in and decidedly as ever asked for his choice Bloody Mary.

"I believe your missus has dropped in, squire," Alex let him know directly.

"My missus?! I must be hearing things."

"You'd better believe what you've just heard. Just turn your head and you won't have a shadow of a doubt about it." His forefinger flicked in the direction of a chubby woman sitting at a table near the inglenook.

"The young lady down there is not my better half and that's that."

"Bless me! Do I hear Solomon pronouncing again?"

"Let the wise man's bones rest in peace, monsieur landlord. To the best of my knowledge, the dame you're indicating is Archie's wife."

"The name rings no bell, I'm afraid. Gee whiz! it looks as if it's up to the law now."

It was indeed! A pair of bobbies came into sight from the door. One of the two stepped forward, and after searching the place with metallic blue eyes he took himself sedately to Walter. Soon afterwards, he was heard to address the performer as Mr Jack Stonecrow and mention the fall in the river of a young pony-tailed male riding a bisque motor scooter.

Walter looked cut to the quick, but, recovering in a flash, he put Roscius's legacy to legit use. "Am I right in saying that you called me Mr Stonecrow, Constable? If I am, you have regrettably got the wrong end of the stick. It so happens that you're talking to Mr Knowell. Edward Knowell," he stated in an impressive staccato. "An actor can live, and die to act a second part," he went on to declaim and then, confronted with the officer's chilly stare and polite but firm request to follow him to the local station in order to help the police with their inquiries, he gave a low bow and joined the couple in blue. Walter, to the last, admirably consistent with his stagy self at the end of a riveting show – or so he seemed to Dino.

Instants later the woman sitting by the fake log fire leapt up and made a speedy exit as if in pursuit.

"By jingo, I must be stoned!" Alex yelled, and the deep hollow sound of his voice mingled with a string of familiar yaps which heralded Pam's entrance.

"Popping in juz to see if Walter was still around, Al," she ejaculated.

"The man you're after has just left, and he was escorted by a couple of bluebottles, woman," the publican croaked.

"Wot?! Nuffink serious, I 'ope."

"Nothing more serious than a young bloke plunging into the river last night, and his motor scooter going down with him."

Pam's eyes coloured with trepidation. "Oi! It wasn't an orange one, for heaven's sake! Not Archie's Vespa!"

"Archie?! And who would this blooming Archie be, once and for all?"

"Archie is me partner all right!"

A sea of lines flooded the man's brow. "Your partner?! All I know is that your partner is the husband of the woman I phoned up for your sake, and she was sitting in here before you strode in. That bloke, not Walter, is, or was, her hubby. Have I made myself understood?"

"Oh, is 'e? Was 'e? Stone the crows, I sez! The cheeky bugger played me false, 'e did!" the towhead shrieked while pinning the inn-keeper down with a steady look. Her well-knit body went into a raucous, convulsive laughter, and if it was a bout of hysterics it was one of little consequence, because within the space of few moments her breast looked level again and she bestowed a dove-like look on Alex. "Archie is me bleeding partner and that's for sure," she reiterated with the intensity of a devoted companion.

The other cogitated briefly and then, "Lend an ear, Pam," he resumed. "What happened on the pier last night looks to me like a thing between your Archie and Walter – I mean Jack – but perhaps it doesn't matter any longer who is who in this bleeding weird story and I…"

"Course it do! Course it do!" she barged in; her breast in a lather again, she dashed to the exit and stopped there. "See the woman on the wall, guv? She's 'aving a dream in a wood in the middle of summer. And so is the man with the ass 'ead, Walter told me. The bloke also said that Archie and I are the likes of that barmy couple, dream an' all." She threw a sheep's eye from under her painstakingly pencilled eyelashes. "I say, where is me addle-pated Archie now?" she squawked and, still balancing on her high heels, her perm in turmoil, dragged a subdued Charlie through the door and back to a no-nonsense world.

The ensuing quiet was fitfully disturbed by the chuckles of detached players and the dull sound of balls knocking against one another in the adjacent room. Alex suddenly overwhelmed the background interference. "Stone the crows indeed, whenever and wherever!" he grunted. "We've come to the closing time of a freakish day, as I apprehend it."

Dino's reaction was to let his eyes turn downwards until they met his shoes: were they still Bernie's memento? Or were they an actor's footgear? He took his cue and said, "I clear all the tables and then I'll go home."

The task had almost been carried out when he spotted, untouched, Walter's last Bloody Mary. He waved a hand to catch his boss's attention and heard him titter, "Toss off the stuff, lad. One for the road. Cheers!"

The novice boozer complied: gripping the fiery potion in his left hand, he took probing sips. His muscles tightened, but they soon eased up. "Just like you said. One for the road," he echoed and, braving the butterflies inside, quaffed the remainder. "I'm off now, Al," he announced and, with a legionary step, made for the door. On reaching it, he came to a standstill. "Did I say 'Al'? Well, no harm in it, I hope. Forgive me, Capone. Prohibition is long gone, anyway," he murmured before marching out.

The street looks deserted by everybody except the fixture with the copper suit, bizarre hat, and streaked eyes. He sits close to him and wonders whether one or other Muse has made him, the visitor from a Muse-ridden land, step into a tavern and watch, as the gentleman probably does when he's not looking at the girl, characters in a play come onto the stage, play their roles, and walk off. The curtain has fallen now, but the actors will doubtless be walking the boards anew and occasionally getting a hit, a palpable hit. Has not a man of the theatre just told him something of the kind?

The shape of a brindled dachshund materialises and stands against a lamppost, wagging its tail. A docked appendage is wiggling on its way to the short-legged creature, and it soon transpires that the item belongs to Charlie. Dino darts to him. "Go back to your mistress, dear," he pleads, but Pam's darling flaps his ears and forges on. He follows the black-and-tan feller, reaches him and goes on his knees for a quick catch, but within an inch of the fair Cavalier he freezes and looks intently through the dimness ahead: Charlie's mistress comes into view as a golden speck on a dark backdrop. He adjusts his specs and makes them aim at a suddenly vacated cobble. King Charles's favourite and his chance sweetheart are now trotting abreast into the expanse ahead, their tails waving to and fro like unequal fingers. His jaws tense up. "What would Marcus Flaccus do? Well, here goes!" he cries into the night, and lunges out.

16

A LUCID DREAM

The heavens are grumbling, but the little boy feels cushioned as he sits at his walnut desk near a coal fire that is dying down in a tarnished brazier. His chubby forefinger slides up to an isle which resembles an emerald teddy resting in a greenish-blue sea. He has just done his homework for his third-form mistress and done it painstakingly, because the lady is a stickler for accuracy. He gets hold of a coloured book and opens it; his eye falls on a black-cowled monk occupied in entering a word with the help of a quill: Briga, he reads, laboriously lengthening each letter. His lips part into a yawn; he stands up and goes on his knees at the bedside. "Angel of God, my good guardian, pray let me have a beautiful dream tonight," he murmurs before diving into bed. The winged spirit, he dearly hopes while his eyes come to a close, will take him to the distant toy bear in touch with the translucent deep…

The long night on the waves was over. In the off-white morning, a grown-up lad stood leaning against the railing on the promenade deck of a puce steamboat, his eyes set on pistachio spots forming a polka-dot pattern on the starboard. "Rosslare," a man announced while directing his index finger towards a large stretch of the coast now emerging in grey patches through lazy sunbeams. Eager for greenness, the youth took a hard look. *Such stuff as dreams are made on,* stole across his mind.

In the evening, he lay in an exceedingly firm bed under the compassionate gaze of a virgin mother. His eyelids moved to a standstill, but they flicked up in sync with a loud knock on the door and a shrill female voice hollering, "Grub's up, lad."

Before long his thumb was swinging metronome-like at the side of an asphalted road while he grinned and bore the enduring presence of the thick oats and the giant egg that, alongside the Land-of-Ire engraving, had offered themselves from a green plate and been speedily accepted. Enveloped in a thin veil of mist, he trod on in contact with feathery ferns alternating with bell-shaped flowers, and at a short distance from tokens of a land of stone. Farther in the fields, the progeny of a mythical fauna was roaming at ease. A mare and foal stood in close nearness under a Cork oak: mother and child in a rufous icon and a world of their own.

"Where are you headed?" The voice sounded silvery, and the face that stuck out of an off-white collar was high-cheeked.

"I'm, er, hoping to reach Limerick."

"Oh Lord, I'm not journeying so far, but surely you want to be out of the breeze. Do hop in," the driver's thin mouth let out.

He obliged and sat close to a black garment which called to mind a wartime soutane. A wiry hand revved the engine and made it cough, splutter, and finally roar. The vehicle trundled ahead.

"In the middle of a trek, lad?"

"It's only a short visit, Father, but I intend to go some distance."

"A cool idea while you are in your prime. When I was about your age I went roving far and wide, and I had a good look at the Continent."

"Glad to hear that. Ever been to Rome?"

A hieratic smile flattened the crow's feet on the man of God's face, but undeviating lines appeared again as soon as he mentioned that he had toured the city at the same time as the Holy Father was staying at his summer castle. A few moments later, his scraggy features filled out as Aida came into the picture: *Celeste Aida* singing at the Caracalla Baths under an overwhelming moon. "It was a fecking thing," he beamed. A silver curl bobbed and bounced on his pasty forehead; a thin arm went up and two reverend fingers gyrated dance-like to bless a pair of cows as well as the curly-haired villager driving them cap in hand. "Welcome to our bogs and drumlins," he whooped; "you're going to see limestone and elms galore in your rambles though." There was a thrill of pride in his fallow eyes.

"Vineyards and olive groves are a feast for the eyes in my parts," gushed the other.

"It must be paradise." One hand slapped against his venerable thigh. "And while we are on the subject of heaven, be good and listen carefully."

The requisite ear was instantly offered and then gradually taken back because the jogging of the vehicle and the warmth of the enclosure lulled the listener to a doze from which he was awoken by the announcement that the destination was nigh. The worn vehicle rumbled along cottages huddled together in shades of grey, white and red until it wheezed to a halt.

"Thank you, Padre," said the passenger while shifting his backpack to the door.

The padre gave a gentle cough, which suggested the soul of a meek fellow liable to inherit the earth. "Feeling peckish?" he inquired, and then, confronted by hesitant nods, "What about a stopover at my little place for a bit of homely fare?" He slapped his thigh again and gave the youngster a dewy look which struck him as free of theological connotations. The backpack rejoined the clutter at the rear of the vehicle.

The parish house lay squatting in a corner, and it appeared

far from grand albeit not lacking the kind of *je ne sais quoi* that obliterates emblems of urban pretensions and, it suddenly occurred to Dino, vindicated the claims of Uncle Raf's farmhouse.

Inside the place, a copper-hued tea poured out of a shamrock-engraved pot and murphies, which created the fleeting image of a girl's breasts drawn by a daydreaming male classmate, popped out of a flat-bottomed pan.

"Surely the bangers don't need a fork. They should go down quite well with the tea," the serving priest predicted, and the guest proved him right by reaching for the beverage as soon as a sausage landed on his tongue. "Anything the matter, son?" came as a solicitous question and the reply was a dubious shake of the head. The host harrumphed. "Now, let me introduce myself befittingly. I was named Benjamin at the font, but I'm known as Father Ben at my parish." His expansive face brightened while he added with a subdued laughter, "I remember that one of my faithful – a man who, bless him, knows verse and chapter – once asked me if he could call me Benoni – that was how Rachael called her son before dying, as you may well know. I felt obliged to remind my parishioner that Jacob, the child's father, had called him Benjamin. "Surely 'son of the right hand' sounds better than 'son of my sorrow'," I told him." His hand reached his thigh for yet another slap. "And how should I call you, young man?"

"Dino's the name, Father."

"Aha, sweet as a nut and sharp as a crack of the whip! Now, have you come to these isles for the other Ben, Dino?' The compact lines on his rural face broke into a smile which appeared imbued with Gaelic humus. "No shame on you if you have," he went on. "I'm talking of the big chiming Ben who, as the rest of the world knows, is never in the wrong." His free hand waved in widening circles. "I'm sure you can do with a little more tea," he added, and headed for the kitchen. His cassock grazed rugged chairs presumably resenting the severance from their native boles. The visitor stared at the aubergine shape of his body before transferring his scrutiny to the wall on which the picture of a man wearing an outmoded jacket ennobled by a cravat and displaying a luxuriant grizzly beard took centre stage. The sitter's large brown eyes and wide forehead connoted a human being with a vision, and it was safe to assume that he belonged to a past generation.

"You're looking at the Father of the Land League," the priest said on re-entering, a pot in one hand, but a prolonged 'moo' wafting through the window made Dino whirl around and close his eyes while savouring the echo of a remote voice. "The girl doesn't mind a dab of brew every now and then," her owner chuckled. "Now, let's give the devil his due: a small quantity of the good stuff is sitting idle in my cellar. Well, there's no time like the present for some of it to make a move, as sure as God made little hops. How is it as a fiendish idea?" With elastic and slightly uneven steps, he reached a set of shelves and picked up a book. "Have a little read while I fetch the unholy liquid," he proposed and proffered a blue-and-white item which dealt with his island's past, as the recipient realised while flicking through the glossy pages with some curiosity until his host returned hugging a big brown bottle. A tumbler full to the brim was solicitously handed over with words such as, "Your Garibaldi and his Redshirts went on a march, didn't they, and it was a long, glorious one." He cleared his throat. "And so is ours, praise the Lord." He attacked his share of the booze. "Yes, we are still marching, no buts about it." He paused for a meditative brief spell. "Well, to tell you the truth, there *is* a 'but'. Trust seems to be burning itself to ashes, and I can only hope and pray that, like the ancient phoenix, it will be born again." He gulped his drink. "Now, do you still intend to march to Limerick?" Dino nodded a big yes. "Fecking right. Have you sorted out where to stay for the night?"

"Not yet, really."

"Well, then. Please be informed that I've got a bed upstairs and it should fit your size, as I gauge it. You'd be quite welcome to it."

The other kept silent except for a couple of hiccups, and then said, "Very kind of you, Father. I'll take a look at the village, and since it's OK with you I'll be back for the night."

"Do as you please, son. And another thing: why don't you cast the net a little wider? I'll be on my way to the north country in the morning, and you could share my jalopy while reserving the right to hop off wherever you like; yeah, that's the idea."

Dino's glazed eyes scanned the room and met the Father of the Land again. "OK, Padre. I'll do just as you say."

"It's a deal, then, but you'll have to get up with the lark: we'll be on our way soon after breakfast." He sounded full of gusto. "Holy Mary, it nearly slipped my mind!" he added while snapping his fingers. "You'll want the privy, I suspect. No cause for fidgeting, lad, you'll find one outside. Thank heaven it's all mod cons at my humble abode. Just be sure to shut the wonky door afterwards, will you." His forefinger prodded the other in the ribs. "There was an old man… but you'll find out about the bloke up in Limerick, son."

The following day brought a pleasurable journey, tight turns, jolts and all. They had covered a few miles past uniformed men securing the border when Father Ben chimed, "Welcome to Beal Feirsde, Dino." It wasn't long before the car came to a stand close to a hotchpotch of swings, roundabouts, shooting galleries, and a Ferris wheel laden with shrieking children. Gracefully tucked behind the funfair was an austere-looking church. "Sure a peek at the interior will do neither of us any harm," said the priest while pointing at the grey façade.

Inside the House of the Lord Dino was assailed by a familiar scent of frankincense and votive candles. Up in a niche the little child who had issued from the womb of a yielding virgin seemed to look pensively from his nest of straw like a Peter Pan cocooned against the perils of growing into manhood. A couple of yards away and standing in front of a carved marble altar, the man of God shot a tender look at the man God who had climbed to naked freedom on a cross; his visage gleamed pale and looked pained against the flicker of the candles; his eyelashes fluttered and his thin hands joined in prayer. Dino's eyes closed on a vision of his father's hands coming to a touch in front of the Liberator.

When both returned to the square, the merry children of the town reasserted their presence while playing a game which looked very much like the *belle statuette* contest he and his playmates had engaged in as they stood motionless on the uneven flagstones of a courtyard to which the sky was the limit. The priest's vehicle chugged away and advanced slowly along grey brick walls; between the nicely sloping ends of gable roofs black-hooded men were pictorially engulfed in a sea of white and blue flags, and in the next street another mural depicted swans floating on water and a gold-haired woman defiantly staring into space against a white-and-green-coloured background. "There she is, Lir's lovely daughter," Father Ben whooped. Further on were walls of iron sheeting, and close to them other children could be seen handling sticks and hitting little balls. "We've reached the peace line," Dino heard at the same time as figures standing inside a lorry like dummies on parade rolled along. It looked like the rehearsal of a harmless pageant, but instants later there was a crackling noise and men in grey-green checked uniforms were spotted taking aim at the chimney on the roof of a discoloured block of flats. Firing from either side broke put, and the rat-tat-tatting noise continued for long tense seconds. From the thick of the skirmish, and yet sounding as if emerging from an unfathomable depth, came the shriek of diminutive creatures scurrying and leaping about like rabbits disturbed in their warrens. Dino glimpsed their small arms picking up what looked like tiny cobbles and casting them at the towering presence ahead, their mouths still wide open for a cry, and the sight brought to his mind's eye the picture of a young man uttering a stifled scream in an office room; at long last he was able to hear it. Glued to his seat he goggled in horror, but, "Never fear," said his guide. "It'll soon be all over." The soothsaying Ezekiel could not have uttered any better, for the crackle of guns ceased as if by magic; the men in uniform stood at ease again, and the children held their sticks just as they'd been doing before the burst: the beautiful statuettes had frozen.

The flivver turned the corner and coughed to a halt. A sizeable handkerchief came out of the man's cassock; a bowl was cutely embroidered on it. Dino pointed at the pattern and mumbled, "I… I like it."

"You're looking at the Sangraal, son," the priest returned. "You know, on this island we are perennially in quest of it, and blood is inherent in our crusade. I see my handkerchief as a reminder of the piece of linen Christ bequeathed to us for our use when grief draws tears or blood." He dabbed his doughy face with the soft item. "The only snag is that the star of old has fallen into a black hole; death comes to us and we accept it as a way to martyrdom and a turning point in our journey to resurrection and life." He coughed a short cough and pocketed the Sangraal. "The wild geese have gone for keeps, but Lir's children are still in the water, awaiting the first mass-bell ring," he resumed in a loftier tone. "But all they can hear is the rat-tat of brigades of some colour or other on the move. The kids recognise them at once. Have you discovered as yet that the name 'brigades' stems from Briga? It's a Celtic word, of course."

The listener's hand moved to the chin and stroked it reflectively. "There was a monk in a book I read when I was a child, and he was writing that word in his manuscript. My schoolmistress never told me the meaning of it," he recalled.

The priest's bushy lashes flickered. "I'm not surprised. Your schoolmistress was not from these parts after all. Strife – that's

215

what the word means, sonny. We know that and soldier on, but the only move left to us is love – love, I say – and not just for those who love us, or what would our reward be? Sadly, hate seems to have been a catchword in our little corner of the world for a very long time, yet we have only to touch our hearts to feel that love is alive and kicking inside." He fell silent briefly and then, "Come to that, only prayer will do; the good Lord will take the heart of stone out of our troubled breasts and give us a heart made of flesh." He paused again for a moment before adding at a higher pitch, "You see, at times I sense that we are having a lucid dream and that the dream is bound to go on." The last utterance mingled with the wheeze of the rattletrap now crossing the peace line. The sputtering engine expired at a short distance from the pastel white-and-grey façade of a stately building. A bizarre rose window and cream mouldings conjured up musical symbols. "Grand but not homemade," was the man's comment while looking up at the noble front. "You'll have time to enjoy it while I go on a most urgent quest. One of my sheep has gone astray, but I'm determined to have the creature back in my flock." His slender forefinger went up in the manner of a judge passing a sentence. "My errand may take quite a while, and surely I can't ask you to wait for me until kingdom come, as much as I'd enjoy staying on the road with you for a little longer."

Dino pondered for a few seconds and then rejoined, "You've been very kind to me, Padre. A thousand thanks for your welcome, and please don't worry. I'll find my way to the railway station."

"Still keen on Limerick, lad?'" The reply was a slow bend of the head. "Super. You've just come out of your vineyards and olive groves. As to me, I've not found a way out of my limestone and drumlins for a long time… too long, I suspect." His voice sounded pregnant with overtones of stones unturned, roses unculled.

"You know, Father," said Dino composedly. "Many years ago,

216

another Padre who happened to be my good parish priest tried to prevent an uncle of mine from falling into a hole. I was at his farm during the war, you see." He took a slight, hesitant breath before adding, "when they found his body at the bottom of a pit, my relative had a black shirt on him."

A question seemed to be filling the priest's dove eyes. The look he gave signalled recoil, reflection, and acceptance before he said, "Try and see it a closed book, Dino. Take it from a man wrapped in an ancient soutane, a paddy who is hoping and praying that we, too, will close the book we're still reading up and down our islet."

The youngster's glasses shifted to the bizarre rose window again. "I've recently learned from a Norfolk novelist that the past is a foreign country, and yet, when I think of my life in the country I've come to, the past is no longer all that foreign to me." A momentary voiceless interval was followed by, "While we were in the street where the burst-up took place I thought of men who have lost their lives in a foreign field, and then of one of them fastened to a cross and yearning for liberty and redemption."

One more time, the clergyman let his hand drop onto his cassocked thigh. "How, where, and why we live and die are not of the essence. Life and death have a relevance of their own, you mark my words," he stated, crinkling his pastoral features. "Well, right, I want to believe that they are my words; it appears that both of us have been digging into somebody else's goldmine, ha-ha." He grasped the wheel as if to give a new direction to his thoughts. "Be streetwise in your travels, Dino," he continued. "Have a great time down in Limerick and as soon as you pop into a tavern for another taste of our good stuff be sure to enquire about Sarsfield and Ginkel... pray make a note of the names." His thin fingers moved to the rear and got hold of his blue-and-white history book. "I just thought that you might want to have a proper look at it," he said with a hieratic smile and thrust the moderately-sized tome into the prospective reader's hands. "It's *arrivederci*, then. See you again in the Eternal City."

Caught unawares, Dino seized the book with widening eyes. "I'm sure the Pope will be there on your next visit, Father Ben," he chimed.

A grin flooded the priest's mobile face, and his beaver head swayed up and down. "Celeste Aida, too, will be there again, I dearly hope. Godspeed, son," Don Benjamin said.

17

A REINCARNATE CRICKET

Clutching a mug of cocoa, Dino managed a rare full smile: he had at long last joined a commune, and the place looked very much up his alley. On cue, the door clicked open, and Lorna and Dan, the co-owners of the place, slid in.

"There will be a massive demo in town tomorrow. Not to be missed, comrade," said he.

"I have a batch of leaflets for you. Handing out a few of them would be a significant contribution to the workers' cause," said she.

"We are mariners braced by the foam of the sea, not bone-dry thinkers," her companion stated.

"And a friendly gust of wind sets a ship in full sail," she remarked.

The listener's mind flashed back to the Chinese chairman, and he had a pleasing image of the great man as someone very much alive and probably swimming up the Yellow River as they spoke.

On the following day, the neo-Communards walked into the square named after the feline king of the forest (a red-haired one, at it happened). Standing on tiptoe, Dino endeavoured to single out the palace of art that a late romantic poet had once chosen as his abode, but all he saw was a feast of clothes and hair of all shapes and colours as well as a number of police vans on standby at strategic corners. A barrage of slogan bawls and catcalls abruptly took the shape of a volley of brickbats in exchange for tear gas, but the communards kept at some distance from the flare-up though not altogether beyond the reach of the law. On seeing a cadet approaching, Dino flattened his body against a lamppost, whereas his flatmates leapt apart thus creating a wide gap through which the attacker went at a tilt. Cool as cucumbers, the couple grabbed his stocky body from behind and pulled it to the ground. As a sequel to the deed, their recently gained comrade removed his glasses, lunged at the captive and ended up touching the head of a young man sprawled out under the weight of the assailants.

"Hold his noddle tight!" Dan thundered.

"Stick your hands to his swan neck!" Lorna yelled.

He went down on his knees and leant over backwards only a couple of inches away from the youth's face now exposed by the falling away of his helmet. Lavender eyes expanded into a metallic gaze, and a crop which evoked an ancestral warrior's hairstyle produced a funny taste in his wide-open mouth. He searched for signs of drilled-in hostility, but all he was able to discern was a hint of denial and determination in a schoolboy face. Was that the countenance of a lackey of the system? Was the wryly-smiling lad a witch-hunter on a spree? Mouthing at him, Dino loosened his grip. A sideways cock of the head made him conscious of the approaching charge of fellow cadets, and, "Let's get out of here!" he squeaked before scuttling off and taking himself away from the perilous spot. Mopping his damp brow, he endeavoured to come to terms with an ego dangling from the branch of a transplanted contestation.

Enveloped in the shades of evening, the lad welcomed solitude. Dan and Lorna were still away from home, and the 'what if' question surged as urgent as ever; he did his utmost to send it back to an unused corner in his brain, but he was hampered by memories of ruthless law enforcers and a handy documentary photo. This time, he feared, no visual evidence would be provided for the benefit of his new flatmates. Shaking his head, he retrieved the details of a vacancy advertised at the corner newsagents. A job as a general assistant in a hotel was available. *Whoopee!* He saw the position as manna from heaven now that his temporary job at Alex's inn had come to an end. Moreover, the name of the hotel was truly imposing: "Imperial," he murmured. The soft utterance went down well with the mellow mango juice he was savouring.

Soon enough he was ensconced in a gunmetal pallet, which strikingly resembled a camp bed. Keeping his legs wide apart, he stared at the ceiling: it formed an utterly immaculate expanse except for a dark blot up in an angle, and he saw it as a sheet covering the silence pervading the room until a small voice gave him a start. "Go home, silly boy; go back to where you belong," it chirped. Squinting, he fixed his eyes on the splodge, and it had the shape of an insect – a big fly, say, or a beetle; or was it a snail? A mollusc of the kind was in a short story he had recently read, and the excellent piece of impressionist narrative had a lot to do with a mark on a wall. He took off his specs and remembered that well ahead of the mollusc a cricket had crept up another wall and spoken to a boy made of a log. What if, then? Again, what if? No, no, it was all tosh! Unless it was, God forbid, a case of micro-hallucination; it occurred to him that his renowned psychoanalyst cousin would probably diagnose his condition as something of the kind. A dull sense of unease made him rack his brains for recollection until he remembered that the man who had entertained children for generations with the ups and downs of a wooden marionette had warned them that in the life of puppets there's always a 'but' and it spoils everything. He snorted, raised his forefinger, and placed it inside the bottom of his serviceable nose. Suppose, just suppose the law showed up and, politely but firmly, obliged him, an undesirable alien, to hop on a plane bound for his native country. Oh, ah, the utter shame of it! His eyes went all over the ceiling and through it. "Angel of God, my good guardian, I promise I'll be a good boy," he whispered, a hand on his heart, and he had a gut feeling that the ghostly cricket whom the impish wooden creature had shamefully squashed would have been happy to hear what he had just said. He took hold of his glasses and let them fall into place: the hideous speck was nothing more than the reflection of a leaf belonging to the aspidistra that sat, supremely unconcerned, on the windowsill. The revelation bucked him up. "I'll hop on a plane as quickly as I can," he said to himself. *Well, on a train, on second thoughts, in case of another roguish pilot; anyhow, without any escort.* Pretty soon he would be back home and free again! He sighed with relief: it was yet another consummation devoutly to be wished. Seconds later, his attention was caught by the wide-eyed stone figure on the front cover of the book concerning the history of Father Benjamin's country. It was high time he gave it a well-deserved read. He lifted the blue-and-white cover and went through the pages: no monk was entering the word 'Briga' anywhere, but a dramatic show was being played up to the bitter end, and the struggle for freedom was its main theme. It occurred to the reader that Immanuel Kant had seen freedom as a boon and added that the nature of moral freedom has always been and will always be a mystery. He closed his eyes and his arm stayed lethargically on the bed cover. "M for Morals," he said to himself and in the same breath, "M for Mors", which was, to the best of his recollection, the Latin for death. Had not Father Ben asserted that love for death was a streak in the national psyche? His eyes reopened wide, and he had a peculiar sensation that he had just had a lucid dream of a kind.

PART III

18

BRIGADES

As good as his word, he was at home. Termini welcomed him back with open arms and he felt the touch of warm streaks inside a heart of stone; the smile of a returning native formed on his pumpkin face. Out of the station, he walked into the office of an accommodation agency and re-emerged holding a badly needed house number. The rush-hour heavy traffic put him to the test, but he negotiated the hubbub and achieved the safety provided by a chubby-faced, fishtailed Triton taken up with blowing his conch shell trumpet inside an ornamented fountain at the centre of a noble piazza. He strode across a patch of classical mosaic. "Here I am, back where I belong," he let the sea god know, and for good measure winked at the lithe naiads languorously dancing in the foamy, babbling water. The image of dust-white cliffs was fast receding into a blur, superseded by the contours of a city soaked in a mesmerising past, shaded by quivering pines impregnated with the scent of richly variegated spring blossoms, intoxicating espressos and masterly baked brioches. "This ancient land dear for her reputation around the world," he recited in an aptly lyrical tone; "This place on earth where enjoying the day is a sacred existential concept; this perennial source of love and understanding!" he continued in a

225

crescendo. A sidelong glance revealed the presence of a comely young woman leaning against the wall of an august building. A posy lay close to her bosom, and how sweet to think of the tribute of a native gallant to beauty and love! It was pleasing to see the maiden turn her dark head sensuously and lift the flowers to greet a man at the wheel of a small car crawling to a halt. In a split second, inferno broke loose: machine gunfire crackled like fiendish fireworks and a hush was promptly dispelled by a renewed round of shots and the roar of a black motorbike in fleeting transit. Bodies could be seen writhing on the ground while a smartly dressed gentleman was being helped out of a long car, gently led into another and whisked off. The wail of an ambulance was heard forthwith and bystanders pointed their fingers as if to give directions. He found himself swept along by the crowd and on impulse fumbled for his watch, but where the dickens was his precious time-keeper? Hopelessly ticking on the island which he had just deserted, perhaps? Albeit in a fluster, he managed to come away from the hullabaloo and walk as far as the banks. The Tiber was flowing as placid as ever and from across the river church bells tolled while a chopper rattled in the sky. Keeping his head bent down and his hands firmly inside his jacket pockets, he made headway inside a maze of streets flanked by grey multi-storeyed houses: no shops, no benches, and no passers-by. When he reached the address provided by the considerate agency, he saw no human beings go into or come out of the block; only a sheep – a ram at a close look – was grazing on a tiny patch of green. There was a kind of surreal dimension to the place, but the name on the door plate looked real enough. Reassured, he pressed the bell.

Long minutes elapsed before an inquiring eye glinted through a chink in the door. "I, er, I'm looking for accommodation," he mumbled. The latch was lifted, and he squeezed in. "The only room available is under the roof – not a large bedsit, but a cosy one," a paunchy fellow with a bulldog face let him know in an incongruously thin voice while his sinewy hand indicated a rugged flight of stairs.

Inside the room at the top, the tiles looked old and tired as though an army of tenants had been marching on them for a good many years; an incongruously polished wardrobe disclosed rough sheets and army blankets tidily stacked on shelves which smelled of mothball; a little red flag and a five-cornered star cut out of an old newspaper lay on the floor. An urgent call of nature made him skitter to a lacklustre loo and slump onto an eggshell bowl. He sat on it befuddled by a powerful chlorine surge, shut his eyes and waited for a soothing release, but there was none. Frustrated, he stood up and, keeping his left hand on his slackened belt, regained his enclosure, sank into a bouncing bed, stretched out his body and, benumbed by exhaustion, waited for the arrival of Morpheus. It wasn't long before the good god of sleep descended upon him.

Daylight had faded away when he was awakened by a dull noise from beneath. It sounded as if a trunk was being lugged along in tune with muffled voices. He jerked up, went down on his knees and stuck an ear onto the floor like a redskin warrior glued to the tracks in a Far West epic tale. Before long, words like 'How are you… cheese… minestrone… whiskey' rolled up in unequal accents but in equally measured tones.

"I need tablets" filtered through in quick succession and conveyed the mellow tone of a well-educated gentleman hailing from the heel of the boot-shaped peninsula. After a short interlude, "Tonight… tonight," surged up, imbued with a strong labourer's tang that indicated a northern region. Their subdued voices suggested friends having a quiet rendezvous; far more intrusive was the persistent whirl of blades in the night sky.

He padded back to his bed and nestled his head against the bolster. Much to his relief, the clatter overhead had petered away, but the bloodcurdling scene at the crossroads was still giving him the creeps: had the extraordinary incident actually occurred? had men fired and other men fallen and stayed down in agony? also, was not the fellow abducted in broad daylight a VIP? He tossed and turned until his wearied eyelids came to a soothing touch.

In the morning, he was out in the street and the spectator of yet another tumultuous event: a multitude was on the move in the fashionable Corso and vociferously calling out for justice and an end to terror; a host of flags and placards were glinting in the early spring sunlight. He gaped at the dismay, anger, fear, but also compassion and hope discernible on countless faces at the same time as police sirens howled and a couple of metallic birds circled and rumbled up in the sky; it appeared that *la dolce vita* had abruptly turned sour. His eye landed on the front page of a tabloid and a photo showing the face of a man encased in a dark frame and staring into space with an air of despondency; his mouth was aslant like a tiny boat in a lumpy sea while long folds ran alongside his nose like furrows in sandy soil and a white streak was pathetically smothered in a matted tangle of silver-grey hair. It was, he realised with a shiver, the self-same face of the fellow abducted at the crossroads and it looked the very likeness of the Premier.

Late in the evening and safely inside his lodgings he heard the voices again as they seeped freely through the boards and wafted on gossamer wings in a world beneath consciousness.

"When I'm close to another man I feel ill at ease," the bloke with a labourer's accent was saying.

"You are close to a man who is your prisoner and is presumed guilty," came up as a rejoinder. "And isn't it ironic that this man should be a staunch advocate of the freedom of the law?" The bland cadence in the utterance would probably have been described by Lorna and Dan as hoity-toity, while Brada and Lando would have welcomed it like the hissing of a snake in the grass.

"Freedom only comes in the wake of a revolution. Am I right, *Presidente*?"

"I doubt it, my friend. Freedom is born out of repentance and forgiveness."

"Not in the realm of politics and legal niceties, as far as I know."

"The history of mankind witnesses to the contrary, I believe."

The sparring match yielded to a momentary silence, and then the conversers were hinting at a losing battle, survival, and the yearning for a unique moment of being. Words and accents met and intermingled as if desirous of losing their separateness.

The voices parted again when the militant worker stated, "As the party chairman, you are the great priest of a militant church and your faithful are legion, sir."

"The faithful don't always follow. I have learned my lesson." The tone would have befitted a resentful student.

"Ah, angry at last!"

"Angry, yes, and with reason: there is comfort in resentment. 'Do not let the sun go down on your anger,' the apostle Paul wrote in a letter. I for one am bound to draw the line at somebody who is acting as an enemy of the State."

"All I can see is a line on a razor."

Silence took over again albeit not for long. "Who killed my dedicated escort?" was the next question, and it sounded like an inquisitor's query.

"Ah, none of us could sensibly claim to be marksmen, come to that, but all of us believe that it makes sense to launch a pre-emptive strike."

"It does indeed. Making the first move is the hallmark of a resolute fighter, but please forgive me for asking who it was that struck first at the crossroads: was this unknown quantity a member of your team and a native speaker of our language?"

There was the quick, sharp sound of crockery being handled, and it was followed by words such as, "The answer is still blowing in the wind. Silence is the only voice a comrade hears while standing with a piece of metal in one hand and a lump of fear inside his heart. Sadly, the dauntless knight of a chivalric age is dead and gone." The clatter of pots and pans continued while the labourer related that the letters their guest had written to his friends on high had been duly forwarded because they were incisive as well as poignant messages of a sensitive soul, not the brainchild of a severely warped mind portrayed by the bourgeois and even the workers' press. It was rather unfortunate that moral responsibility was no longer an issue out there, whereas inside padded walls the two of them were civilly doing their best to maintain their respective identities and beat Death at its game. A deafening silence fell anew, but it was soon swept away by the professorial voice. "I believe that you and I are playing the devil with our souls; the last move in our game ought to be one for salvation." A clinking sound made the eavesdropper imagine that the debaters had been hitting their glasses together to toast salvation. Bowled over in mesmerised immobility, he kept his head in touch with the floor, but when his mind cleared up, he thought hard about his next move. Should he make his landlord privy to what was taking place at his place? Doing so would undoubtedly stand to reason and probably bear fruit; only, where on earth was the mastiff now? A couple of growls had been the last of him. *Aha, about time I had an espresso!* he silently exclaimed.

Entirely unforeseen, a young and agreeable female voice claimed his undivided attention. "I've been looking for ways of changing the world, of turning my dreams into reality," it was saying.

"You are still in time to step back from the abyss, *signorina*. Do so while you can." The modulated pitch befitted a person of rank.

"Awfully sorry, but leaving things undone is not in my book."

"Now then, take a long look at our palaces, churches, and

fountains. I'm confident that doing so will give you pause. Whenever I gaze at the grandeur that is a component of our national heritage, an inner voice tells me that the good people of this Imperial as well as Christian city would conscientiously balk at rallying behind a blood-smeared banner."

"*Professore*! Blood is a crucial ingredient of the Christian success story, as you are undoubtedly well aware of. At times I ask myself if Christ has really saved us from our cannibalistic instincts by virtue of offering his wine and his bread. No offence intended, of course."

"I'm not hurt, young lady. Love covers all offences as well as a multitude of sins. Keeping in mind the words from the Book does a power of good."

There was another quiet interval before "I see the story of Christ as that of a revolution, and I trust you agree. In this day and age the masses must be brought to believe, as I firmly do, that another revolution is possible, and that the time for action is now. My awareness has reached this point, and it keeps me going. In fact, my personal revolution has already begun." The female speaker sounded adamant. "May I tempt you to a cookie?" she was then asking in the endearing manner of a girl alluring her boyfriend.

"Oh, just the kind I like! How did you know? Womanly intuition, should I say? Or would you, arguably a feminist, object to my sexist assumption?"

A rippling laughter broke through the ceiling. "These biscuits made my mouth water every time my grandmother opened a shiny tin and proffered a cookie to her little granddaughter. That's all I can safely say about my feminine intuition."

"They are my grandson's favourites, too." A gentle clearing of the throat intervened. "I'm certain that he misses me as much as I miss him. He is a quiet nipper, you know. No budding Che, I daresay."

"Come to that, I am no Dolores."

"What about your family, say, your parents?"

A low-pitched cough was a prelude to "Oh, they are fine, thank you, and as integrated as bourgeois folk can be. I, too, was fine as a home-and-church girl until I opened the house door and ran into the world out there. It looked as if it had been waiting for me. There's no way back, now." Her voice sounded a tad emotional when she added, "I had a fiancé once, and I did care for him until I fell heart and soul in love with a beautiful idea." Her peculiar timbre rose whilst she disclosed a recent dream of hers, "I was walking in a very long tunnel, but I was seeing the light at the end of it," she related.

All of a sudden there was a renewed whirring of metal blades, and were they churning directly above the house? When the noise faded away, the woman's voice reasserted itself. "He has got the sulks now," it said. The 'he', the eavesdropper confidently assumed, was the abducted professor.

"What about us? Are we parents or children to him?"

"Come on, comrade! Would it be out of order if we let the chairman go? It might well be a stab in the heart of the system, or it might send the message that those guys at the Palace can't be beaten." A silent spell reasserted itself, but not for long. "They have taken away the woman in your life, I know, and I'm in no doubt that the pain is still with you though you keep mum about it," she was now saying and after giving another discreet cough, "The chairman says that he misses his grandchild enormously."

"Does he? Well, well, well. It seems that he and I are in the same boat: I, too, miss my only boy. Mind you, he was only a toddler when I last saw him." The labourer sounded like a sensitive actor in a moving domestic drama.

No better time than this to walk away and dream up a happy ending, the hidden listener felt, and yet he kept rooted to the spot as if impeded by the tentacles of a giant octopus. Before too long the captive professor was on stage again and articulating his faith in a dialogue between classes and, more than that, between humans.

"Ha, a dialogue conducive to a historic compromise with the proletariat, you mean," the militant worker scoffed. "I see it as nothing short of a last-ditch attempt to prop up a crumbling fort." The pitch went up by an octave while he expanded on how the Establishment had reacted to the removal of him as a chairman of great tactical skill taken up with an exceedingly subtle plan: the powers that be had resorted to vituperation, calumny, reticence, and, crème de la crème, a vile betrayal. In response to the onslaught he, as the leader of his party, had written increasingly bitter messages, which had touched a chord with him, his captor and an enemy of the state.

"Christ himself was not able to bear the weight of the cross all the way," was the prisoner's comment on that, and it sounded rueful.

"How finely put. I am always at one with a hapless loser."

"Perhaps we are all losers in the ongoing battle."

"Not to my eye. There are winners, and the memory of their feats lives on."

"The memory of your feat will be dead and buried in the fullness of time, I suspect."

"Never! It may be twisted, exorcised, banished. But buried? Not for the world. Memory in a condition of freedom is what you and I want, isn't it?" It sounded a conciliatory statement.

"It's hardly my condition, I'm afraid. A man in captivity can barely hope to enjoy the pleasures of free reminiscence." There was a hint of rueful rejection in the subdued tone of voice.

"The captivity is over, Chairman – for you, and for me. I am a child of hope again, and there is freedom in that." The utterance was conveyed in an agreeably sostenuto manner.

Another soundless moment intervened before the abducted gentleman said, "I heard a canary sing the other day, but there hasn't been a single warble since then."

Regrettably, the little bird had availed himself of a moment of carelessness to desert its cage. "It would appear that freedom is a historic necessity for a canary as well," his guard remarked.

The utterances abated to barely audible whispers and then to nothingness like logs overwhelmed by breakers, but they soon re-emerged. Fragments like "The Court of the People... guilty... the sentence is final" bubbled up until the young woman's voice came through again, and it sounded as clear as a bell when she said that the gentleman they were holding was just about her father's age.

"Try and see him as the begetter of a dangerous idea or a child of Machiavelli. Offspring like him make an ideal offering," was the other's suggestion.

"I hope that it's a peace-offering and that the ram I've spotted grazing outside is still there."

"Nobody has asked me to fetch him, I'm sorry to say. I've been left with the sacrificial son – and with you, of course. Will you still be with me?" There was a sound suggesting a long sigh and then, "I shall be at your side all the way, *compagno*."

The eavesdropper fidgeted and made an effort to come away from his uneasy position, but to little avail. He surrendered, crossed his arms and kept waiting, straight as a ramrod. Polite, chilly, inexorable, the labourer's voice put an end to the wait. "Sorry to wake you up, sir. The moment of truth has come. You and I must move on, I'm afraid."

"It's time to say our farewells, then. May I thank you and the young lady for lending an ear," was the gentleman's response in the fashion of a leave-taking lecturer. His acknowledgement conveyed the awareness that a regrettable task had been accomplished.

"No, you can't do that to him!" the secret hearer burst out. "I know who you are. I, too, was at the crossroads, and I saw you – oh yes, I did. And then there was this man, flitting by on a motorbike and holding something that looked like a weapon.

Was the mysterious rider one of yours? I saw the whole shoot; it was no mirage." He paused for an instant before adding, "you claim to be champions of the proletariat. Very good. Go no further, you men of the people; revolution springs from collective consciousness, not from the individuality of a self-contained brigade; therefore, stop now! Let me hear the cry of the free, not the moan of slaves!"

There was no feedback to his vehement plea. No more voices were heard. As if touched by a magic wand the listener turned actor in the drama now about to close sensed that he was free to move. He rose, lumbered to the window and looked down: the ram was still within sight and feeding nonchalantly in his green corner.

Dino sprang up in his bed and sat upright on it, peering at the sunbeam that had found its way through the windowpane and, on hitting the ceiling, laid bare the reflection of the aspidistra leaf. Then he spotted the book of John's lyrics that was a major ingredient of his daily diet, and opened it. 'Now more than ever it seems rich to die, to cease upon midnight with no pain,' he read with bleary eyes.

When he went down into the communal hall, a letter was waiting for him, and its continental stamp prompted him to open it without delay. Aldo – for it was none other than he – was writing in reply to the lines from him containing news about the remarkable commune he had just become a member of. 'Wonders will never cease. Still, nature makes no leaps' – this is how his former classmate felt about the move; besides, it was a good opportunity for letting his long-standing comrade have his views about the abduction *en plein jour* of their head of government. 'It does violence to the rights of the individual in a free society, no denying that, but even if I don't see eye to eye with the brigades that have done the deed, at the end of the red-letter day it seems to me a blessing in disguise. I trust you will agree with me that our wonky country must be dragged away from the edge of the precipice, whatever the cost.'

The reader sniffled and skipped the rest of the letter, but the name of Brada in a P.S. made his eyes linger on it. The girl had made tracks for Vallombrosa in search of her old flame Gero. 'My little sister has taken leave of her senses, I suspect,' her brother was commenting, and the incisive viewpoint provoked another snuffle. Apropos, where was Vallombrosa? And what sort of place was it? He rubbed his abruptly itchy forehead and acknowledged that, wherever and whatever the place chanced to be, it had an umbrageous name.

A few minutes later, he was out of the building and walking at a good clip. As he passed by a newsagent's stall, his eye fell upon the picture of a man folded in a car boot like a doubled-up rabbit: 'DEATH OF A PREMIER', he read. Hanging his head, he trotted away, but he halted as soon as the position at the Imperial Hotel flashed into his mind. Despite the majestic name of the establishment, he raised his eyebrows: the prospect of offering his services to a *maitre d'hôtel* had lost its shine; no longer did it feel like a consummation, etc., etc. "Where do I go from here?" he asked himself more than once while making a beeline for his diggings. The telephone was ringing insistently when he re-entered them, and he dashed to the receiver. Husky and perceptibly aged, his mother's voice pierced the silence inside him: "Your father is feeling rather poorly," it was saying, "and he'd like very much to see you again. Please come home as quick as you can, son."

19

A WICKED STONE

The pear-shaped body of a young woman emerged from the sea and ambled by a circuitous route to a large flowery sunshade fastened to the golden sand at a short distance from the chalet. Her slim hands slipped a bizarrely coronet-shaped cap off her cutely oval face and mopped her cascading russet hair with a gesture that implied obliviousness of the cutely bearded young man patently savouring the fierce sun in the nearby deckchair. Moments later his sonorous voice interwove with the swash and backwash of the waves: "Excuse me, is your tongue English?" Her little nod entered the slit in his semi-closed eye. "Just as I thought. G'day. On hols, I guess."

"An excellent guess, I'm bound to say." Her smile brought out a feast of dimples.

"I'm a stranger myself. Been hopping about all the way from the Antipodes if it's a mile."

"Well, I never! I hail from the Fens beyond the Channel. Does it sound familiar?"

"Well, after a sort. And what made you pick this nook of the world?"

"The local plants, most of all. I hope to be a marine biologist before too long."

His other eye jerked open. "Sounds grand. Been to Cumae in your travels, Sheila?"

"Marion is the name." Her shapely lips stirred in minute folds.

"You're talking to Rudy, Marion. I wouldn't mind a tip or two from the sibyl down there – if the old hag's still hanging inside the green bottle in her grotto, of course."

The vibrant sound of an accordion floated along and both turned to watch a silver-haired, corpulent man playing the instrument while he waddled ahead of a batch of dummies along the water's edge.

"Wow! A carnival or something is coming our way," she whooped. "The dragon is my pick; he's breathing fire all right."

"No wallabies in the bunch though. But never mind that. The little mermaid will do nicely." He stirred his long hairy legs. "My turn for a swim," he added while moving away and advancing on the fiery sand by leaps and bounds.

"Down under all the way, mate," she called out in an undertone before casting a look in the direction of the chalet; immune to the caustic heat of the sand by virtue of her carroty flip-flops, she padded to it. "*E' possibile* a little *vino rosso*?" she asked the young man standing at the bar.

"Quite possible," he replied with a sparkling smile. "Dino is at your service, miss."

"How nice of you to use my language. Please feel free to call me Marion."

"I lived in your country for a couple of years, Marion; I went to college every day and studied flat-out. I came back mainly because of my father's poor health. Poor papà passed away soon after my return." He nodded repeatedly. *That's life,* he meant.

"I'm really sorry to hear that, Dino." Her hand moved to the counter ledge and lifted a glass brimming with carmine wine. She took a sip. "Whew! It tastes nicely old."

"Naturally. It's ancient. Julius Caesar drank this very wine, you know."

"Super. I'll savour the great man's tipple under my sunshade, if you don't mind." Awkwardly balancing the imperial potion, she flip-flopped back to her corner.

Julius's tipple had been taken care of when her next-parasol neighbour hopped back to her, dripping with pearly blobs of water and inviting her to a walk on the shore.

"Not a bad idea," said she, and off they went, inhaling rather warm whiffs of wind as they strolled on. "Feeling the heat as much as I am?" she inquired. "The sirocco is to blame, I suspect, and it's rubbing me up the wrong way. This kind of hot air belongs to the desert and should stick to it," she stated in between laborious breaths.

He remarked that it was only an apology for the blasts Aeolus had puffed out while Ulysses and his mates were sailing around not too far from where they were.

"Look!" she cried, extending her forefinger toward a woman's dark head jutting out of the water in a little pool, her long pale face confronting them with weasel eyes and the ghost of a smile which grazed the corners of her protruding lips. "Her features remind me of a Herculaneum mask I spotted in a holiday brochure the other day," she related with the smile of one to the manner born.

"The pool she's squatting in works wonders for females itching to have a bambino," he let her know.

Her cornflower-blue eyes widened. "I'm feeling peckish. How about having a bite?" His swaying head signalled agreement. "Let's go to the chalet, then. I'm sure Dino's keeping some nice grub in store for a Fen girl."

"And a darned good stubby for an Aussie," he chuckled.

Unfortunately, Dino was not to be seen at the chalet: he was at his mother's pink cottage aptly situated at the edge of the pinewood facing the lido and standing in front of the lady seated bolt upright on a tiger-striped sofa, her gimlet eyes glued to the small black-and-white screen that had only recently made its appearance as a thing of marvel in their southern corner of the peninsula. Balloon-like, her black gown covered her substantial yet shrinking body while her head offered a display of snow-white flakes interspersed with a few dark threads. Time had nibbled at her angular face, but it had spared her moist smile. "Go and eat, Dino," she said imperiously, but he shook his head. "Let's have a coffee, then," she suggested by way of a compromise. He obliged, and it didn't take long for a monk-shaped coffee pot to take pride of place on the table top. A large dose of sugar dropped into her tiny cup and then she launched into a recollection of the man who had been Dino's begetter. "Your father had a soft spot for blonde Valkyrie," she recalled with an abortive grimace. "He chased them like crazy and did so even after we were engaged to marry."

"Yes, Ma, but in the end dad chose you."

"Well and good, but I must say that marrying me was the lesser of two evils." As a matter of fact, she was carrying him in her womb, and her father was a man of the old mould; in addition, it was a question of olive groves, vineyards and cattle. All elements of the same equation, as she put it. Her small lips sucked in a few black drops. "A man died at the airport the other day," she drawled on. "A stone from the quarry near the castle fell off a lorry and dropped bang on him, poor Christ." A checked hankie surfaced, and she blew her nose gently. "And fancy that! He was the very man who came to the farm where you and I…"

"I was happy at Nut Farm, and I felt sad when Uncle Raf disappeared," Dino chipped in.

"Ah, poor Raffaello! Have you been told that they found him at the bottom of a big hole up on the hills?" She gave a long sigh. "My wretched brother was lying in there, his right arm still up." She let out a longer sigh. "I still remember Padre Orsino telling me that no angel had flown down from heaven to help him. Do you remember the parish priest, son?"

"Ah, Don Orsino! He always gave me a heavy penance when I went to confession."

She borrowed one of his half smiles while saying, "Don Orsino had a heart of gold. He hid a few partisans in the crypt. Just think: had they been tracked down he'd have been shot on the spot – he and all those he'd been keeping out of sight."

The piece of info came as a surprise to the listener: had not the same priest blessed the dark shirts on parade in the village square? However, he was a man of God, and how unlike the ogre who had entered the farm one hot afternoon and caused havoc! "I do remember the man who cropped up at the farmhouse and did what he did. He was big and looked down-at-heel," he said.

A distant look came into her eyes. "Ha, you do have a good memory. The brute came at you for a bashing, but Eulalia cropped up and you slipped between her legs and out of the room. However, that fellow was after your father, you see, and I'm still in the dark about the reason why: your father was doing his duty, wherever he was." Her ageing breast ebbed and flowed. "Busy as a bee, the man helped himself to our food and wine. In no time at all, he was soused and hot as a mandrill, and all my efforts to reason him out were of no use. Then my sister screamed; he lunged at her and threw her onto my sofa, I scuttled out for help." She put her sizeable rag to good use again by wiping a stealthy tear. "Her shrieks still ring in my years, and now... now you can see yourself how poorly your aunt is doing, all alone in her loft."

Dino moved his forefinger to the bottom of his nose and then, overpowered by the woman's piercing stare, placed the digit under his chin. On one occasion his auntie had snivelled at the sight of the onions he'd taken to her: "Bring me onions, not eggs, next time, or I'll feed my piglet on your little balls, ninny," she had said, cackling kind of funny. He gave his mother an inquiring look. "I say, couldn't Aunt Eulalia come out of the loft and stay with us? I'd be very glad to have her around."

She shook her head. "It can't be done, son. Exposing your aunt to prying eyes would add insult to injury and be no good for the honour of our family. Have you forgotten what your cousin Lando went through?"

"Ah, Lando! Before I went away, the two of us spent a few days together on a houseboat. He had changed, and in a curious way."

Her regretful smile in response added to the significance of the nods she produced in an impressive sequence. "Your ill-fated cousin was caught on the hill; he and his mates. They were all shot, and he was kept in an underground cell for a long time; he was spared only because my brother reminded his supporters that the lad was part of his own flesh and blood. After coming out of the dungeon, he started having bad dreams and took to rambling in the woods, weeping like a baby, poor Lando." She made a momentary pause. "Not many days later, Raf was found down in the pit.'"

"But papà, where was papà then?" After all those years, he was still clueless about his father's whereabouts in wartime.

Long seconds ticked away. "Well, since you are keen to know, I'll tell you straight: he was being detained at some place where they made rifles for our blond allies. I tried to explain that to the scoundrel who came to the farm, but he wouldn't listen; he went berserk." The strains of an accordion wafted through the balcony just as she was adding, "When he burst into Nut Farm I… I called out for Eulalia, and…" Her head turned sideways. "Aha, Grassone! I must have a word with this man now," she continued in a suddenly enlivened voice while a few more drops of coffee and an even larger dose of sugar fell into her cup.

Dino stood up. "I must return to the lido now," he said, and moved to the door. Halfway, he turned his head to face her again. "What a pity though. You and I were having quite an interesting chat, Ma," he said. "And oh, I remember that papà liked his coffee bitter," he added, an impish smile creeping over his roundish face.

The smile she gave in return looked uneasy. "Ah, you've just brought in the other side of the equation, son," she said.

He whirled his hand, gave a wink, and clopped to the door.

In the morning, he was standing at his post of duty and having an argument with the espresso apparatus when Marion appeared togged up in flaming red Bermudas which made him cast a dispirited glance at his dun baggy shorts. Flashing a smile which brightened the paleness in the sky, she pointed at the truncated frame of the castle squatting on the top of the hill which lay at the back of the village and was patchily discernible through the rising mist.

"Ah, you are looking at my castle," said he. "Once upon a time a dragon lived in it. He breathed fire, as all decent dragons were expected to do."

The quaint frame disappeared inside a cloud. "Ah, your desolate castle, vast empty desert, is no more," she recited, and there were overtones of commiseration in her voice. He went through a couple of facial contortions. "It's only a Chinese wail, mind you," she let him know.

He shot his forefinger at a line of fishermen dragging a boat ashore, their olive brown twill trousers rolled up to their knees, and chanting "*Issa, issa*" while they pulled and pushed. "Those men have been fishing all night long," he informed her. "And I'm sure they've been rowing above Sinuessa." A string of nods gave him the air of a bearer of momentous news. "I'm talking of a village under the sea, my dear."

Her face glowed with anticipation as she asked, "Has any of your fishermen ever heard church bells ringing down there?" He thrust out his lips. "At times, chimes do come from Dunwich, a village near the Fens from where I come," she related with chilly mildness. "Unfortunately, it was swallowed up by the sea ages ago."

Aha, the wonder of the thing! It was as wondrous as the ancient woman he spotted sitting not far from them and holding two hanging pans in her hand. He looked harder, and – damn! – the scales appeared to be uneven. "Some fishermen swear they have seen a little mermaid swim around the village," he divulged and, yes, the balance was now tilting in his favour!

"I'm not surprised. I could swear I saw her walking ashore with a dragon the other day," she returned deadpan.

He squinted at the scales: sedately but inexorably, they were turning against him for a second time. "Sinuessa is not too far from the beach. I can take you there… even now if you like," he blurted out.

"I can't think of a better time for an outing, Dino. Take me there, please," she pleaded, her face afloat in a sea of dimples.

He saw the weighing come to the hoped-for end. "*Tekel!*" he squeaked, echoing the howl that one Christian Brother or other would unleash on catching a pupil in the sinful act of cribbing.

They moved to a rowing, flat-bottomed boat bobbing at the water's edge and soon were off. Puffing and panting, he kept pulling hard on the oars while she sat on the keel, her face divested of all expression and her aquamarine eyes fixed on the blades splashing in the azure liquid. No doubt some young lady from the Tiber had heard a similar sound while lying on the deck of her slave-propelled barge, and now this girl from the Fens looked as if she expected the resonance to go on and on and the precious moment to last forever. His laborious exercise came to a halt. "When I was a little boy my father took me to the sunken place once," he recalled. "In case the little mermaid came up, you see."

"Fantastic! And did she ever come up?" A brief silence reigned before she added, "well, men will be boys upon occasion. Was your dad a young prince with large black eyes?"

"He was my father all right," he replied curtly. "'If you are in with a chance, take the plunge, Dino,' was one of his recommendations shortly before he passed away." The oars went up.

Marion stirred. "Are we on the very spot?"

"Just look at the colour of the water – weird, eh?" He embarked on tentative dancing steps.

Looking amused, she dimpled again, but as soon as his prancing turned into a cheerful tarantella the hilarity and the ingrained dents on her face vanished. "Oh," she murmured while staring at the heavy rolling of the boat; a few moments later, "Stop it, darling," she entreated and immediately after, provoked by deaf ears, "cheese it, dimwit!" she cried with utter resolve.

Her fellow tripper's reaction was barely of the quality she had hoped for: in a sudden Dionysian mood, he hit the plank with rhythmical bits until his god-inspired performance came to a premature and ungodly conclusion on his plunging into the sea. The boat reacted by tilting and taking an upside-down U shape, but the orgiastic dancer resurfaced in no time, flailing his arms like a manipulated marionette and spitting salty driblets. From behind glasses obstinately clinging to his distressed nose he zeroed in on the lady mariner and saw her sit on the upturned hull in less of a Roman maiden's posture, her fox hair blowing in the sudden wind. He knew at once what his good cousin Lando would have done in his shoes, or fins though they might be: a good deal of furious swimming brought him to her. "Don't panic, dear! You'll soon be okay," he stated emphatically and, in keeping with his word, got firm hold of her ankles as a preliminary move in a gallant rescue, but, "Let go for God's sake!" the stressed damsel shrieked before diving into the water. He saw her swim with graceful strokes towards the beach, and acknowledged that the fishermen had told him no fib: a mermaid *was* alive and roaming at Sinuessa. Appeased, he stayed with the ill-starred vessel as a duty-bound captain would with his sinking ship; or like a seal having a rest at the end of an exhausting exercise, as Marion told him after the event with a voice that sounded as if coming from the sunken village in her godforsaken Fenland.

The heat of the early afternoon was almost unbearable. Cooling her face with a pizza carton, Marion repaired to the pine grove facing the sea. On reaching the canopy of needle-shaped leaves stirring in the light breeze she sat on a bench and helped herself to plenty of suntan oil until Dino sidled up to her, making his arms swing in sync with apologies for the mishap at sea. Her blue-green eyes flashed with forgiveness while she said, "I've got a startling piece of news for you," and asked if he'd been at the procession in the old quarter of the village. His head swayed in the negative. Well, she had. The azure-and-white statue of the Virgin looked rather nice, and who was standing not far from her but the funny woman she had spotted sitting in the pool close to the lido a couple of days before? "The oomph of the band cheered me up," she continued, "but suddenly there was a crack in the air: fireworks, I thought and then I caught a glimpse of the woman flicking something into her pouch." Within the space of a minute she'd found herself fighting her way through a forest of flailing arms and en route espying twitches of pain on the face of one of the statue's bearers while his fellow carriers kept moving at a brisk pace which made the Madonna lean one way and the other, her sombre features towering above musicians in disarray and notables in black up to their elbows in a spirited debate. The narrator looked willing to elaborate on the dramatic episode, but the listener got hold of her suntan-oiled arms and gently yet firmly dragged her in the direction of his mother's cottage.

Before long they were in the presence of the lady. Ensconced in her sofa and fanning her face with a flower-embroidered fan, she motioned Marion with a reassuring smile to come closer, and the pleasure signal flashed on and off while her son, after duly introducing the guest, animatedly passed on the news of the accident at the procession. When the report came to a close, "*Destino, Destino* is the boss," the matron stated, making the best of her wartime smattering of Marion's tongue. "But Dino say, 'No, *we* make *Destino,* he say.'" In an operatic flash, her son saw her transmogrified into Alvaro's female counterpart lamenting the overwhelming force of Destiny; then he heard her make in a matter-of-fact way a request for a refreshing cup of coffee. He obliged, and the burble of the manly potion presently reached his ears before merging into the chirpiness of mingling female voices.

"Yes, we shape our own destiny, I believe," Marion was saying.

"No, I not understand my son," his mum was echoing with a sigh.

"If I have a son one day, maybe I won't understand him either," the girl conceded.

He returned to them with the bearing of a well-trained waiter and handed in the steaming cups. Sugar cascaded as it usually would into his mother's open piece of china. "*La vita è una tazzina di caffè*," she articulated in the assured tone of a connoisseur of life and coffee while adjusting her oyster-shaped hair slide; "you move the *cucchiaino* and *tutto lo zucchero* come up." He was conversant with her choice metaphor about life being like a tiny cup of coffee and all the sugar coming up while you stirred the potion with a little spoon. A probing look at Marion allowed him to see her and his mother exchange an intense look. Whiffs of zephyr exhaling from the lady's large fan were redolent of her native soil; the slow, regular rise and fall of the girl's unobtrusive breasts sounded like the soughing of an exotic breeze; the smile that tentatively issued from both was awash with the intimation of a tacit mutual understanding.

The night was young, the sand warm, and the lido had the contours of a lampshade in an Oriental tale. Marion's light dress glinted in the blood-red light of the moon; her hair twinkled with diagonal bands of light and shade.

Holding a straw-covered flask in his arms, Dino clopped to her. "I'm carrying a few drops of royal nectar for a fair princess," he said under his breath.

"It's your Caesar's tipple, I bet. How nice of you. I could do with it before having a splash," said she while getting rid of her flimsy dress.

He flashed an appreciative smile at her bikini-clad tapering body. "On a night like this, Valchirie ride up and down the beach," he whispered, "with their long legs and…"

"Short clothes if any at all." A quizzical smile formed on her cheeks.

"My poor father liked them very much. And, frankly, I don't mind them either."

"Unfortunately, I am not a Valkyr. I don't ride. I run – in my local park, mostly."

His short-range eyes glided along her sylph-like frame and came to a rest above a splodge in the middle of her belly. "What do I see here, Marion? Is it an oyster or what?"

"Only a tattoo, really." She sat on the sand and imbibed her share of the noble potion he had chivalrously proffered. "Your turn," she added while returning the flask.

He took a full slug. "Your turn again," he murmured with an amazingly full-blown smile.

The narrow-necked bottle arched over her lips and stayed there for longer than it had done before. "Back to you, now," then she breathed with a slight hiccup.

The straw-covered container went to and fro more than once, and there was scarcely a trace of the nectar inside it when Marion rose and leapt away, flapping her arms. He went in pursuit.

They chased each other like frolicking swallows until she let herself go down onto the velvety sand. He leant over her body and made contact with the bluebottle streaks in her eyes: in the shimmering light, they seemed to be taking on an almond hue. His lips grazed her hair and the copper locks felt like the maize in the wartime farm field where a little girl had been standing at ease. He detached himself and teetered to the shoreline; suddenly his trunks looked redundant, and he disposed of them; then, with arms akimbo, he waddled in the twinkling water, elatedly spattering the foam-flecked liquid all over his body. "Here I go! Here I go!" he called out. When he cast a misty glance at the beach, a Valchiria was riding away beneath the bloodshot moon.

The morning after, Marion wanted to know if ancient fauns had a habit of exposing their not altogether divine bodies. He mustered all his strength for another fully developed smile but come a cropper and contented himself with the available half.

The beach was ablaze with sunlight. Unfazed by the fieriness from above, Marion lay comfortably on the sea lion enmeshed in her towel, lending a sympathetic ear to the enthused cries of children moulding doomed castles out of the sand. A young couple launched into a tambourine game, and the monotonous thuds of the little ball being bounced forwards and backwards made her lift her head and look at the players from behind the fashionable sunglasses she had purchased as a souvenir of the luminous Med. Her small lips puckered up with a wry smile; her upturned nose, dwarfed by the stylish specs, creased. Encircled by the brilliance of the granular expanse, a bay horse galloped up, pranced, accomplished an acrobatic pirouette, and landed in style. The young lady gazed at his sinewy shape made gentler by a star-shaped patch on his upper head and smiled on seeing the long-haired darksome rider take off his conical hat and wave it with a grin. The quadruped let out a whinny and trotted on, but the steady pace seemed on the verge of turning into a gallop again when a tiny girl deserted her little fort on the sand and bolted into the stallion's path. Flecks of fear surged up and froze the child's enlarged pupils while streaks of alarm flickered on the rider's pockmarked face as he endeavoured frantically to rein his steed back. "Oh no-o-o!" Marion wailed, but the musical waves of an accordion submerged her outburst. As the sound turned poignant and increasingly soporific, the horse slowed down and, inches away from the nipper manifestly in the grip of terror, reared up, his large nostrils flaring, his fierce eyes aglow and his long tail flapping. An instant of panic was swept away by the drop of brawny legs onto the sand and, finally, rest. "I really wish I wasn't so fond of horses," she let Rudy know as soon as he approached her.

"His long bacons were no joke," he growled. "I'm raring to go and have a word with Orpheus down there."

It wasn't long before he learned from Grassone, to the accompaniment of finely tuned bars and explosions of facial twists, that the man on the horse was a clown and he had met his father, one Rudy who had opted for a new life in Canada – or was it Australia? – and never returned. The tubby man descanted on a tale of displacement, marriage with a local pigeon-fancier and, in the long haul, integration. When the spin came to a stop, "It's a funny small world, sport," Rudy commented, a grin weaving its way through his bushy beard.

The fiery afternoon was yielding to a balmy evening when the Fenland girl reached the pink cottage and pulled the cord of the copper bell hanging on the door. Within seconds Dino's sundried, bowled-over face showed up on the threshold. The puzzled expression faded away as soon as he was told that she was visiting in response to his mother's kind invitation. Sad to say, the lady was out, but "Do come in", he jovially added before leading her by the hand into the lounge. With a gallant bow and a full extension of his arm he made her sit on the sofa his mum ought to be occupying, fan and all; a sombre countenance prefaced the news that the man fired at during the procession had breathed his last in a ward.

Her sea-green eyes sparkled with horror. "Dear me, but why was he shot?"

"Ah, you'd better ask the woman you caught in the act," he replied with a sigh. However, the long and the short of the story was that she had so far failed to provide her husband with a badly wanted heir and soon other males had been intimating over a glass of wine and a card game in more than one bar that her consort left something to be desired on that essential issue. The rumour had inevitably reached the maligned chap's ears and he, a man of honour up to the hilt, had promptly put his manliness to the test with a little help from another woman. His better half had paid him back in kind: a bullet into his heart had footed the bill, and the street ceremony in honour of the Madonna had been a most fitting occasion because husband and wife were devout churchgoers.

Marion received the tale with a few slow nods and related that she had caught sight of the culprit crossing herself while squatting in the pool by the sea: it was known to be a wonder pool, Rudy had told her, and now she was feeling very sorry for the unfortunate lady.

"Don't worry," Dino countered without delay, "a crime of passion warms the cockles of a judge's heart in these parts, and nobody could deny that she is a passionate woman." *No, she will not languish in jail for the rest of her life*, he stated, and breathed deeply in and out. "Shall we do something more cheerful now?" he suggested before moving quickly into the kitchenette. He reappeared holding a tray with a coffee pot, two tiny cups and puff pastries on it in one hand, and an olive twig in the other. "I'm sure you don't have anything of the kind in your Fens," he boasted, waving the twig. She gaped at the arrow-pierced heart pinned on the stem before colouring with hues of embarrassment. Were flecks of the sun that was his own now touching her cheeks? He gazed at the tapering shoulders and curved eyelids of the damsel from a low wet land, nuzzled his forefinger against his nose, moved to the cabinet and put a record on. As soon as a male voice crooned, 'I want to live with you forever and ever and ever', he closed his eyes and offered an impromptu translation of the lyrics in a voice that he endeavoured to bring up to the crooner's standard. When his eyes reopened, her inborn dimples were in full swing and she was slewing in the settee. His mother's fan dropped to the floor with a gentle thud. "How silly of me," he heard her grumble while bending to pick up the silky item. Soon afterwards, he saw his guest pad to the balcony and en route sneak a peek at the face of the tortoise-shell haired girl printed on the record sleeve where the name 'Ange' had been written in red ink. Keeping his eyes on the coffee, he slowly poured the thick liquid out. Moments later Marion re-emerged and announced that she would be making tracks soon.

"How soon?" asked he.

"Immediately after I've visited your castle. Rudy's taking me up there; it's very kind of him, I must say."

He glanced at the lingering folds in her cheeks, her boiled lobster face, her snub nose, and finally at the glint of purplish-blue wavelets in her eyes – a reminder with a difference of the summer cornflower tint that had unsettled him all those years ago. "Mind the dragon when you go up there," he warned her gruffly.

"Any snakes?" was her response counterpoised by an enigmatic smile.

"Only a few lizards, to my knowledge."

She gave a shrug.

"I wish you a merry trip," he intoned. Twice for good measure. It sounded like an unseasonable carol.

The early morning hour found Dino beset by misgivings about the misty expanse above: did it forebode a quick change in the weather? He looked intently at a bunch of olive-brown fishermen back from the sea until he saw his mother come to him slowly, making her large handbag trail on the sand. Her long dress formed a large blotch of ink against the shiny fence; her angular visage bore the marks of a laborious progress, and her hair was unusually loose.

"A little bird told me you were coming," he called out.

"I've come to tell you that I'll be away for the day; going to pay a duty call to the family of the man killed by a stone at the airport," she let him know on reaching the chalet.

"Fair enough, Ma. See you tonight, then."

"Ah, I almost forgot. Have a look at what I've found in an old casket." Her hand fumbled inside her handbag and brought out a photo: a comely country girl and a little cock were in it, the one and the other blurred with the haze of time.

He observed the picture pensively. "She saved my life once, you know, and then flew away like… like a butterfly," he said in an undertone.

Her piercing eyes darted a look around. "Where is she? I mean, the other 'she.'"

He raised his eyebrows as if trying to make sense of the question before replying, "Ah, she! Somewhere around, but not for long now." His eyes turned up to a plane flying through the mist and leaving a pencil-shaped trail of vapour: being on one of them again struck him as an interesting prospect, come hell or high water.

"Well, a bird in the hand is worth two in the bush, isn't it? Do take care, son," she said, and plodded away, but soon wheeled round and added in a gently commanding tone, "Go home for your lunch. Something's waiting for you on the cooker. I hope you'll like it," she said.

"I certainly will," said he. Her shapely head seemed to be swaying up and down as she trod on the fine golden grains. A white scrap of paper which had presumably fallen off her gown caught his attention, and a spur-of-the-moment decision made him pick it up and shove it into his pocket, but instants later the item was out again. It was a chit and his widening eyes went through lines jotted down in large and curiously oblique characters. 'I came to your door to beg for forgiveness. I couldn't bring myself to ring the bell, but I hope and pray that this bit of paper will do just as well. War is war; when it comes, the dragon comes with it. Well, I think I've said more than enough; there's no doubt in my mind that you will understand.' There was no signature. He scratched his head, folded the chit, unfolded it again and had a second read. "The dragon, still the dragon, forever the dragon," he hissed through gritted teeth. "*Bon voyage*, Ma!" then he cried, but she had already reached the far end of the lido, and was now fading into the encompassing glare. Slowly, he waved his hand.

One day later he was walking homewards, enmeshed in shafts of the setting sun, when the wench who had belonged to a distant farm came to mind again. "Women tend to enact their mimetic identification", this much a lecturer at his college on the island beyond the Channel had stated, and the theory made him assume that Ange had, by entering the world of a butterfly, symbiotically linked with animal pains and pleasures.

When he got to the cottage, softly pink in the gleaming of the sunset light, Grassone was coming out of it. "Hurry up, Dino! Your mother's waiting to see you," the man boomed, and he charged inside and up into the bedroom.

Sitting in the middle of her one-time generative bed, his parent was propping herself up with a large bolster and wheezing, her eyes open to a mere slit. In the subdued light provided by the bedside lamp her angular face looked inordinately wan and distorted, and the long hair that had made a dense dark mass in bygone days was now tumbling down her shrinking shoulders in the shape of a grey-silver whorl. His eyes panned across the room. From inside the silver frame on the cabinet his father seemed to be fixing his eyes on his spouse with the sad expression of an impotent onlooker, and at a short distance from both the young parish priest was reading out of a purple little book in his otherworldly manner, his chapped lips pulsating as they would in a shadow play. Huddled up on her own in a corner, Aunt Eulalia was staring vacantly at the floor and wailing in an ancient strain – her small breasts concealed by her arms and her body swaying rhythmically from one side to the other. He advanced to the bed gingerly and placed his hands on the patently ailing woman's thinned arms. "You are behaving like a naughty mother," he whispered. "Lying in while a delicious meal is waiting for both of us on the table. How dare you?"

She raised her head sluggishly, and her gimlet eyes appeared to be struggling for contact. "I fell, son," she let him know in a raucous voice. "I don't know why. Maybe it was the shoes I started wearing when the war was still with us." She rolled out a hollow cough. "They were only available on the black market, you know, but they are so comfy!'" she added with an exceedingly laboured drawl.

Out of the glowing mists of memory an image rushed to his mind. "Do you remember the day I was awarded three golden medals in the courtyard of the Christian Brothers School, mamma? You came to me in order to pin them on my chest, and, damn it, you fell. But you got to your feet in a flash and fastened the medals one by one. Your eyes sparkled." He kept silent for a moment and then, "I haven't won any more golden medals since then, but please get up as you did on that occasion. Please."

A narrowing of her eyelashes made him suspect an effort to bring the scene back to mind. A rueful smile suggested that his mother had succeeded in her attempt. "I hope I've put on a good show all my life," she said in the mode of a stage manager ringing down the curtain. "I'm feeling a bit dizzy right now, but don't worry. It will soon be as it should be," she assured him.

"It will, mother. I'm going to make a strong coffee at once, and I'll put loads of sugar in it," said he with a laboriously achieved smile. "I'm sure it will all come up." He fell silent for a few seconds and then, "listen to this: only the other day I heard a crooner on the radio, and he was telling his sweetheart that she was like a cup of coffee and he was going to stir the sugar in it until it would blend with the potion and drop into his mouth. Doesn't it sound like what you said the other day?"

The smile she produced by way of a reply implied that her views on the issue were at one with the crooner's attitude, but a streak of regret in her gimlet eyes conveyed a sense of discomfort about the way her own philosophy of life had been plagiarised by a mushy singer. Her hands moved with some difficulty to the rear of her neck and returned tremblingly to the front: her hair slide was in them. "Look here, Dino," she said with her ingrained drawl, "this was your father's first gift when I said yes to him. It's not much in fashion these days, I know, but please take it. I've made good use of it all these years; somebody else may find it handy now." He got hold of the object with a slight nod and a grateful smile. "You must be hungry. Go and eat now," she continued in an abruptly upbeat tone. "There's a time for everything, my son. Never forget that."

Her words came to him as an echo of the reply of the sibyl to the children who had asked her, as she stood inside a green bottle at her wonted grotto, to disclose her heart's desire. "I wish to die," the answer of the immensely old woman of Cumae had been. His head swayed incessantly while he slouched into the kitchen, glowering at the last rays of the sun he saw filter through the red-rose-embroidered curtains at the window. He moved to the table and sat down. The bowl in front of him was laden with pomegranates and he grabbed one, broke its tough rind in half and sucked its red juicy flesh: it had the sharp yet mellow taste of a nourishing source on the wane. He goggled at the crunchy core of the globular fruit until he felt Grassone's big hand on his shoulders. "Go to her, Dino, go," the man said in a surprisingly

256

caring voice while shreds of the dark earth materialised in his pupils. He leapt up and rushed into the bedroom. His mother had fallen in a heap on the pillow, her hands touching her forehead as if endeavouring to retrieve discarded thoughts. He dashed forward and lifted her up. Her body, remorselessly levelled by the might of Time, came into contact with his, yielding yet firm like a clod of the fertile loam at Nut Farm; her piercing eyes fixed him with an intense, lingering stare; in the next breath, they glazed over and fled into the void ahead. As he encircled her in his arms he perceived that the fullness of time had caught up with both of them. The fount that he, as a child, had grudgingly shared with his father was now beyond the reach of both. "Yes, there's a time for togetherness and a time for severance. There's a time for everything, mother," he whispered into her ear. A full smile formed over his round face: in his heart of hearts he knew that that she had heard him.

The departed woman had been lying at rest beside her husband for a week when Dino looked intently at the steep Dragon Hill and embarked on a climb. By dint of a two-hour effort largely on all fours he made the summit. Puffing and panting, he inhaled the drone of an army of cicadas and shot long looks here and there in case of a golden medal up for grabs, but a pair of puce, heart-shaped clods came into sight in lieu and he seized them. "Yes, the good earth remembers," he murmured while lifting the brown load skywards. "It's just like you said, Uncle Raf," he added while holding the boob-shaped lumps against a beam of light.

As he put the fragments back where they belonged, the squat frame of the castle, or of what was left of it, met the eye and he hurried to the relic, grinning like an owner gaining belated access to a cherished piece of inheritance. A pleasant strain took him by surprise, and a fleeting look made him aware of the presence of Grassone sitting at ease in the shade of an olive tree and pressing his plump fingers on the black-and-white face of his regular companion whose obliging response was the puffing release of a tune. He recognised the melody at once because it had been the winning entry in the latest national festival: it told the story of a young man entreating a white dove to fly to his sweetheart and announce his coming back to her in hopes of love and understanding. Was the portly accordionist playing the song simply because it was on everybody's lips? Or was his performance the outpouring of a gentle soul inside a rough body? 'God in heaven, would I were a dove!' the performer seemed to imply in tune with the lyrics, and the listener's heart melted while he had a vision of the hefty man taking off in the guise of a winged messenger. He drew closer with an appreciative smile. The music ceased.

"Quite a scorcher, eh? Yea, much better to be at the seaside on a day like this," the musician growled and without a moment's hesitation plunged into a recollection of cool starry nights at the castle when he was a shepherd boy. "Now I have a roof over my head," he disclosed. "I've built my little house with my bare hands, brick by brick, Dino. Those layabouts at the town hall must give me a licence now, he-he." The hearer bowed his head in sympathy and pointed at a posy of chrysanthemums quaintly arranged on a piece of rock. "Ah, that! I've just paid my respects to the poor soul who's resting under the stone," said the accordionist before bursting into a belly cough which brought about a string of ripples across his barrel-like frame. "You know, we were both young when the thing happened, and death-squad men were lurking about. Your Nut Farm uncle was with them and knew where on the hills the partisans were hiding. The chap lying here was in the resistance and…"

"No need to mention what happened on the hills," Dino cut in. "My mother put me in the picture. All I can say is that I was very sad about my uncle staying away from his farm."

"And how could he possibly return? What kept him away for

keeps was tit for tat on behalf of the lads caught in their caves." Darkish streaks cut a swath through the bloke's ripe features while he pivoted to face the castle. "See the skeleton over there? Bad bones it has." There was another, devastating, fit of coughing and then, "yea, this is a rotten stone, a wicked stone. Wicked as the dragon that haunted the castle," he affirmed in a waspish tone; his big hand jerked up in a spanking gesture while his crooked, unevenly spaced teeth went into a bout of clenching and unclenching.

Dino raised widening eyes to the relentlessly blue sky. A church bell tolled from below, and "Is it ringing from Sinuessa?" he inquired quizzically.

The beefy man stared at him with codfish eyes. "Now you're talking of another skeleton, lad. No, no. It's the 'Ave Maria' the good monks ring when evening comes." He crossed himself with an ample motion of his hand. "I had a word with your mother, God bless her soul, not long ago, and she said that talking to you was like talking to the wind. There's no breathing hole in the wind, says I." A melancholy smile fought for a way through his massive features. He got laboriously to his feet and stepped away, but swivelled round at the bend of the track. "Mind the stone, son," he hissed and trudged forward like an elephant on its exclusive jungle path.

Dino moved to fill the vacant space under the olive tree, sat under the canopy of branches and cast another look at the remainder of what had doubtless been an imposing building. Then he thought of the dragon: had he been the great red one with seven heads and seven horns that, as Don Orsino had told him, had appeared to the apostle John? That dragon had been thrown down to the earth and gone on to cause havoc; so why had Grassone been carrying his image at the carnival procession on the beach? What had he to do with the monster and the wicked stone? His left hand sank into his trouser pocket and re-emerged holding a piece of paper: it was the last message from the wartime trespasser, the odd character who had recited his epilogue and left the stage. He looked around: a lizard was resting on a slab and flicking its tongue. "Pipsqueak; travesty of a dragon," he scoffed before aiming an imaginary arrow at the little reptile. Then, with a sigh, he adjusted himself to the uneven shape of the bole. Little by little, his eyelashes came to a touch.

A vibrant, "Wakey wakey, sport", along with the feel of a tiny wig on his conspicuous nose bridge restored him to the world and to Rudy bending over him while saying with his exotic accent, "I've come to rescue you from the dragon, mate. I really felt I had to give it a burl." Then the saviour from Down Under gave a long look at the vestiges of the haunting castle and added, "seriously though, I've heard about your mother and it was devastating news; and so it was for Sheila."

"W-where is Marion?"

"Hanging about the lido. She reckons you would want to be on your own at a time like this." He turned to the relic again. "I see a rotten thing over there," he muttered.

"You talk like Grassone, ha-ha."

"You must be kidding! I know the geezer; he's told me a few funny stories." He shuffled to the cliff edge. "A cute lizard's squatting on a stone, Dino."

"Aha, there were many of them when I was a child. But my chums and I had arrows and a jar ready for them; and the jar was very hot sometimes."

"Shame on you and your chums! We left our geckoes well alone, cobber. We went after wallabies for a change." He rolled out a sardonic laugh.

Dino gazed at the youth standing between him and the sun. "Ever gone bush?" he uttered with a rambling sound and, his hands up and stretched out, he headed for the bluff, but, within an inch of the youth's massive shoulders, he swerved to the lizard. "Go to the devil!" he cried as he reached the nearest slab and, a pebble in a hand, stood on it with a vengeful frown. "It was no fun for you, eh? My turn now," he shrieked, and started jumping up and down at the edge of the crag.

"Watch out, drongo!'" his companion yelled.

The antics came to a halt. Standing akimbo, the bold performer peered ahead in the manner of one expecting visitors. And up they came, one by one, as if in a succession of cinematic clips…

***

Ahead of the batch, Uncle Raf is flaunting a glossy pitch-black shirt and keeping his right arm up at an angle while he croaks a hymn to youth, spring of beauty. Close at heels, Aldo goosesteps and laughs in his sleeve while, in line with him, Ron is shouting, "So long, Puppy kid. *Io amico.*" Within easy distance of him, Gigi gushes over the soldier-boys who are about to come and buy his cigarettes; lanky Romeo hints at death squads prowling about; Aunt Eulalia rejects the onions he has brought to her because they are not onions and his philosophy teacher is feeling his way as the blinded Cyclops did in his cave. Brada is then heard urging a good kick in the buttocks of the System and Lando is running about in the buff and waxing sadly lyrical about his old self. Close to her, Medo states that there's no way of beating the establishment and Ange asserts that love and war are nought but frenzied range. Soon after, an iridescent butterfly is seen fluttering skywards. Farther away, his father points at the Man God who had liberated humanity from the dragon for whom wartime is a magnificent time and Aunt Hilde is spotted playing with the ring her little nephew has failed to find. Behind her, a young barman is heard chortling, "Real shit, ha-ha-ha!" and Herbie is pleading, "Come back, Robin." At a short distance from them, Maria is engaged in a Galician dance and her one-man audience is shouting, "Bravo! Bravo!"; a few moments later Bernie titters, "She's after my body," while Linda is suggesting that he could do with a little help. A small space separates her from Gavin occupying his desk and writing about copies of copies while Stella complains about an awful mess and Leo is talking of gods that kill human beings for their sport. Adjacent to him, Michael twiddles his thumbs and from a poster on the wall a young man lets out a scream. In close succession, Fiona is enthusing over her lovely puppets; Elena and Francis are having an intimate chat close to a flowerbed; Marna is saying that we are all penned in our cages and Walter is stating that life is a tiny ball of strings while Alex maintains that everybody mucks about at a pinch. Hot on his heels, Pam shrieks, "Stone the crows!" From a distance, Father Benjamin slaps his thigh and speculates on a lucid dream. Who's following him? A young woman is close at hand, and she is heard to disclose her love for a beautiful idea; behind her, a labourer hints at winners and losers in the ruthless game we often play in life, and a captive Premier warns that at the end of the day we may all turn out losers in the game. Shuffling away from both, Grassone hugs his musical buddy and curses a malignant stone close at hand. On the beach below, Marion is skipping under a blood-red moon and saying, "Unfortunately, I'm not a Valkyr" while, inside her cottage and ensconced in her flowered divan, his mother is reading a letter from a former intruder to the effect that when war comes, the dragon comes with it; then she is diligently stirring masses of sugar in a tiny cup and drawling out that there's a time for everything...

Keeping his hands steady on his hips and his elbows projecting outwards, the on-looker mopped and mowed. Uncalled-for, *una furtiva lacrima* wormed its way through his horn-rimmed glasses and trickled down his face. He tried to wipe the tiny blob away, but it escaped into the pellucid air and soon looked like a topaz glistening on its way down to the star-studded waves. He stamped on the stone and whooped, "Here I go! Here I go!" Obligingly, the piece of rock gave in.

"It's a weird world, fair dinkum," he heard Rudy growl before toppling over.

For a few exhilarating moments, he drifted at ease as though tied to the string of an adroit puppeteer. Maintaining control over tightly closed eyes, he hovered in mid-air, strikingly resembling the character depicted in a popular strip cartoon as a chap in free fall and yet successfully resisting gravitation by virtue of not looking down; then his eyelids fluttered of their own accord and his face swayed in a vacuum: consonant with his destiny-conscious mother and the hapless Alvaro, the high flier yielded to the irresistible force of destiny.

***

Young Icarus soared to the sun but, deprived of his wings made of wax and feathers, plunged into the arms of the sea god Poseidon for an everlasting embrace – or so the ancient story goes. "I haven't been so daft," Dino says to himself as he lies on a chair in a somnolent hospital. "I defied the dragon and got the better of him. My swift descent was due only to a silly stone." His free hand taps on his plastered arm, disappears into a pocket of his dressing gown and retrieves a pink envelope. He unseals the flap with care and brings out a mauve little sheet. After restoring his uneven specs to equilibrium, he catches sight of the signature at the bottom of a letter and with a whirl of the head dashes to the top.

'I felt rather sad when I heard of your mother's sudden demise, but it was good to know that she went peacefully and you were at her bedside. The accident at the castle was completely out of place, of course, but what matters is that you are recovering speedily,' the sender has written. He sniffles and reads on. 'As to me, I'll be searching for plants and animals somewhere else before I make my way back to the Fens, but I must admit that coming to your corner of the world has given me a great thrill. Well, I am not surprised: as you probably know, my name is associated with your ancestor Marius and I welcome the connection a good deal more than the one with 'marionette' suggested by somebody.' A little blank is followed by, 'I'm sure you'll be pleased to know that I've visited Sinuessa and found I was in no danger of drowning. You see, the relic was in the middle of an olive grove and appeared to be as dry as a bone!' The reader's mouth opens into the shape of the Giotto's O that had once ennobled his primary school classroom and his eyes press on to the following lines. 'I've even managed an eleventh-hour paddle in the wonder pool. Fancy me doing a thing like that! The water was warm and for an instant I even heard a breathing sound. Good gracious! Has your awesome dragon finally borne on me? However, I felt pretty good while splashing in the pool, and that is a fact.' A half-smile materialises before the last lines are reached, and they are about Rudy. 'The young Aussie is about to make tracks as well, and when the two of us had a farewell rendezvous last night he asked me to call him Rodolfo. Goodness knows why.' Almost missed, there's a P.S.: 'I've seen fit to lay a posy of red roses at the door of the cottage that was the abode of your mother – a real mamma and no mistake.' He gives a slow, prolonged nod before his left hand slides to the trouser pocket inside which the oyster hair slide had been treasured up to the moment when his flight down the cliff had confided it to good Mother Earth. Then he gets up and traipses along. His eye falls on the wall where the brainchild of a schoolgirl displays a boy standing in front of a mirror with a look of contentment on his small face. Down in a corner another boy, one made of wood, leans, aslant and dejected, against a chair. Words scribbled at the bottom of the cartoon read, 'How ridiculous did I look when I was a puppet!' "Out with it!" he blurts as he aims a finger at the little lad facing the mirror. "Having the life of a real boy is no piece of cake, is it? You knew that only too well and did your best to keep in one wooden piece as long as possible, eh?" He

264

pauses briefly and then, bittersweet, "The truth is that you have had a dream, dear kid, and I can only hope that it was a lucid one. There's always a 'but' in the life of a puppet, and it spoils everything. I've no doubt you know what I mean. There are no buts about it, puppy boy."

He moves back to the window and peers at the world outside: perched on the hill, a skeleton is looking down on him, and he glares at the ungainly shape. "Dragons can't fly, ha-ha," he cries tauntingly, "only angels can." He is sure about it because an angel with flaxen hair has come down from her celestial sphere and flapped her wings in a field of wheat before turning into a butterfly. Down below, a sun-parched maize field comes into view and a tall, big-boned man wearing a very dark shirt is advancing on the withered grass, waving his arms. A booming "Dino-o-o!" hits his ears. The voice is coming from behind, and he turns to the sound: a stocky chap in a white coat is waddling in his direction, all smiles and a syringe in hand. He heads for the nurse with measured steps, but halts in front of a map on the wall: Europe is on it; his solidly framed eyes glide over the multi-coloured picture and land on the green isles on the other side of the Channel: their shape evokes the waist-coated, pink-eyed White Rabbit scurrying about in Alice's wonderland. At its southern tip cliffs stand glimmering and vast, out in the tranquil bay. "A thousand thanks, Matthew," he murmurs and shuffles on, but he pauses anew in front of the next window and fixes his attention on the street: 'Brutus's Motorcycles', he reads and it occurs to him that such was the name of the young statesman who had prevented the ambitious Caesar from reaching the fabulous cliffs for a second time. Regrettably, the deed of a batch of conspirators had put an end to Julius's travels; yet, to be fair about it, the valiant leader had gone too far, hadn't he? "At the end of the day, Brutus is my man, and why shouldn't he be, for surely he was a rebel with a cause. Yes, from now onwards I shall soldier on under his banner," he vows. "In the spirit of men

265

there is no blood... Brutus will start a spirit as soon as Caesar," he pours forth in tune with the Swan of Avon whose song he has put to good use time and again. His forefinger reaches the bridge on his Roman nose, and he sees fresh and exciting possibilities ahead. Indeed, time is the fabric of human life, and space is the dimension we need in order to locate our position and make sense of our behaviour. "If that is the case, all I have to do is to move forward in time as well as in space on a shiny bike, and then I'll be as safe as the stocks." His unfettered hand jerks downwards and comes up holding the Omega Grand Prix 1900. Against the lingering lustre of the late summer day, the valuable antique is showing his father's time. He raises it aloft. "In a tunnel again, am I? Oh well, I feel it's my duty to walk on in expectation of a luminous flow of luminous energy at the end of it," Dino Puppi says emphatically and marches on to meet the man in white, an undivided smile glowing like a lump of coal on fire all over his legionary face.